Published May 2022
Copyright © 2022 Brian Tim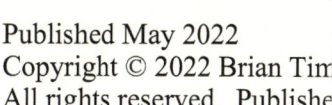
All rights reserved. Publishe

Paperback version available on Amazon.com and worldwide stores (if having trouble finding it on Amazon search, then go to lightworker17.com for the exact links).

Ebook version available on lightworker17.com

Audiobook version available on lightworker17.com

Other offerings by Brian Timlin:
Quantumlearning.info
Nocaloriecounting.com

Chapter 1

Geoff looked over at Michael. They both wore the same expression, one that said *what on earth is this?* Even Michael was chilled to the core — and he had seen it all.

They were looking at cloned humans in tubes and organ harvesting ovens. Torture cubicles sat next to them, old blood seeping from their entrances in the underground darkness.

They would remember this forever.

Six months earlier, when life was "normal"...

All his life, Geoff has been compliant. He was the one to bring joy to people - to tell a joke, to act the fool. And when it came to toeing the narrative, Geoff was the first one to say, "yes, sir."

The only thing that ever annoyed Geoff was those that dared to think outside the norm. Yes, he was one of those guys.

Yet Geoff was quite easy to endure because his foibles were so predictable. Within regular society, Geoff was a good, fun guy who would act exactly as expected; despite how boring it was, people liked that. But throw in a few good jokes, and you had yourself a guy who could fit in — and even climb the social ladder.

You might not have connected with or respected him, but you would have liked him in a superficial sense because he went around with a smile on his chubby face and never posed a threat to anyone.

At school, Geoff was in the second-best class of five in his year. Though fairly average in intelligence, he worked reasonably hard — since the tests are basically 95% memorisation, he got into a decent business course in college.

As one of his teachers told him, "If you have your eye on the prize, you can move up through the college grades fairly easily. It doesn't matter if you start with a lower course." Geoff worked hard and got his diploma, then moved on to a degree, and finally, a master's in business.

While not grossly fat, Geoff had always been plump, and as he got older, he developed a nicely rounded beer belly. It neatly suited the insurance trade he had entered, where meetings with consumption of food or drink always seemed to be on the agenda.

At work, Geoff was in his element. He loved to know everybody, eat and drink all day, fire out the plans, and get his commissions. It was hard not to like the enthusiastic glint in Geoff's eye when he was downing another coffee with some Joe Schmoe and outlining why he had the best quote, the best bonuses, and the best payment plan available in Cafford, Texas.

Leaving aside the rat race materialism and completely hideous nature of roping young families into all sorts of car, house, health, property, mortgage, utility, and TV schemes that were supposedly in their best interests — but actually designed to benefit those at the top of the pyramid — Geoff was working his trade nicely. In fact, he was quite happy to be both a pawn and a player.

"You're driving that Ford pickup," he'd say to a prospective client. "Lots can go wrong accident-wise or damage-wise with those automobiles, but I'll give you a great deal of six hundred dollars a year. I'll even throw in a one hundred dollar rebate if you maintain the no-claims bonus. Plus, I'll let you pay just ninety-nine dollars upfront and the rest over ten months in instalments. Easy peasy lemon squeezy." He made the sale almost every time — a master at work.

Given his single status, it was easy for Geoff to work long hours, make money, and impress the bosses. It wasn't long before he was a manager in Leroy & Son's Insurance.

But this didn't satisfy Geoff. On the surface, his only real complaint was about the traffic in Cafford. However, there was a more profound dissatisfaction in his life: he was lonely.

If he was skilled in sales, he wasn't nearly as skilled with the opposite sex. Geoff's options mainly consisted of women he didn't like and hookers.

On their Friday trip to the bar across the street, Geoff told his colleague Syed, "I want to take over this company or go into politics. I want more from life."

Syed knew that Geoff just wanted to get laid, meet high-quality girls, and ultimately find the one — and figured power was the answer. Geoff already had money, a nice apartment in town, a membership at the golf & country club, a Porsche, a Cadillac SUV, and a few great holidays a year. In Syed's mind, there wasn't much else Geoff needed.

Syed had been down this path — not quite to the same end, but he recognised the pattern. Unlike Geoff, Syed kept himself in good shape and was pretty smooth with the ladies. He had been lucky enough to meet his good wife already.

"It's all well and good for you with your gym body and brown eyes," Geoff said as they sipped Guinness at the bar, "and the fact that Indian girls look for Indian men." Syed smiled knowingly, as his suspicions had just been confirmed.

Syed only ever drank one Guinness before moving on to Captain Morgan, but Geoff would stay on the black stuff for as long as he could hold the bloat and weight of it. In his mind, Guinness was the magical Irish porter of his ancestors; the saying that Irish Americans are more Irish than the Irish themselves held true for him.

Stuffed like a Christmas turkey, he would move on to Captain Morgan or gin and tonics, depending on his mood. And it could take only four or five pints before he got to that point; Guinness was a filling drink.

Tonight, they had been invited to a party hosted by one of the city's foremost socialites: the mayor's wife, Priscilla Stewart. Although both men were making a name for themselves in the city, they were curious, if not apprehensive, as to why they were invited to a social gathering littered with very powerful individuals.

Geoff and Syed took a taxi to the Stewart's illustrious estate house on the edge of town. Geoff didn't sober up a bit on the ride there, as his body was still catching up with all the alcohol he'd already consumed. He'd get an extra hour or two of inebriation before calling it a night.

And he would need it.

Priscilla and her husband, Mayor Brad Stewart, greeted them on the way in. Brad was a proper frontman: he looked the part and did what his wife and the Democratic Party told him to do. Brad was your typical grey-haired, tanned, black-suited politician with a Hollywood smile. He gave Geoff and Syed a stiff handshake and welcomed them to the party with a cheesy grin. But it was Priscilla that truly handled things.

She was unusually stunning with her natural blond hair, symmetrical face, and sleek, youthful curves that belied her years. Beneath the party lights, her silver sequined dress shimmered.

"I would like to talk to you later, Geoff, if you have a few minutes," she said to Geoff as they walked in, showing not nearly the same interest in Syed despite his similar rank in the company.

"Of course, Priscilla," Geoff replied. After their short exchange, Priscilla promptly but smoothly went back to welcoming the incoming guests.

As a powerful woman in a small city, Priscilla was sharp as a dagger, her charm only matched by the uneasy feeling she inspired in others. But if you wanted anything in the system, you had to deal with her.

Geoff's eye wandered more toward the social ladder, but Priscilla had her eye on Geoff for quite some time. She had specific requirements that Geoff could undoubtedly fill; that perfect yes-man that could hold his own on any presentation, social gathering, or media conference.

Their eventual meeting was inevitable.

As Geoff and Syed entered the main dining room, they couldn't help but marvel at the decadence inside: wonderfully large rugs of the best fabrics and designs dressed the wooden floors, and the fine leather seating was interspersed with oak furniture and crystal ornamentation; the décor was an appealing and affluent throwback to Classical or Gregorian design.

The room was full enough to have a good atmosphere but not so busy that it became uncomfortable. Beyond the crowd, there was a string quartet featuring a tuxedo-clad singer, his flowing locks perfectly complementing his smooth voice, his timbre that deep, contemporary conversational style. Though the quartet had a distinct jazz feel, the string instruments added a classic quality that satisfied the more stiff-upper-lip audience members while providing a snappy beat and modern cadence to appease the casual party-goers.

It was a nice mixture.

As the night went on, Geoff and Syed mingled among successful business people, politicians, and other movers and shakers, often ending up back where they started and recounting interesting interactions with each other. But the evening was about to get a whole lot tastier for Geoff.

While moving through the party, he finally bumped back into Priscilla. After some small talk, she asked him to come to the office for a brief meeting. Geoff wondered what it could be about; though he was excited, he didn't want to get ahead of himself by speculating too much.

The office matched the rest of the house: it was large, furnished with beautiful leathers and oak, with a bookshelf fitting for an Oxford University library. One would have required a ladder to get to the higher shelves, and the dark brown wood framed the books in the most alluring and presentable way.

Geoff loved this room in particular and said so to Priscilla. She thanked him appreciatively as she swept her dress back to sit down without creasing it, gesturing with an open hand for Geoff to sit on the couch across from her.

After planting himself down, Geoff said, "Sounds important," with a smile, looking more relaxed than he felt.

"I've been watching you for a while now, Geoff. Our mutual acquaintance Bob Coates brought you to my attention, " Priscilla said.

"Oh really?" replied Geoff, a little taken aback. Bob was a democratic politician in Austin that Geoff had donated to when he was an elected official in Cafford.

"Yes. How well you've done for yourself hasn't gone unnoticed," Priscilla continued. "Not only are you very successful, but you also seem to be able to mix in all companies."

"Thanks very much," Geoff replied.

"I can't help but think you could be destined for greater things."

"You mean like government and so on?"

"Precisely," Priscilla said in a tone you'd expect from a Supreme Court judge. "The thing is, it's hard to find people cut out for it. There's a lot more to working in public office than meets the eye, Geoff," she finished, sending him a pointed look.

"I'm sure," said Geoff.

Priscilla stared him down. Hard. "You have to have the right person to deal with all the complexities that now separate you from the normal populace," she continued. "It's a society within a society; you must be able to act a certain way, to show discernment in what you say, who you say it to, and what you are willing to do for the greater good." As she broke her cold stare, her expression shifted to a pensive smile.

Geoff, not knowing what to say, simply nodded.

Priscilla started to wrap things up by saying, "Come to one of our meetings next Tuesday evening, eight o'clock at the townhouse, and you'll get a flavour for it."

"I will indeed," said Geoff.

And with that, Priscilla stood, prompting Geoff to do likewise and move back to the party.

"Chat on Tuesday," she said as he left the room. Little did Geoff know how pivotal this small meeting would be in shifting his path in life.

Geoff went back into the crowd and immediately began searching for Syed. He found him on the far side of the dining room, just inside the large front window. His lovely wife Isabella had joined him; she was dressed very eloquently in a sleek purple gown with slight padding on the shoulders.

Geoff welcomed Isabella with a kiss, complimenting her attire before adding that Syed was punching well above his weight.

Syed always enjoyed such pokes and showed it with a smile. Even if he felt it was only half true, it somehow made him feel more masculine and confident that he had the mojo to land such a woman.

"So, what was that about in the office?" Syed said straight out, not caring about being blunt in his curiosity.

"Interesting stuff," Geoff replied with a pleased look. However, he stopped short of elaborating, and Syed picked up the silent cue.

Geoff spotted Bob Coates in conversation over the other side of the room and they gave each other a nod and smile.

The party continued, and at just past one o'clock, guests began to depart in a continuous stream of tailor-suited men and ladies dressed to the nines being picked up by chauffeurs and town cars.

This was nothing new for a powerhouse couple like Brad and Priscilla Stewart. They had forged their position over many decades, and they had all the luxury to show for it.

Priscilla Maidstone grew up in Los Angeles and was an only child of two famous actors: Tom and Sherri Maidstone. She had a torrid childhood, as her parents didn't care much for her; instead, they were more concerned with public appearances.

Traumatised by the Hollywood circle, she wanted to gain her parents' approval by becoming a successful actor. Although she looked the part, did well in acting school, and gained reasonable acclaim in her minor roles, she found it wasn't for her. For one thing, she didn't feel she would succeed due to a lack of passion for the craft.

However, that path led her to discover what truly satisfied her: flaunting her looks, gaining power over men, and manipulating situations to get what she wanted.

This realisation thrilled her. Priscilla knew her skills could take her to very high places, even without an acting career, so she dropped out of college, moved to Austin, and enrolled in a political science undergraduate course at Austin University.

It was there that she met Brad.

Brad was from a political family in Austin. His father was a Senator, his mother a successful fundraiser for the Democratic Party; as a result, Brad had been groomed from a young age to move into political office.

In college, Brad drove a nice Cadillac and wore sweaters over his back with the arms draping over either shoulder. He sauntered around campus like he owned the place — to an extent, he did, as his family was one of the largest donors to the university. Since first stepping onto the campus in freshman year, Brad had been the head of the students' union; one got the impression that this was by design.

Brad could, however, deliver a speech.

His parents had sent him to public speaking lessons and debate coaching for years, so he carried the surface attributes of the role pretty well. But he left the real union work — meeting the student's needs, improving the infrastructure and experience of college life — to the committee, which he chaired in a very hands-off manner.

Brad had his pick of the pretty girls at parties. And he had fun with them, but it seemed more for show than anything else. He was a spoofer, unlikeable due to his falseness and the position of power given to him because of his family's wealth rather than skill and ambition.

However, Priscilla had her own goals, and she saw Brad as a hot ticket to her end game. She began to bring herself to Brad's attention by joining his classes and societies; she even got herself on the students' union board. It appeared to Brad that Priscilla was everywhere. Brad began to feel that her being his girlfriend must be fate — if he only knew the planning that went into it.

It wasn't long before Priscilla had wrangled herself into being the assistant to the chair. Now she could see Brad almost any time she liked. At this point, they weren't exchanging mere pleasantries; they were starting to work closely together. Now, Priscilla could really get her hooks in.

Brad began to rely on her for all his meeting prep, minutes, and reviews. He was starting to feel they were two peas in a pod, which was oddly fitting due to their upbringings and their unknowingly distorted view of success and the world. Although they didn't feel an amazing passion for one another, they became a couple. Their goals aligned all the way, and their families approved.

From there, things moved quickly. A year after they graduated from the political science program, they were wed in a ceremony in Rome before their parents and friends.

Never the type to slack off, they had two children in the next five years. Priscilla raised the kids with the help of a nanny while supporting Brad's career progression in the Democratic Party; in reality, she was still organising and planning everything for him.

Decades passed with Brad acting as a county official, mayor, and senator. He was learning the ropes as any younger politician needed to, but his main goal was to be the Governor of Texas. After twenty years, he finally reached it.

The Stewart name and Priscilla's hard work got him there despite battling the same shortcomings he had in college. After a remarkably unspectacular four-year stint as governor, Brad happily added the title to his resume and returned to more minor mayoral duties, this time in Cafford, Texas.

In 2008, they setup the TACFA foundation for helping children in need. By 2009, they were in the most powerful position they had ever occupied, becoming famous for their charity work with tsunami victims in Malaysia.

The day after the tsunami hit, Brad and Priscilla were on the biggest cable networks in America, pleading for donations. It wasn't long before astronomical sums of money came in. Plans were drawn up to allocate the funding as schools, businesses, hospitals, shops, and homes needed to be rebuilt. It wouldn't be an overnight job, but they were determined to do it.

Early in their charity efforts, Brad and Priscilla travelled to Malaysia themselves to see the devastation. They shook hands with state officials and talked to children, wondering if they knew a word of what was being said to them. But, once they had their feet on the ground, they realised they would need much more help than they had initially anticipated, and getting all the needed volunteers wasn't going to be easy.

Brad and Priscilla travelled the globe to plead their case to distinguished officials, convincing world leaders to back their efforts in Malaysia, raise more funds, and encourage the necessary workers to make the trip.

It wasn't long before they had all manner of people taking six months out of their lives to help the people of Malaysia. And it also wasn't long before five hundred million dollars had been raised — an astonishing achievement.

However, TACFA's success wasn't repairing the cracks in their marriage. Despite going through the motions to have children early on, the sex had very much dried up, and their marriage had become empty; both began to seek pleasures outside of their relationship.

In the beginning, they tried to find mutual satisfaction by Brad watching men have sex with Priscilla. The men were of all types and races, but they were all younger and more attractive than Brad.

The whole problem with this setup was that Brad wanted to be in Priscilla's position. Brad was a homosexual. He eventually confessed to Priscilla, but she suspected it all along.

They went through a short phase where they would switch between voyeur and participant, but Priscilla grew tired of seeing her husband in such compromising positions. So they began to do it in separate rooms — they would still share the same men quite a bit because that satisfied their need for kinky deviance.

However, they were becoming more discreet and accustomed to their arrangements. No longer were they trying to figure out what they liked and whether or not they could have a sex life together; it had become evident that wasn't going to happen.

Eventually, they began seeing different men altogether, as it was far less complicated that way.

But Brad had many more issues than discovering his sexuality. He had been pampered all his life and had everything handed to him on a platter. As a result, he was arrogant despite having no achievements of his own; he had never worked hard and suffered to reach difficult goals; he lacked character and morals.

Brad was like a walking amalgamation of other people's ideas. He was empty, a sociopath. So it was no surprise when he went completely off the rails.

It happened one weekend when the children were away with his parents for a few days. Brad had one of his male escorts over, and after an Italian dinner with too much wine, he brought his companion to the bedroom.

Priscilla was on the other side of the mansion, keeping away from her husband's proclivities, when she heard shouts and screams. She ran upstairs to the bedroom to find vast pools of blood all over the bed and floor and the handsome young man's body lying dead, still bleeding out from the neck. It was horrific.

"What happened?" shrieked Priscilla.

Brad, emotionless, admitted that during sex he had decided to smash his partner over the head with a glass vase and slice his neck open with one of the shards.

"Are you completely f*#king stupid?" screamed Priscilla.

He didn't answer but kept his head down like a spoilt child being absconded.

She knew this would take a lot to get out of. But, of course, since she was also devoid of any real humanity or sense of normalcy, she didn't feel anything over the loss of life — only pressure to fix the mess her husband had made. She told Brad to shower, change his clothes, and go to his parents' house in Austin for a few days.

Priscilla immediately got on the phone with an FBI secret service team she knew of through the Democratic Party. Within twenty minutes, the agents arrived, and Brad was already gone.

"It's upstairs, the third door on the left," Priscilla said, directing the two plain-clothes agents to the crime scene.

"Jesus," said the first agent. "Holy shit!" exclaimed the other.

"What happened here?" the lead agent enquired once he had collected himself.

"Brad slashed him on the neck," Priscilla answered. "I have no idea what was going through his head."

"Well, that explains all the blood," replied the second agent.

"I need this scene completely cleared and clean as a whistle," Priscilla said, shooting the agents a firm look. "Get rid of all the evidence. I want it to look like this never happened."

"Understood."

The room was stripped within an hour, the carpet cleaned, and all surfaces bleached. The agents bagged up anything that couldn't be salvaged, prepared to dispose of it where no one could find it. They wrapped the body in black bags and carried it out to the back of the black Range Rover they arrived in. As they sped away, it was like nothing had ever happened. Priscilla breathed a sigh of relief. She didn't want to look at Brad for at least a few days.

However, it wasn't over.

The man who had been murdered, Lucas Brevea, was popular, and he had friends looking for him. One friend knew he was seeing Brad that night.

This was big trouble for the Stewarts. The police arrived at Priscilla's door a couple of days later, enquiring if she or Brad knew anything about Lucas' disappearance. She said she didn't know anything about it, that Brad was in Austin and had been there the night Lucas disappeared.

Brad was taken in for questioning in Austin, and his parents corroborated his story. The Stewarts told police that sometimes they are targeted for money.

It wasn't long before the higher-up police told the investigators that there was nothing to this claim and to let it go.

But Lucas's friend Marcus wouldn't give up. He was back at the police station, insisting that something had happened to Lucas. The investigative team came down to meet him, took him aside and said they were sorry, but they had exhausted all leads, that Lucas was gone — a fairly common occurrence in his line of business — but he might show up at some point.

This didn't feel right to Marcus, though. He knew Lucas wouldn't have high-tailed it without so much as a word to his friends. He wouldn't have left them to worry.

Marcus went to every newspaper in town with Lucas's disappearance and his suspicions about Brad Stewart's involvement. No editor would touch it. However, one rogue investigative journalist wrote and published the story, going with the shakedown angle. Though he didn't believe that himself, he knew that was the only way to get it published. The small story got tongues wagging about Brad Stewart's sexuality, and suspicions about that night arose.

Priscilla was furious. She put every squeeze possible on the paper in question, the *Cafford Herald*, and the journalist who wrote it, hoping that they would never publish a story about it again.

It was too late, though. This journalist had started digging into Brad Stewart and discovered that what he found was only the tip of the iceberg.

However, even with what he had, he knew he still had a million-dollar book on his hands regarding Brad's sexuality, the lies surrounding it, and of course, what happened to Lucas Brevea. It was too big an opportunity — he was going to publish it.

Priscilla could handle one article spun in their favour. Of course, she would have preferred none, but at least they could pass off the accusation of Brad being gay as silly rumours spread for monetary gain.

But an entire book on Brad's life was another matter.

A few days before the book's deadline, the journalist was found dead in a ditch at the side of a road just outside Cafford. The incident only made it into police reports — no newspaper or television station covered it, not even the *Cafford Herald,* where he worked. He just disappeared.

His regular readers assumed there had been a falling out at the paper, that he had been fired or moved away to Canada. After a while, no one thought anything of it. And in light of this, when Marcus knew this journalist was also murdered, he backed off completely. He now knew for a fact what had happened to Lucas, but he also realised just how powerful and ruthless the Stewarts were and that he would meet the same fate if he pursued the matter any further.

The issue went quiet for a few years before it came back with a vengeance. Files from the Stewart's emails, texts, and phone conversations had been leaked all over the internet by Dmitri Olen.

Dmitri Olen was a brilliant hacker and freelance investigative journalist from Ukraine who championed the principles of real journalism and being truthful. No spin, no mistruths, and no misinformation. He was a beacon who had been working away anonymously. But he had made himself into a massive target for the deep state, as he had material on many others as well.

When he first released his information, mainly private corporate and government intel that showed some powerful people in a bad light, he received prestigious titles and awards like Journalist of the Decade. Some damage had been done, but the institutions got past it the way they usually do: spinning it to go away.

However, when he didn't stop, it became a problem. While there was no way Dmitri would have been taken out for exposing one person — or even one family — alone, the fact that he was going after all of them meant he would be discredited and shut down by whatever means necessary.

It wasn't long before a murder allegation surfaced against Dmitri. He maintained that he was completely innocent and moved out of the country. He sought political asylum in Vietnam, and it was granted. However, they withdrew it some years later, and he was extradited to the Ukraine, where he was sentenced to ninety weeks in prison for skipping bail.

In the meantime, the murder charges had been dropped due to a lack of evidence.

However, six years later, he was still incarcerated.

No one knew why; according to the official explanation, under a government act similar to the Patriot Act in America, the president could deem any person an 'enemy combatant ' and detain them indefinitely.

Priscilla and her corrupt colleagues had once again gotten around their issues, but more damage had been done to their reputations. Plus, it had made more people realise who they were and how they operated.

Despite it all, Priscilla and Brad continued with their political and business ambitions. Her philosophy was that the majority would forget the Stewart's transgressions with enough media pieces on how great they were. Then, they would be conditioned into thinking it was just another political argument.

Unfortunately, she was right.

Chapter 2

Time flew over the weekend and through Monday for Geoff; before he knew it, he finished work on Tuesday and prepared to go to the city townhouse.

Geoff entered the grey stone building. A porter waited in the wood-floored lobby, ushering him down carpeted stairs to one of the smaller private rooms; though the building had formal and informal uses, the rooms had a homely feel.

As he entered the room and the porter left, several people — including Priscilla — greeted him. The room resembled a mix of a sitting room and a gaming room, with a large conference table in the middle. A lovely fire roared in the fireplace, the warm glow accenting the lightly varnished wood.

Everyone returned to their seats, and an older man told Geoff to sit near the middle of the table. Never being too shy, Geoff put himself down one seat closer to the top of the table than the centre.

What he didn't realise was that this gathering had been entirely setup for him. It was essential to ease a new person into the circle with carefully crafted introductions followed by months—and perhaps years—of step-by-step processes to engrain them within the system.

"Well, it's great to have you here, Geoff," Priscilla said to begin the meeting. "Thank you for coming."

Geoff said, "My pleasure." Priscilla ran through the names of the eight or nine people at the table, each one introducing themselves to Geoff as they were announced.

"As you may or may not know," Priscilla continued, "everyone here tonight is a Democratic Party councillor or representative in some shape or form.

"We have all come in through various avenues, but we do have one thing in common: we are always here to help one another and our communities."

After a slight pause, Priscilla carried on. "We feel you would be an excellent candidate to join us, Geoff. You have the credentials, contacts, and ability to enter this world. It's truly about helping others and each other. If you need something, you have your friends and the power of the Democratic Party behind you.

"We know you have a friendship with Bob Coates; that you have voted for him in the past and donated to his election fund. So you're aware of how business works alongside our interests.

"You've helped Bob, and he has helped you acquire properties. Nothing wrong with that. Well, in working with us, you are expanding your network further. We may ask you to act a certain way or say certain things to protect the interests of this group and your constituents. It's a give and take, naturally."

"Sounds logical," replied Geoff, never averse to schmoozing his way up the social ladder. That was the way the world operated, after all.

If, when dissected, this whole paradigm could easily be shown to be a poor choice for the people, Geoff's idea was to bury that fact, as he believed nothing could be done. He told himself, *this is the game, and you can't change the rules; you just play it.*

And it was an easy excuse to give himself since this was really about serving his own interests.
Geoff often thought that life was competitive, but nothing was wrong with that. He knew he might be twisting a truism, and in this case, it had gone past that point — in reality, he didn't know where it ended.
But he stuffed that feeling into his substantial midriff and tuned back to the meeting.

Priscilla, slightly softer tonight, looked at Geoff as she continued, "We would like you to be a local assistant councillor to start. How does that sound?"

"What does it involve?" asked Geoff — he didn't have objections; he just wanted to clarify.

"Well, you would have to attend regular meetings on matters related to your area regarding health, business, education, policing, and decision-making. Aside from helping your community, you will also gain influence and widen your network."

Geoff responded, "That sounds like something I'd like to be doing; I feel I could do some good."

An older gentleman sitting across from Geoff looked at him thoughtfully and said, "This is not about you, sonny. It's about the party."

Priscilla moved on quickly.

"Well, that's just fantastic. We will announce our newest assistant councillor in the *Cafford Herald* tomorrow morning. And we will see you at your first council assembly next Monday, Geoff. "She added, "I hope that suits you," in a tone suggesting it would have to.

"Yes, Monday is good," said Geoff, knowing he usually did a management review at Leroy & Sons on a Monday evening but having the sense to reschedule.

Geoff got the feeling, like many before him, that Priscilla was not a lady you said no to easily.

He arrived at his first council meeting the following Monday. Things were relatively standard, but what happened afterwards piqued Geoff's interest.

Once the meeting was over, the off-the-record discussions could begin. The official minutes were generally just to dot the I's and cross the T's, moving ideas forward so quickly that no one ever thought to question them. And if someone did, the party line had already been fleshed out in a bubble of political double-speak and possibilities within the mesh of details.

It was only when you zoomed out that you could see what was truly happening.

After the fourth meeting, Pavlek, another esteemed councillor, felt comfortable giving Geoff more of a low-down on how things ran in the city.

Pavlek was a rotund man of Eastern European descent. He wore thick glasses and fancy three-piece suits to every occasion, even on the way to watch a movie with his grandkids.

Sipping his Cesu Latvian beer, Pavlek said, "Geoff, this is a Democrat city. But what we say to the people and what we do have to be very different things. The tax rate is, on average, the same as the Republican cities. It won't work otherwise. You won't have businesses here; you won't have spenders, and you won't have facilities, as there won't be enough money coming in.

"We have to bullshit the populace. If you distract, scare, and divide them enough, you dumb them down so much that they won't even question it.

"I hate to say it, but you even have to allocate more funding to the better areas rather than spread it out evenly. I mean, haven't you noticed the difference in the public schools and hospitals in high-income Redman and Silvercross compared to lower-income areas like Pittlong and Eastern?"

Geoff blinked and nodded in agreement before Pavlek continued:

"There's no social housing in certain parts of town. Despite how much we talk about affordable housing, we don't build it. Affordable means apartment complexes; it means moving away from single-family housing that people have already bought at reasonable prices and don't want to leave.
"They like their areas not overcrowded, and not with people lacking income. It's sad, but it's true. These are the realities. Every time a bill goes in for affordable housing where there's room to build in the city, like in single-family home areas, it's shot down in minutes — even in a Democratic city.

"People don't even question it! And they will vote us back in next time!" Pavlek said with a quiet laugh.

"It's crazy," he continued. "The whole system is crazy, but it's about power, maintaining the status quo, and eliminating questions. Liberal ideas are lovely in theory, but this is the reality. What we really do is control the mass media.

"And they think all of this doesn't happen in the socialist democracies of Western Europe. They might do it slightly differently, but the rich don't pay much tax there, either. They just use crafty accountants and pay off the politicians." This time, he let out a hearty laugh.

Although Geoff was climbing the ladder he had a growing apprehension of the endless deceptions and where the boundaries of this game were, if there were any at all.

It was Friday night, and Geoff and Syed were revelling in their usual routine.

Geoff was getting to grips with how things were in the political sphere. He was a little shocked by a lot of it, but at the same time, it became apparent when he thought about it.

The way he saw it, he was taking a place someone else would occupy otherwise. Plus, he was happy to use his position to get involved in charities to give back. This would be his way of feeling good about things.

He told Syed, "This political game, it's not what most think. It's all smoke and mirrors."
"Aren't you doing some good, though?" asked his friend.

"Not really, aside from the outside charities. You're pushed and prodded from every angle, and you lobby for interests you've been tapped for. There's no real time for morality — it's all who can get what. It's all a system.

"You hash things out to find what will work for everyone in the network while still keeping the powerful ones outside happy, and then you pass that motion at the meeting before anyone can question it.

"If they do challenge it, there are standard ways to twist it, make it sound rational and plausible. If you can't do that, you deflect, blame someone else, and distract. The playbook has been perfected over time.

"In the fast-paced environment, no one has the time to zoom out and put a spanner in the works. Plus, if they do, they get labelled a conspiracy nut, or there's another motion already on the table.

"The longer you're there, the more you realise the Republicans are on the same side. The enemy is the people, as they can stop the bullshit. They are the ultimate losers, but they are also the ones that they don't want questions from...

"Because, ironically, the people have all the power — they're a huge group controlled by the few.
"The Second Amendment is what scares the living shit out of Democrats and Republicans — despite their public policies — as it was put in place so a civilian army could bear arms if the government had gone rogue. And rogue we are." Syed looked at him with surprise and asked Geoff if he regretted joining the council.

"No, I don't regret it at all. I'm not harming anyone that wouldn't be harmed otherwise. I'm just being smart." There was a fair amount of pragmatic truth in that sentence, but it rang hollow.

The two lads pushed that to one side, nodding their heads upwards in a way that suggested, *Well, what can be done?*

"Yeah, it's a media game, Syed. Everything else is a doddle," Geoff continued. "We have to construct a party line for this and that to control the narrative. If you say it enough times, they believe it because you're supposed to be there to serve the people, and you wouldn't be doing anything else, now, would you?" He smirked at Syed, and Syed felt being close to the network gave him some superiority and made him in the know.

"Listen, man, I'm going to devote loads of time to doing charity work," Geoff said. "That's me giving back, and it gives you credit too."

Syed agreed and said, "Yeah, you are using your position for good, then."

The very next morning, Geoff has one such charity outing. As a representative of the council, he had the blessing of Priscilla and the others to get out there, shake hands, and provide service.

TACFA had helped many children over the years, and Geoff had setup fitness runs and cycling events every Saturday to raise money for the organisation. It aimed to raise funds for shelter, food, education, and opportunities for children in need — a tremendous cause.

If Geoff had to roll through all the other nonsense to get ahead, this made him feel good about himself.

He arose out of bed the following morning in his penthouse apartment at half-past eight, allowing himself a bit of extra time to sleep in. He could afford it — the charity run and cycle wasn't starting until half-ten, and the starting line was practically around the corner.

Geoff slept in a t-shirt and boxers. Going sockless was mandatory in Geoff's eyes, as it let your feet breathe. He would admonish anyone going the foot-warmer route. However, the t-shirt depended on the season; during the peak of summer in Cafford, just about anyone would say you'd be mad to wear more than skimpy underwear to bed. Geoff was no different.

As always, he first went to the window to draw back the curtains. The daylight beaming in gave him an extra boost of energy and helped to wake him up. He had netted blinds that he could see through but made it impossible, especially a few storeys up, for anyone else to see him. With that knowledge, he could stretch out in all his glory.

When he bought the apartment, he had worked with an interior designer to put a very nice place together. What Geoff lacked in time, he had in money, and he could delegate to get things right. He didn't have much interest in designing his place past practicality and a 'nice' impression.

He gave Mary, the designer, a rough outline and let her do her work. She came up with a modern squared layout that she felt suited the rooms. The furniture was large with sharp angles; only the cushions gave rounded punctuation to the contemporary white rooms.

In the bedrooms, the curtains were navy, and the cushions matched them. The main rooms followed the scheme in light lime, but that was the extent of the colouring. Mary felt that Geoff liked neat, simple, and clean — she framed this as 'uncluttered modern' to Geoff, and although she thought he wouldn't be hard to please, he was genuinely pleased with the job.

After that was all done, Geoff hired a regular cleaner to come in twice a week from Clean Queen, a company that worked with Leroy & Sons. The place was always immaculate; keeping a manager at Leroy & Sons happy was a good idea since he was in charge of one of their largest contracts.

Once Geoff had attended to his bedroom curtains, he did what he would always do: shave. He had a large, pleasantly spacious walk-in bathroom, the type where you could count your steps going from toilet to sink.

Geoff would spruce up his facial hair first. He always had a little bit of a ginger whisp, which he tidied with his face trimmer set low to give him a distinct look that was just a cut above designer stubble.

He then hopped in the shower, did his business, towel-dried himself, and slapped some Old Spice aftershave on. And when Geoff slapped, he meant it — the sound echoed off the bathroom walls with each smack.

It was another way to wake himself up in the morning.

Geoff wasn't a designer dresser, but he was snazzy. He had the good sense to know what worked for him and what matched, but he mostly played it safe. He went a size bigger if needed because it didn't matter to a man of his shape, and he was aware that nothing looked worse on a rotund man than a size too small.

Today, he was going with a knitted mustard sweater and regular-fitting grey dockers trousers. To complete the look, he put on a nice pair of brown Ecco shoes. It was casual, but it fit the occasion.

As good as Geoff was at organising events and getting other people moving, he didn't move much himself. Geoff never enjoyed exercise — plus, he never thought he was doing it right. Over the years, he told himself he just wasn't athletic. Other than that, he was also much too busy to work out and had no inclination to make time for it.

After a breakfast of cranberry and orange juice and freshly cut fruits, Geoff arrived at the Prime Health centre just in time to set up shop. His word-of-mouth and leaflet promotions had worked — the effect had snowballed, and now he had hundreds of people showing up each week from all over the city.

Every person had a sponsorship website connected to TACFA for what they aimed to raise, culminating in a long-distance run or cycle. The Saturday training was an organised way to meet others doing the same thing; a wonderful initiative all around.

The course headed straight into the nearby park and woods in Centre's Grove, a protected area of greenery and walkways in the city centre. Two main roads intersected at right angles in the middle of the park with a two-laned ring track around the perimeter specifically for cyclists and runners. The perimeter was 10 kilometres and passed through forest, parkland, and streams. It was a very scenic, natural, and healthy getaway right in the middle of a city of a quarter of a million people.

For the charity gig, people could walk, jog, or cycle. Every person had a chip that beeped as they crossed the starting and finish lines. Then, using a website Geoff had hired someone to develop, the participants could track their times.

Geoff began to look forward to Saturday mornings more and more, as he could feel proud of himself for organising charity events for children in need. Over some time, the Saturday mornings raised over five hundred thousand dollars, an astonishing achievement.

With the money, TACFA built a child and teen support centre in Eastern, one of the poorest areas of town.

Geoff was making further strides in his life, and the charity work brought out more of his authentic character. However, he was still searching for the right girl.

He decided to join a dating app. He had been on Tinder before, but he wanted something with more features that would be based on personality.

He came across a platform called CupidHeart that fit the bill perfectly. People had to pay to join, so it was less likely to have time wasters. It was highly customizable with a built-in video call software, which was very helpful since they were still in Covid lockdowns.

Geoff set about making his profile. He put up his best pictures and ones that showed his personality and lifestyle: on holiday with friends, playing golf, going to house music gigs, doing his charity work, driving in the countryside, having dinners and parties at his apartment.

While Geoff was a bit overweight, he was still a decent-looking man, dressed well, and had a personality and lifestyle attractive to women. As a result, he began to get many matches.

When he went through them, he wasn't impressed by many, as they seemed a bit shallow and dull. He also disliked how many younger women made too many Kardashian-type poses with their lips and flicked their hair; it felt fake to him. Geoff was starting to realise that, even on paid sites, an obviously affluent person would attract unwanted attention.

However, as he flicked through the many aspiring reality-TV stars, he did come across one profile that caught his eye.

It was a girl from Canada called Denise Buthyran. Denise was a beautiful, outdoorsy, girl-next-door type. All her photos were authentic, and she had an attractive personality. She was into climbing and canoeing, and she worked in a health food store. Like Geoff, Denise was also a big fan of house music and loved to go to gigs and festivals.

The backdrop of her photos was spectacular, as she also lived in a fantastic part of the world called Banff, Canada. It was a picturesque landscape intertwining snow-tipped mountains, tall trees and winding rivers.

Geoff was smitten. Although the distance between them was an obvious problem, everything was on lockdown anyway, and there were no signs of the governments relaxing their stance anytime soon. It was a common thought that people might need to find other ways of dating and even starting relationships for the foreseeable future.

He decided to contact her. His opening line made Denise laugh: "Hi Denise, master climber here. I spent my formative years on the top bunk over an aspiring WWE wrestler."

She replied, "You must be elite ☺."

"You've no idea how good I am at hanging on for dear life." She sent back a laughing emoji.

They were off to a good start, and Geoff asked her if she'd like to set up a video call. She was delighted and said yes.

Their first 'date' was to be a few evenings later. So Geoff put on his best outfit and dimmed the lighting on his computer. He wanted to appear like he was in a restaurant rather than a dentist's office.

Denise already knew all about lighting, having figured it out decades ago; when it came to looking your best, it was fair to say the female learning curve was far shorter than the male one.

Geoff was a tiny bit nervous because it was a screen and not real life, where he was used to being put on the spot. When she popped on the screen, those nerves took another spike — she was even more attractive live than in the photos. And if she looked this good on a video call, she must be a stunner in the flesh. Her brown hair was shoulder-length, straight, and styled perfectly. Along with her brown eyes and sweet smile, Geoff was captivated.

He gathered himself, and her friendly smile eased his nerves.

Denise, too, was put at ease very quickly. She found him very interesting, humble for a man with an influential career, and she liked his jovial personality. And there was definitely a spark between them.

During the call, they talked about all manner of things and got along great, connecting over their hobbies and mutual love of house music and going to see great DJs. They resolved to teach one another about organising events, marketing, climbing, and eating well. For the next several weeks, they arranged a date every few days.

Geoff and Denise were getting to know one another much better and learning each other's views on the world — but that was where they differed. Denise felt that Geoff was still finding himself, and she got the impression he would agree with one person's view and then do the same with another person with the opposite view; he was on his own journey that would prevent things from going further at the moment. It disappointed her because she did think they had a deeper connection.

As a result of Denise's hesitancy, Geoff also started to feel things fizzling out, not to mention the issue of distance and whether or not the relationship was realistic. However, that wasn't actually the main problem; it was more that they knew something wasn't quite clicking.

They agreed to let this one go. However, they both felt it could be revisited later.

Geoff felt that familiar deflation of failure, but something had happened when he met Denise. It was part of a deeper catalyst that he needed. Though he didn't realise it yet, she had helped spark something in him, and he was more prepared for what lay ahead.

Chapter 3

Though the charity work was his own, Geoff still had to attend meetings with TACFA. During the construction of the teen support centre, many people were involved in the proposals, setup and funding.

Of course, Priscilla helped, but Geoff also met other socialites, politicians, judges, bankers, solicitors, and more. All were associated with the foundation. With his pride overflowing, Geoff revelled in the attention he received for his hard work during those meetings.

Not long after his latest successful Saturday event, Priscilla invited him for another meeting in her office. Sitting just as they were the last time, she began to flesh out a new plan for Geoff.

"It's not gone unnoticed what a good job you're doing. The charity work is very impressive. Your reputation is highly regarded, and I believe the constituents will vote you into a high-ranking position." She paused to let that sink in before she said, "How does County Executive sound?"

"Sounds great," replied Geoff, "but will I be able to carry on the charity work?"

Priscilla answered, "Of course, but maybe in another capacity, like an overseer. You could get one of the town official assistants to do the day-to-day organising."

"Oh, okay," said Geoff, slightly perturbed that he might lose the best part of his week. "I guess I can do the same thing, just in a different way."

"Exactly," said Priscilla, her tone understanding yet severe. "That's that, then. My assistant will get you briefed on all the meetings, presentations, speaking engagements, canvassing, and advertisement campaigns that will make sure to get you over the line. It's a bit more work in the short-term, but you can leave your current job and have a fully-paid, better role here."

"Very good," replied Geoff. He had expected this day would come; as Priscilla rose from her chair and prompted Geoff to do the same, he sensed she was a woman of routine.

Another Monday rolled around, and Geoff met with Priscilla's assistant, Sandra. They sat in a small office in the townhouse as she rolled out the complete plan.

"That's a beautiful picture," commented Geoff on the large panoramic painting of a Texan expanse and mountain range hanging over the mantelpiece. "Yes, it's one of Priscilla's favourites, she only put it up a few weeks ago," replied Sandra.

Sandra was highly organised and on point, and after some anticipated preludes, she moved on to the meat of the sandwich, "Now to funding... These campaigns don't pay for themselves. To give you an idea, a presidential candidate spends one billion dollars on average. However, we don't need anywhere near that. We do, however, need a county-wide presence and advertisement campaign.

"You will get a certain amount, maybe half of what you need, from the major lobbies that patron the Democratic Party as part of the standard rollout. However, the rest you will need to obtain from patrons in town. There are people and businesses that will help out."

That was the first port of call for Geoff. Next, he had to give presentations and speeches to guests and as many potential donors as possible.

It was a speech targeted at their needs, wants, and special interests. The system was already pretty much there for a Democrat in this city, so Geoff didn't need to work particularly hard for the money.

The regular donors would give a certain amount to stay in the loop or garner favour if they needed it. One or two that had a particularly special interest would often give triple or more to the coffers, knowing the Democratic candidate was a shoo-in come election time in Cafford.

It added up to the funds required, and Geoff merely had to turn up and give assurances of business as usual. The rates, taxes, ways to get around taxation, allocation of public funds — all of that would be the same. And he would meet with them individually and give them his card to let them know they had a powerful friend at the end of a phone line.

This was a very different set of meetings from the public-facing conferences he'd have later on, the ones reciting Democratic policies while virtue signalling to the masses about his character. Since no one cared to check, they would just agree with how the media presented him, knowing that he had done great work for charity.

Although a wide-eyed person would cringe at the false promises in the public speeches knowing they would never be carried out, the Democrats knew their audience and targeted them as required.

As the process continued, Sandra told Priscilla she had made a good choice with Geoff. He had raised the funding quickly, and the advertising and public speeches were already being rolled out; You couldn't go anywhere in the city without seeing Geoff's face.

He was popular, and his campaign was effective. When election day rolled around, Geoff won by a landslide. But that had always been a sure thing — he was a Democratic candidate in a Democratic city, and he knew how to hit all the right buttons.

In the town hall building, as the blue and white balloons and confetti exploded across the stage, Geoff and his team were all smiles. But it was short-lived. As the balloons hit the ceiling, Priscilla was already taking Geoff aside to plan their next course of action.

She walked away from the crowd, and Geoff followed. Once they were out of earshot, Priscilla cut to the chase.

"Geoff, an offshore account has been created for you with a large investment. You will have access to these funds via card and online. Spend it as you wish. You could even buy property."

"Oh," replied Geoff. "Thank you."

Priscilla continued, "Think of it as a perk of the job. You have to demonstrate your luxurious lifestyle to fit in with the powerful people you're dealing with." She gave Geoff one of her trademark stares, dwelling for a moment of firmness before shifting more to proud mentor, kissing him on the cheek and whispering in his ear, "Well done today."

Geoff didn't waste much time finding out how much was in the bank account. The next day, he had logged in and was immediately searching for available properties. Within a week, he had purchased a commercial complex in Cafford that rented out units to shops and offices and a seafront home in the Bahamas. He figured he better not look a gift horse in the mouth for too long.

Everything else in his new role was quite similar to his previous one, but he had a higher position in the meetings and exerted more influence. He also had to be seen to be at his desk for a certain amount of hours per week, presumably responding to public questions and requests.

Priscilla had warned him that his charity work would change, but Geoff never expected what she truly meant. She invited him over for another meeting, but Brad was also present this time.

"Have you heard of the Free Masons?" Brad asked in his smooth, velvety voice.

"Well, only on *The Simpsons*," Geoff replied, giving the three of them a chuckle. "I don't know much about it."

"It's an organisation that helps us a lot," Brad continued. "It's a superb network with many advantages, ones we need, particularly for the job we're doing. When you're a Free Mason, you're above reproach. Free Masons control the media, the FED, the IRS — even the CIA and FBI.

"Given the complexities of our work, we need that protection from scrutiny. We have to keep the peace and the structures intact; otherwise, we won't keep our patrons happy. And if they aren't happy, the money doesn't come in. The money must keep coming in. You understand?'

"Yeah, I get it," Geoff answered, looking slightly bewildered as to why he might have to join this group. "But what does it involve? And isn't it a bit of a cult?" Brad and Priscilla smiled.

Priscilla took over and said, "No, it's not a cult. It's just like being a church-goer. There are familiar routines and principles, and it's a way to socialise and create connections.

"As we say, it's like a family that looks out for one another. When you get closer to the top, you need the support of your peers. Of course, we still do charity work, so you'll enjoy it. You'll start to see why we do things the way we do. It'll all make sense."

Priscilla got up, prompting Geoff to do the same. He was slightly confused, but he trusted that the Stewarts knew what they were doing. Brad shook his hand, smiled, and headed off to the kitchen, letting Priscilla walk him out to the front door.

On the way, she disclosed more information he wasn't expecting. "We don't publicise that we are Free Masons for many reasons, but we are the real power. I worked my way up in this organisation, and I'm now the most powerful woman in America." Geoff's eyes widened. He knew Priscilla had a commanding presence in Texas, but he didn't realise how far her influence extended.

"It's deliberate that we are located in a smaller city and that my husband is at the front while I'm in the shadows. That lets me work more easily.

"But I'm the one with access to the FED buildings, documents, FBI teams, CIA intelligence. And I'm at the top table when the biggest decisions are made."

"You work with me, and you'll go places," Priscilla said with an authority that confirmed what she was saying was genuine.

Geoff hadn't expected any of this, but he convinced himself it was proof he was moving into the upper echelons; he even felt a bit special for being invited to a private club to be mentored by such a highly perched individual.

His first meeting and initiation ceremony was this Thursday at the Lodge. It was a large wooden building in a secluded forested area about forty minutes outside the city. Apparently, Free Masons had facilities like these in private areas worldwide.

Geoff rolled up to the mansion's front gate in his Cadillac Escalade SUV, rolling down his window to provide the password he had been given to enter.

After punching it into the keypad, the gate began to pull back and open. Geoff went through, feeling like he was entering a farmland version of the Augusta National Golf Club's famous Magnolia Lane driveway.

He stopped at the motor court where several cars were parked. Geoff loved the sound of his SUV's large tires crunching over the gravel as he positioned his car into a spacious gap between two other premium vehicles. With the car beeping to indicate he was close to the wall in front, Geoff put it in park and lifted the handbrake.

As Geoff entered the loft, he was greeted by some familiar faces from TACFA, receiving warm welcomes, hugs, and handshakes alongside congratulations about his election win.

They brought him into a circular room with old wooden chairs built into the walls in a semi-circle. He was asked to take the robe off the centre chair and go to the adjoining men's locker room to change.

The locker room was more typical, with modern lockers and sections like the country clubs he was used to.

He returned wearing the hooded dark red robe, the rope around his waist keeping it belted to his body. He sat on the centre chair.

"This is your initiation, Geoff," said Brad Stewart as he approached him straight on with a large mace. He brought the large, heavy-headed metallic rod to each of Geoff's shoulders in an arc over his head before hanging it back in its proper place by the doorway. Brad passed him again, taking an ancient looking vessel from a table near the back of the room.

He brought it to Geoff and asked him to drink from it. Geoff could smell alcohol and took a small sip.

"Very good," said Brad as he took the chalice back, and the men and ladies present all broke into song. From what Geoff could guess, it was some kind of old fable. Of course, it was all a little weird, but Geoff figured he was just part of an exclusive club, and clubs needed traditions.

After the singing, everyone broke off to the jacuzzi and steam rooms to drink the night away.
He was invited back next Thursday. And the Thursday after that.

A few weeks later, he confided with Syed during one of their Friday nights. "Keep this under your hat, but I was asked to join this private group," Geoff began. "It's like a secret society — we help protect each other since powerful figures like us can come under attack."

Geoff would often tell Syed private things with the idea that Syed would soon be joining him; it had always been like that between them.

Syed asked, "What's this secret society called?" and wondered if it was one he had heard of.

"The Free Masons," replied Geoff. Syed's face fell.

Syed leaned a bit closer and said, "I've heard really bad shit about that, Geoff. I'd give it a wide berth."

"What do you mean by that?" Geoff asked, knowing that Syed wasn't so naive to think politics didn't have its discrepancies.

"I heard they are paedophiles," Syed began. "Even worse, they drink kid's blood and do other wild, disgusting shit!" Syed kept his voice low, looking around to see if anyone was in earshot.

For a moment, Geoff was stunned, but then he massaged his ginger whiskers with his thumb and index finger and said, "Nah, can't be. It's the guys that help TACFA, and I haven't seen anything remotely like that."

Syed gave him a sceptical look and commented, "Well, if you see any kids where they shouldn't be, or they hand you a cup of blood... remember what I said."

Geoff looked at Syed as if he were insane. Wanting to put it behind them, they quickly moved on to their more usual subjects.

Geoff kept attending the Free Masons meetings every Thursday for the next few months, enjoying the time and comradery — every couple of weeks, he got a new button sewn on his robe. During this time, they had raised more money through various projects and events for TACFA and another charity called Cancer Call. Geoff firmly believed he was doing a good thing.

However, something was about to happen that would change the course of Geoff's life forever...

Chapter 4

This wasn't a regular Thursday at the Lodge. This was a nightmare.

Things had shifted, and Geoff's Free Mason buddies had torn off three layers of the onion in one filthy swipe.

Throughout his rise up the ranks, Geoff had a nagging feeling of uncertainty, not knowing where it would end. However, never in his wildest dreams would he have thought the rabbit hole was this deep and dark.

It started on his way into the Lodge when he saw two children being escorted from one room to another — they were no more than eleven, and he recognised them from the TACFA foundation. He was startled when they looked back and had bruises around their eyes.

He went in and sat down in the locker room — slumped and distraught, he didn't know what to think or where to look.

"You okay there, Geoff?" bellowed Fred, a loud Texan Republican with a large belly and a fat cigar permanently drooping from his mouth.

"I'm not sure I am," replied Geoff.

Fred was fresh out of the shower with only a towel around his waist. He moved closer and put the perennial cigar in an ashtray to his side. Geoff could smell the steam coming off this giant slab of meat.
"Talk to me, brother," said Fred.

"What really goes on in this place?" Geoff enquired, looking at him with desperation; he needed to know the answer but wasn't sure if he wanted to hear it.

"It's all fun and games, my man. We are the powerful ones," Fred boasted.

"I just saw two children I helped in TACFA. What are they doing here, and why do they look like they've been struck in the face?!" Geoff asked, glaring at Fred as he appealed for an answer.

"Life is not all a bed of roses, Geoff," Fred began. "You know that. The men here are above the law. The ladies in the Order of Free Masons are above it too. They can do what they like. Some have proclivities that might not be so palatable to all the members, but they turn a blind eye. It is what it is."

Despite what he was saying, none of it seemed to bother Fred.

"How can I be okay with that?" asked Geoff. "It's f*#king sick and abusive!"

Geoff's raised voice and the serious nature of their interaction drew glances from the other side of the room. Brad and Pavlek were momentarily curious, but they soon returned to their conversation on the Lakers versus the Celtics.

Fred picked up his cigar, not wanting it to all waste away before he'd taken his fair share of enjoyment from it.

"Let me tell you something, kid," he said. "Many a person has entered these lodges with ideas about the world, about morals and all that. But you parked your morals the day you took money for your campaign and made promises to people instead of serving the communities that elected you to do so. You're in a bind now, so you better start making your peace with being powerful and being around other powerful people that do what they want. You don't bother them, and they won't bother you.

"The ones at the top have certain tastes too, so not only is it allowed here at these slightly lower levels, but it's also quite common. Orphans and kids in need always get abused anyway. You need to shut up and get on with it."

"F*#k me," said Geoff as he held his face in his hands.

"Look, Geoff, it's not my bag either. Youngest I'll go is fourteen," said Fred without a hint of shame. Geoff gathered he better not object to that jarring declaration if he wanted to get through the evening and back home.

"They obviously think it's time to let you see a few things since you've been here long enough," Fred continued. "This'll also be the night they give you the power drink. It's an anti-aging cocktail that gives you the best high you'll ever have. It'll be shipped to you in monthly supplies after this.

"You have to think about being successful, powerful, and having a great life. Just go with it. Just take it."

Geoff's eyes widened as he asked Fred, "It's not child's blood, is it…?"

Fred laughed and said, "Nah, don't be crazy. It's just a type of special juice from the Amazon." Of course, he was being deliberately disingenuous not to raise suspicion before Geoff got into the program.

"Okay, I think you're right," said Geoff, playing along and wondering what excuse he could use to have a look around the main room, which was still dark.

"I'm just going to go for a walk to clear my head," he told Fred.

"Okay, bud, you do that," said Fred, thinking he had talked some Free Mason sense into Geoff and that the new guy just needed time to take it all in.

Geoff slipped out into the main corridor, and no one was around to see him sneak into the main room. He put the lights on dim and went in to look around. He saw the ancient jug on the table and checked what was in it.

It was full of a red liquid. *Oh Lord*, thought Geoff, apprehensive to find out if this was what Syed had warned him about. He leaned in to get his nose as close as possible without touching it. He sniffed it, and it had that smell of pulp and iron — blood.

Geoff recoiled; this was the straw that had snapped the camel's back. *I gotta get out of here.* He headed for the door, switched off the lights, and made sure the corridor was clear before slipping outside.

He immediately got in his car and reversed out, gravel quietly crunching beneath the tires as he compromised speed for silence.

He had never been so relieved to leave a property in his life.

When Geoff got home, he flung his keys onto the glass table and pulled up a seat, placing his elbows on the transparent surface. As he combed his fingers through his hair, he wrestled with his thoughts. How could this be happening?

He would have absolutely no part in this evil.

However, he knew he had to be smart, as he was dealing with very powerful people largely above reproach. Geoff's whole idea of the world and life was falling apart, but he couldn't sulk; he had to do something.

First, he called Syed. Not in the mood for small talk, he got straight to the point:

"You were right about the Free Masons!" declared Geoff.

"What happened?" asked Syed.

"Exactly what you said to look for: paedos and blood drinking," Geoff explained with shame and disgust. "How did you know about this? Where do I find out more?"

"I'm going to send you a video file called *The Fall of The Cabal* — it will explain a hell of a lot. I wasn't sure if it was only a small group at the very top, but obviously this is more pervasive than I thought," advised Syed.

"Okay, thanks." Geoff took a moment to catch his breath, then said, "My head is in a spin, Syed. How did I not see it?"

"Everyone is on their own journey," replied Syed, the wisdom of his homeland coming through. "The important thing is you have been forced to really look. Research this, and you will find more truths.

"Many people kid themselves in life and refuse to look at uncomfortable things, but that's not conducive to goodness. Critical thinking is logical thinking; it's not emotional. Burying yourself in the hustle and bustle until you're too busy to think about anything is even worse."

Geoff had to respect these words because Syed was no airy-fairy spoofer — he was a pragmatist, and he cleverly assembled details into the big picture.

After hanging up the phone, Geoff immediately went on his laptop and watched the whole documentary on the Cabal. He was floored by what he saw, and he knew it was all true. It resonated with all he had experienced.

What on earth do I do now? he thought.

He felt the urge to call his mother's best friend, Martha Radlowski.

Martha was an energy healer, a tarot card reader, and a very wise woman. Geoff had always liked her.

She had a very tough life. From a young age, she was abused by her dad both physically and sexually. This went on for many years; by the time she was fourteen, she didn't want to live anymore and was in a perpetual state of depression and anxiety. She had no idea that the life she had was abnormal — she was too young not to blame herself and understand it from a bigger perspective.

When she was sixteen, she ran away. However, life was tough. Martha wandered from one shelter to another, searching for food and a bed.

Eventually, she ran out of options and ended up on the streets. She was there for a few years, eating restaurant garbage out of bins: a slice of pizza, half a steak, a few sausages — whatever she could get her hands on. It would only take three or four restaurant dumpster dives to get a full meal, though it was never as tasty as she might have liked. If she came at the right time, the compassionate closing staff would come out and hand her the leftovers.

Even with those pockets of kindness, it was always a battle on the streets. There was conflict with the weather, finding a place to sleep where you weren't going to be moved, finding a place where you weren't at risk from rats, people, or junkies... Life on the streets was risky enough to turn many to drugs, using substances to deal with the stress and get some sort of pleasure from life, even if it was fleeting and fake.

After years of resisting, Martha took a crack pipe from a homeless friend one night. Within a couple of days, she was hooked.

This brought with it another set of problems. It was expensive, awful for her health, and dangerous to get — the type of person who sold crack to the homeless was a particular evil, a true cretin who preyed on society's most vulnerable. And Cafford was full of them. Martha had to pay for the drugs somehow; to do so, she had to beg, borrow, or steal every day.

The dealers preferred putting their customers outside supermarkets where people would give them cash — as opposed to committing petty crimes — because it meant their cash stream wouldn't be taken off the street. They would even come to check if that was being carried out, and if the beggars hadn't made enough money, they would get a few hard slaps. If the dealers heard, through bent coppers, that they had been out robbing people, they would beat them as punishment.

Of course, there were exceptions: the skilled pickpocketers were discreet, and the good musicians made more than enough by busking.

Sitting on her ass begging and worrying all day outside a supermarket was hell, so Martha decided she needed a good skill. Her friend Rosey — who gave her the hit of the crackpipe — started to teach her to sing and play the guitar. They would spend all day playing music outside the mall.

Rosey had been on the street for twenty years and knew every trick in the book. So naturally, she was a master pickpocketer. Rosey showed Martha that pickpocketing would work in only two situations: the first was in a super crowded area, and the second was with no one around. Otherwise, unless you were a master, you would get caught.

It was all about distraction. The easiest lifts were in a crowded space with pushing and shoving going on. All you had to do was learn three things: positioning, diversion, and the subtle removal of the wallet.

Men with a large back pocket and an even bigger ego were the easiest and juiciest targets. A person pretending to push into them would deflect their attention while the other set of dextrous digits was removing their leather pouch. By the time the victim noticed anything was missing, their bill folder was already in the escapee's jacket pocket, far and away.

"Easy peasy, lemon squeezy," Martha would say after she mastered the art of pickpocketing. Geoff had first heard the saying from her before using it as his own when he secured an insurance deal.

The odd time, some sharp-eyed onlooker might get the right angle, witness the lift, and let out a shout, but that's where running away quickly and knowing all the back alleys would get them out of dodge before getting caught — most of the time.

It wasn't long before Martha was skilled at playing music and dipping into shopper's pockets. She took turns playing the guitar with Rosey because they only had one, but after a particularly good wallet day, she purchased her own. She guarded her stringed instrument as her prized possession and hid it very well whenever she had to make an excursion free of baggage.

Things carried on like this for a while, and Martha was making more money, but it was a vicious circle. The more money she got, the more those scumbags would charge her for their drugs and 'protection'.

More money also saw stressed-out street-dwelling addicts like Martha wanting more and more uppers. When those stimulants made her antsy, she took opiates to take the edge off. It got to the point where she was too strung out to play music or pickpocket. But she still begged for drugs, couldn't pay for the last batch, and got a beating within an inch of her life.

She knew she was at a crossroads: she could carry on like this, be found dead of an overdose or murdered, or find a way out.

Martha had always been a very spiritual person, and she knew she had to reconnect with her inner guidance, her inner knowing. So she sat and breathed deeply, accepting the pain and resolving to find her higher self, her connection to the source, a universal consciousness. A part of her knew life was an illusion of duality, and she was seeking a deeper truth.

After a while, she felt more centred than she had in a long time.

Martha began to pray for answers — not to something outside herself, but through her connection to the universal. She did this for two solid days.

Even if she didn't accomplish anything, it was helping her stay away from crack and letting her body heal; she had been through so much trauma in her life that she could tolerate extreme pain, and in some ways, having so much outer pain was distracting her from the withdrawal.

On the third day, she found the answer. She recalled something a wise primary school teacher told her about feeling gratitude for several things every day, explaining that it was the key to happiness and success. Martha resolved to listen to this wise advice. She began practising gratitude every hour so that it would become her default.

After a few days, she felt better and was cleaning up her drug habit, having made it through the worst of the withdrawal. When the drug dealers showed up, they were shocked when she told them she didn't want any more drugs and would have them paid off in a few days when she could walk again.

They must have had some tiny semblance of good in their dark souls because they respected the toughness of someone who pulled herself out of this cycle – barely anyone could. They left her alone and said they would be back in a few days.

Martha busked at the mall and made enough to pay them off. However, they still wanted money for 'protection' going forward, and she had no choice but to agree. At least the rate was better, but it would be challenging for her to save up enough money to get a deposit for a place to live.

Accumulating cash on the street was a dicey game with so many vultures floating about.

However, Martha had another idea come to her, one that she had read in a book written by a very spiritual and successful man who wrote about visualisation. He visualised where he wanted to be in sensory detail and highly recommended it.

So, Martha dedicated herself to that practice too. She saw herself healthy and happy in her own home with a good job. All day every day, she was practising gratitude and visualising where she wanted to be between her busy busking stints. Though she still had to pay the parasites to keep them off her back, she gradually saved up.

After a few weeks, she was one-fifth of the way to having enough for a new set of clothes and a deposit. She planned to buy an outfit, get to a shelter, and talk a volunteer into getting her a hot shower and a chance to rent a room somewhere.

But disaster struck again.

A newly homeless teenage boy woke her up one night, harassed her, and gave her a few kicks while demanding money. He was out of his mind and wielding a knife, so she gave him all the cash she had.

Just as he got the loot and took off into the night, a shout came from afar: "Hey, leave her alone!" and a man ran over.

He was a handsome man in a suit and tweed hat, strong, with well-defined features; he reminded Martha of a character from the old movies.

"Are you okay?" he inquired. The boy was long gone and uncatchable at this point.

"I'm fine. I just have to start saving all over again," she said, hiding the fact that she was a little shaken up.

"I'm Michael Clarke," he said. "What's your name?"

"Martha Radlowski."

"Tell me, what you are saving for?" He was genuinely curious because he had been walking past Martha on the street for the past year on his way to work. Recently, he had been so struck by her; unlike other homeless people, she was fully lucid and genuinely wished everyone a good day — he could tell it came from the heart and that Martha had no ulterior motive. Her kindness made him want to get to know her, but he hadn't worked up the courage to do so. The time was now.

"I'm saving up a deposit for a place of my own," she told him.

Michael knew she was serious — he was a detective and had been reading people for years. She explained that she had been one-fifth the way there, but the protection racket made it difficult for her to save.

"You're likely to be robbed again once word gets around you are saving," he said. "It'll happen over and over." He considered this and paused before saying, "Okay, come with me."

Martha was a little startled. Michael knew he had to put her at ease and said, "I've been walking past you here for a while. I know you want to get off the streets and have the resolve to do it — I can see it. I can help you do that, no strings attached. Of course, my wife will need some convincing, but she will come around to the idea."

The mention of his wife put her at ease. In her life experiences with men, she thought she would be used for sex and then turned out without any place to go. Martha didn't have much to lose at this point, and she felt he had good energy, so she decided to trust in what she had been imagining.

"Tell me more about your plan," he asked as they walked to his car. He carried her bag of belongings as she strapped her beloved instrument case over her back.

She outlined exactly what she wanted to do. Michael told her it was a good plan, but if he helped her, it would be much better: she wouldn't get robbed again, would have an existing address, and get a reference from him as a previous landlord. That was very important, he told her, in getting a job and securing rented accommodation.

When Michael got home, he told Martha to wait in the car while he went in and talked to his wife. Shortly after, Diana came out alongside Michael with a welcoming smile on her face; it was clear from her expression that Michael had told Martha's story well and spoke highly of her. As they welcomed her into their home, she was close to tears — she had never experienced such kindness.

Diana got her some food first. Martha tried to be polite and not eat too fast, which wasn't easy, especially since it was the best meal she'd had in years: steak with vegetables and potatoes topped with gravy. Being around such luxury made her conscious of her raggedy look and musty smell.

Diana didn't want to pressure her with too much talk, as it was late and she had just arrived, so when she was finished eating, Diana showed Martha to the spare room and told her to make herself at home. Martha eagerly hopped into the shower as Diana looked through her wardrobe for spare clothing.

When Martha came out of the shower, fresh and in good spirits, she was surprised to find stylish clothing lying on her bed: a white polo shirt, a pink knitted jumper, blue jeans, socks, underwear, and a pair of trainers. The trainers were a little tight, but everything else fit perfectly.

The bedroom table had a large mirror, and once she was all cleaned up and dressed nicely, Martha was eager to see how she looked. The polished reflection staring back at her, which she hadn't seen in years, made her smile. Martha had natural fluffy, light brown curls, blue eyes, and a wide face, her lovely personality written on her facial features. She was also trim and shapely, having fought tooth and nail to stay alive in recent years.

Tonight, Martha exercised her gratitude with increased positivity. For the first time since she started the list, she had replaced some of the old items with new ones.

When the couple got up in the morning, Martha was already downstairs. She looked and smelled great, but it wasn't only her — there was also the smell of Irish breakfast wafting through the kitchen.

"Breakfast is served!" she exclaimed.
"Look at you — don't you clean up well," Diana said excitedly, admiring how her clothes looked on Martha.

Michael savoured the moment. *Great start*, he thought to himself. In fact, he felt like he had known Martha all his life — he instinctively trusted her.

Michael sat down with Martha after breakfast, and they wrote up a resume. They had to fudge the last few years, and he put down a few of his co-workers as references. But they were already in on it; he told them to do him a favour, and that if anyone called asking about Martha, to pretend they employed her.

For the rest of the week, Martha applied for jobs. When she came home, she cleaned every room except Michael and Diana's bedroom.
And when they arrived home from work, dinner was already made.

They were starting to love having Martha around; her spirit, energy, and housework were all wonderful. Every morning, she would feel gratitude for each thing on her list, and several times a day, she would sit down and visualise her next step in life.

51

Within five days, she had a job at the local supermarket stacking shelves. It was mundane, but she was thankful for the work and did her job earnestly. She was making great progress, saving every penny she could.

She continued to clean the house and cook meals as often as possible. Diana had given her two more outfits, as she had too full a wardrobe anyway, and a small loan to go to the dentist, as Martha needed a few fillings and a general cleaning.

With her lovely personality, Martha was the perfect houseguest. Despite her street smarts, she still possessed an endearing and non-judgemental innocence.

Though Martha had saved up enough money for a deposit after eight weeks, the Clarkes insisted she stay. They loved having her, and it would give her a chance to save even more, so Martha agreed. In fact, she was happy to stay. She loved the Clarkes — they treated her better than anyone ever had.

When two months had passed, Martha felt it was time to go. She began searching for a new home and found a quaint, shared accommodation: a two-bedroom apartment with a roommate, a female nursing student. It was ideal.

Martha finally had her independence and a foundation she could build on.

Michael called every week to check in on her and have a chat. He asked her what she would like to do if she had all the money in the world; she told him she would love to be a healer, read tarot cards, and give people advice.

"Go for it," said Michael, though he advised her to continue her day job and work towards her dream in the evenings. Martha did just that, and her visualisations were now focused on bringing her new career into her life.

She found teachers she admired and took online courses; she learned to read the tarot from Janine in Canada, and she learned healing from both Dr. Alex Loyd of The Healing Codes in the US and The Heyoka, David Ian Rogers, in the UK.

Most importantly, she was learning how to heal herself. Over time, her traumatic memories melted away, as if they had happened to someone else. With her gratitude and visualisation practises, she felt like she possessed a full repertoire of resources to help herself and others.

Six months flew by, and Martha was having a blast. She almost couldn't believe how much her life had grown. She had a circle of friends she played music with every Friday, did healing sessions for people most evenings, and did tarot readings for friends.

Within a year, she had so many clients that she knew she could do it full-time. Her roommate had since moved out, but Martha knew she could now afford rent on her own. As a bonus, she could use the second bedroom as her workplace.

Four years passed.

Martha's business was thriving. Through helping so many others heal and find their purpose in life, Martha felt like she'd become a new person. But her friendship with Michael remained, as they had grown very close over the years, treating each other like siblings.

Michael had spent the last three years in South America working with the CIA and Navy SEALs. He had been trained by the CIA and Navy units as a detective and agent so he could work in multiple areas — the skills were necessary for the type of work he did. He had been drafted in for this secret service work, and he wanted to experience it, so off he went.

However, it took a toll on his marriage. He was away for very long periods and only saw Diana once every six months. After two years, she had an affair with another man.

After she admitted it to Michael, he was distraught. He spent a few hours at the bar downing shots of whiskey before stumbling to Martha's apartment late that night — he wasn't much of a talker, but he knew he had to get help from someone. He wanted that someone to be Martha.

Of course, Martha would never turn him away. So when he showed up on her doorstep, she ushered him in and sat him down on the couch.

"What's wrong?" she asked.

"Diana cheated on me," he said straight out, trying to look more sober than he felt. Even when drunk, Michael could keep a straight face and play it cool.

Martha gasped and covered her mouth. "That's awful!"

"Yup, she got lonely when I was away — took up with the local golf pro," he continued.

"You poor thing," Martha said, bringing his head to her chest and running her fingers through his hair to comfort him.

Michael kissed Martha's cheek. She pulled back, not wanting to take it further.

"I don't think that would be a good idea," she said.

Michael sat up and said, "Yeah, you're probably right."

Though Martha had always had a bit of a crush on Michael (because he was a strong, silent type who had saved her from the streets), she knew nothing could ever come of it. In the end, they were more like close friends. Even if Diana had broken up their marriage, anything sexual between Michael and Martha just wasn't a good idea.

Chapter 5

"Hello?" Martha answered as she picked up the phone.

When Geoff gave her a quick greeting in return, she said, "Hi, Geoff!" Before Geoff could get another word in, Martha continued, "I had a feeling you were going to call me. Of course, I'd recognise your voice any day of the week. You found out who were you working for?"

"Yes... Did you channel that?" asked a surprised and curious Geoff; Martha never did miss a beat.

"No, I just saw you had gone into some political circles and won a county seat."
Geoff nodded, "Ah."

Martha continued, "I knew you wouldn't be happy there; your heart is pure, and your real purpose has begun to come forth. Since you were a child, I've sensed that you possessed a pure aura — dormant but ambitious as hell. When you combine that with your compliance, you would inevitably collide into something that would jolt you awake like a bolt from heaven. When I saw you celebrating your election victory on the TV, I knew that day was coming."

"You know me better than I know myself M, which is why I need your help," Geoff confessed. "I need your guidance on what to do next."

"Okay, come to my place tomorrow, any time in the morning," Martha offered.

"That's fantastic," said Geoff. "I'll come over just before noon."

"Great," said Martha. "See you tomorrow."

Geoff would sleep a lot easier tonight, knowing he had a plan.

He got a decent sleep, but he was in for another shock by breakfast. Just as he sat down, his phone started ringing. It was Priscilla.

55

"Hello?" Geoff's heart beat hard and fast as he answered.

"Hi, Geoff." Priscilla's voice sounded smooth and relaxed on the other end of the line. "Don't be alarmed, but we need to have a serious talk. Could you make it to a meeting at our house this morning?"

"Sure," replied Geoff. "See you there shortly."

His mind raced as he raked it for answers, wondering what she had planned for him. Worst-case scenarios were pouring through his mind — he'd be blackmailed into silence forever, thrown into prison, or found dead at the bottom of a lake. But surely, things wouldn't come to that; at least, that was what Geoff kept telling himself as he tried his best to calm down. He was smart enough to realise he was going to be threatened. Hopefully, that was the worst of it.

Geoff ran through play-by-plays of potential conversations, going over endless possibilities in his head on his journey to the Stewart's house.

As he arrived, the gates automatically opened for him. He drove his classy SUV up the gravelled driveway and parked several metres to the side of the fountain of youth statue — a working ornament in the centre of the motor court.

A menacing black motorbike occupied one of the parking spaces on the opposite side of the fountain. It didn't fit with the Rolls-Royce and Jaguars, so it caught Geoff's eye.

"Good morning, Geoff," Priscilla said, coming out to meet him with a smile. "Come in." Her calm and courteous demeanour put Geoff at ease, but he knew he couldn't let his guard down too much.

This time, she brought him into the sitting room. Brad was there with another man Geoff didn't recognise.

"Hi, Geoff," said Brad in a relaxed, understated tone. He gestured to the man next to him and said, "This is Miguel." As Geoff reached out and shook Miguel's hand, he felt uneasy and intimidated. Miguel was wearing all black leather, his high cheekbones and deep-set brown eyes framed by his dark locks.

"Take a seat," Priscilla said, gesturing everyone toward two perpendicular couches cornered off by three chairs. Miguel took a chair on one side, Priscilla a chair on the far end, and Bill and Geoff sat on the separate couches. Everyone had their own breathing space.

The fireplace opposite Geoff crackled as Priscilla broke the tension. "Geoff, we know what happened last night. Don't be alarmed — you aren't in any kind of trouble. We just need to have a serious chat about it."

"I understand," said Geoff, doing his best to hide his nervousness.

"There had to be a point where you were introduced to the realities of high-end life. We don't make up the rules; they just are. The ones at the very top are all into this sort of thing. It's simply the way it is." Priscilla explained while studying Geoff's reaction. "New recruits either go with it or turn a blind eye, but most take the adrenochrome for its many benefits."

"Is that the blood?" Geoff asked tentatively. "Yes, it is," said Brad. "Look, it seems weird at first, but you have to think of it this way: those kids get abused anyway, and the powers that be decide how the world is. You may as well be a winner in that system. You get me?"

"I don't know if it's for me, Brad," Geoff said, deciding it was better to come straight out with it.

There was a long pause. Brad took a breath and decided Geoff wasn't going to be talked into changing his mind.

"Well, that's okay... but if you don't do it, you can't be Free Mason," Brad continued, "and you can't breathe a word of this to anyone else. Priscilla is very powerful, but she's not at the level of the European families; or the next rung down, the paymasters. We are the third rung, a bridge to the public. If the higher-ups trace anything back to you, they'll skin you alive. Do you understand?"

"Yes, I do," said Geoff, unwilling to dwell further on the thought. "However, I have something to say as well. A friend of mine warned me about your activities when I first joined the Free Masons, and I told him about my experience. So if anything were to happen to me, if Miguel there were to bury me in a forest or fake a suicide, my friend would know. And he wouldn't stay quiet."

Shocked at Geoff's immediate resourcefulness after being thrown into the deep end, Priscilla was almost impressed. "If you don't cause problems, nothing will happen to you," she assured him. "And if you do, it won't matter how many friends you have. We own the press, the police force, and the courts. Just the same as we own you.

"These organisations fall into two camps: either they're on our side, or we have compromising information on those in charge and hold it over their heads; everyone below simply follows orders, and we get what we want.

"There are rare people in high positions that stay clean, but they also know not to rock the boat too much lest they spur us into action. Well, apart from that cretin Trapp who seems intent on ruining his life, his family's life, and ours."

Brad took over and added, "He doesn't seem to realise that if you can't change it, you may as well thrive off of it. But we will destroy him, just like we destroyed JFK when he talked about secret societies, dismantling the CIA, and going to gold-backed money.

Though we're disappointed you aren't going to be as successful and helpful to us as we would have liked, you're still a good politician who can get the job done." Brad paused before he finished by saying, "Just remember who you're dealing with."

"I will," replied Geoff feeling calmer that he wasn't in any immediate danger.

The meeting was promptly wrapped up. Geoff stole a glance at the Stewart's henchman as he was leaving, feeling he was a dangerous individual.

Although this went about as well as expected, he knew well he'd be under strict surveillance for quite some time. And part of that would no doubt include being tailed by that mongrel Miguel.

Miguel Vasquez was from a city in Cuba called Matanzas, one of the poorest areas in a poor country. As the third eldest of seven siblings, life was tough for him from the start. His father left when he was only eight because he couldn't take the pressure of caring for his many children in an unforgiving country.

Esteban Vasquez left Cuba on a boat during the night with no notice and no real plan. Maybe he intended to dock in the US, get a job, and send money home, but he never discussed it with his wife, so no one ever knew. In the end, she was left with seven hungry mouths and very little income.

Matanzas was a rough city. Like nearly all smaller kids with no older brother, Miguel used to get beaten up at school.

That was what got him into boxing when he was nine years old. It was obvious right away that Miguel had natural talent. He got good very quickly, and it wasn't long before he was winning medals in his age group. As an added bonus, he'd always get big meals at the boxing club because the government liked to sponsor them. But since the sport was taken so seriously, few stuck with it due to the severity of the training.

Despite the rigorous schedule, Miguel liked it. For a few years, he was doing much better, and he dreamed of helping his mother. But Miguel's dreams were dark ones.

He fantasised about being a crime kingpin and making his mother his benefactor, slaying as many as necessary to give her a better life.

When his mother died of cancer when he was twelve, Miguel slipped further into his feelings of indignation and anger. Without her influence, his mind became chaotic. However, he was still putting it all into boxing. And because he had nothing else but an extreme desire for success, he became the most ferocious boxer many had ever seen.

Outside the ring, he got into trouble for stealing and beating up his old bullies, but as far as the boxing club was concerned, he was too talented, too much of an asset to let go. So they did just enough to keep him in line.

Through it all, he was winning all the titles in his age groups across the country, winning dozens of matches with rare knockouts that riled up the crowds. Their enthusiasm drove him to continue training and, most of all, to continue winning.

One of his trainers was fluent in English and began speaking to him in the foreign language everyday. He told him that he would be a star, that he would need the main language of the world to promote himself and make money one day. Miguel liked that idea a lot, and it also helped him to stay focused.

By the time he was nineteen, he was a shoo-in for the Cuban Olympic team going to the London 2012 Olympics.

At this time in his life, Miguel was on top of the world, and nothing and no one could bring him down. He was heavily muscled from years of intense training, his hair kept short for his time in the ring. His sharp features bore an expression that exuded confidence and intimidated anyone he passed.

When he stepped off the plane after it landed in London, even his walk down the steps was that of a man who would win gold in the welterweight division.

He breezed through to the semi-finals with a series of easy points victories and a few knockouts. The amateur game had far fewer rounds, so not only was the equipment prohibitive to knockouts, but a fighter didn't have much time to get one.

That's what made what happened in the semi-final all the more unbelievable. Miguel was fighting a Russian, Sergei Talov, with a reputation that rivalled Miguel's. However, Miguel was very much in control going into the third round.

Boom! Out of nowhere, Miguel was knocked down in a daze. Sergei had jabbed, jabbed again, and then stepped back, preparing to throw a big right.

Miguel dodged and slipped in for his own attack, but it was too late — he was in Sergei's range, about to take a massive counter. Miguel had fallen for it.

He took the full blow on the temple, his legs buckling immediately. He was down, and the referee was just about to wave it off on the count of two when Miguel regained his senses. As he pushed himself up, the countdown stopped.

In those few seconds, Miguel found the will to bring himself back fully in the moment and was lucid enough to continue. He stared resolutely into the referee's eyes and raised his gloves.

"I'm okay," he said. The official nodded and allowed the bout to continue.

Sergei, sensing blood, stepped on the gas with a flurry of blows, which Miguel defended well. Sergei was putting so much into a finish that wasn't happening, and he was tiring. Miguel sensed an opportunity; he came at the Russian hard, pushing him back onto the ropes and teeing up huge right hands with his jab.

In his confusion, Sergei didn't know how Miguel would follow up: with another jab, a straight right, or a right hook followed by a left hook. The body shots hurt, and the head shots were huge, but not getting all the way through.

However, Miguel was regaining his wits at precisely the right time. He took a step to the left, spun clockwise on that foot, and hit Sergei with a massive left hook before he knew what was happening. Sergei tried to defend with his right glove, leaving a gap that Miguel promptly exploited, his powerful straight right going in with all his weight behind it.

Sergei took the full force of that punch and crumpled to the floor. This knockout was one that he couldn't come back from. Sergei was planted face down for more than ten seconds before he was back on this planet, and it would be a further fifteen seconds before he had control of his legs and knew where he was.

However, the referee had already waved it off as soon as he hit the canvas.

Miguel was through, and the Cuban team celebrated. But soon, their attention turned to the finals.

Three days later, he was fighting an Irishman named John Hughes. Every move in this fight would be a chess match; when two very skilled fighters came face to face, it was a game of inches. As part of the dance, every move was efficient and specifically crafted. They could even be setting something up for much later in the fight by reading their opponents, playing with their expectations, and then switching it up. It only took one mistake or stroke of genius to make or break a fight.

And until midway through the second round, that's exactly what this fight was like: cagey.

Miguel was reading something in Hughes: every time he did a one-two jab and right hand, Hughes would immediately counter. Miguel felt if he did a double jab at the right time, Hughes would momentarily be flummoxed, expecting the right and getting stiffed with a jab down the middle instead. Then, a follow-up right hook could be very much in play.

But Miguel didn't know the wily Irish man was a step ahead of him. He was making this predictable move because he knew that, at some point, Miguel would double jab and try to launch something on the third punch.

He was totally focused, anticipating the double jab. But, as soon as he saw a second jab coming, he parried it and slipped away from the oncoming hook and launched an overhand left at Miguel's unguarded jaw.

Miguel was stung and stumbled to the floor. He was hurt, but not like in the last fight. Instead, he sprung up and took a count of eight as the referee studied him before resuming.

Being a proud fighter, Miguel somewhat lost his composure after being knocked down. He started chasing Hughes in a flurry of knockout attempts, but he was uncharacteristically loading up too much. A skilled boxer could see those punches coming a mile away.

Miguel threw a thunderous overhand right, but it met Hughes' left glove. He was tiring from throwing such big shots, and he'd left himself open. Hughes put a right hand straight down the pipe, smacking Miguel on the left side of his face and leaving him disoriented. Another sharp left hook put him down for the second time.

But Miguel recovered quite quickly. With only twenty seconds left in the round, he made it back to his stool. His coaches were frantic, telling him in quick-fire Spanish that he had to compose himself and keep boxing, that he was going to lose unless he stayed calm and waited for a knockout punch. With two knockdowns against him, there was no other way.

Hughes would know this too and would most likely fight a very technical and conservative last round to stay away from trouble. The odds were very much against Miguel.

The bell rang for the third and final round, and each fighter stepped towards the centre. Miguel resolved to wait for his opening, hoping he could execute a perfect punch when the time came. It was his only hope.

Miguel breathed deeply, entering a focused state. He knew he could find his chance if he cleared his mind.

Hughes tended to drop his left hand just after a combination. It wasn't much, but if Miguel could exploit that tendency, he could create an opening. He hadn't used a body jab yet, so if he threw that punch, it just might throw Hughes for a second and give Miguel the opportunity he needed. But Miguel wanted to create a flurry so he could execute this move in close quarters when it wasn't telegraphed. There would have to be some chaotic back and forth first.

In the second minute of the round, he stepped in and upped the pace; jab, right cross, left hook; a classic combination, but with enough venom that it had to be defended against, and it pushed Hughes back. Hughes stepped laterally to his right, but Miguel expected it, as he'd been doing it the whole fight.

Miguel was ready — he intercepted Hughes straight on and forced him back onto the ropes. He piled in with some body shots and uppercuts, and soon, Hughes was turtling up and trying to get some pot shots in.

Miguel stepped back and then pounded another jab and cross combo to stop Hughes from getting off the ropes or throwing a good combo back. But Miguel still hadn't done any real damage. It was just a good flurry. However, it was just what he needed to outsmart Hughes.

No sooner had Miguel finished that combo when Hughes fired something back in the chaos — followed by the predictable drop of his left hand. Miguel, wanting to increase his opening, jabbed Hughes' left ribs, getting in under the elbow and forcing him to drop his whole arm.

Ready for his split-second opening, Miguel's right hook was already in motion, swinging from his hip with the full force of this muscular body behind it. It would have knocked out a heavyweight.

Bang! The punch landed against Hughes' temple with a thud that echoed all around the ring. Hughes' legs stiffened, and he went over like timber crashing to the deck.

For a shocking moment, everyone in the audience was flabbergasted. Then they realised what had happened — all of a sudden, they were jumping around, shouting their praises for one of the greatest knockouts they had ever seen. Meanwhile, the ref was waving the fight off as finished. Hughes was out of it, but he managed to stand. He would be alright, though thoroughly disappointed. And he'd have to admit that he had been bested.

Miguel Vasquez had won the gold medal for Cuba!

His team, the trainers, and the coaches that had nurtured him since he was young were ecstatic. They could barely hang on to their hats, and the champagne was already flowing into mouths and over heads. After raising Miguel's arm to signal his win, they put him up on their shoulders.

His smile was wide as he raised his wrapped fists to the sky. This was the photo that would beam back home and adorn newspapers worldwide; this was the biggest, highest, and greatest moment of Miguel's life. He came home to a hero's welcome.

The high continued for weeks. However, despite the brilliance of his achievement, the reward felt fleeting to Miguel, as the realities of life hadn't really changed. It started to hit him hard. He was an Olympic gold medallist, but he was still on twenty dollars a week like everyone else. *This is bullshit*, he thought.

At first, Miguel had only sought a way to hold his own, get back at the bullies, and become respected in his community. As a kid and teenager, that was what success meant to him. But beyond that, he hadn't worked out a full plan. He had seen crime as another avenue, but being young, he didn't need wealth in those years; he just wanted to build his ability to fight and be the baddest guy around.

However, now he was turning twenty. He had become a great fighter and won respect, but he was still broke. To the real players in the city, he was only slightly above a bum in social status. Miguel, ambitious as he was, wasn't going to stand for this.

Though Cuban athletes could compete professionally, they had to remain on their stipend from the Cuban government. That certainly didn't appeal to Miguel. But the only other option was to become a citizen of another country, fight under their flag, and pay that country's taxes. It was not ideal for a patriotic Cuban, but he felt he had no choice.

Miguel was going to defect to the United States of America. Sometimes, the Cuban amateur boxers went to events in the US, and it just so happened there was one coming up in a few months in Texas. So, Miguel began to plot.

He went to the tournament and competed, winning the welterweight category. Everything seemed to be proceeding as normal, but when the Cuban team was boarding the plane to go home, Miguel was nowhere to be seen.

He had passable English and found a way to sell his Olympic gold medal for a few thousand dollars — that would give him enough for a fresh start. He knew it was worth a lot more, but he wasn't in a position to haggle, and the owner of the Pawn City Shop knew that. Though Miguel had no way of knowing what became of his medal, the pawn shop owner would later auction it for thirty-five thousand dollars to a rich man who wanted it on his wall collection of sports memorabilia and valuables.

Miguel had enough to put a deposit on a one-bedroom apartment and begin looking for a job. Apart from boxing, he was very good at fixing cars; he'd done that on the side in Cuba when he wanted to earn a bit more, so that was how he started his search.
He was quickly brought on for a trial position at a local garage. When he walked in, the owner said, "We're very short-staffed and have a car lot full of engines that need repair before selling them. We also turn away car owner repairs everyday because we don't have enough time or workers." He threw a pair of overalls and a towel at Miguel and said, "Get to work, kid. If you do well, you'll get the job."

Miguel got three cars back up for sale, and because of him, the shop didn't turn away one customer all day; he took the easy jobs, like fixing lights, wheels, and wipers, freeing up the more experienced mechanics for heavier repairs.

Before the day had ended, Miguel had a new job.

Now he just had to find a gym to continue training after work. He had a look around, chatted with some locals, and found one that seemed to fit the bill: Viper Gym. They had trained some top fighters in the past, like Earl Graham and Willy Handeras, who had both become world champions. It would be a great fit.

The trainer there was Tom O'Reilly, and he was only too delighted to welcome Miguel into his stable. He knew exactly who he was, of course, and felt he could make it to the top in the pro game. So Miguel began training at Viper, and it was immediately clear how classy the Cuban boxer was. The younger fighters marvelled at his technique, rhythm, and power.

By day, he continued working in the garage. It was a tough regime, but Miguel had his eyes on the prize.

One day, a boxing promoter named Roma Reinhart approached him during his training with an exciting proposal: he wanted to set up a fight with a journeyman from Philadelphia, John Thomas, and he'd pay Miguel in cash and get him on the fast track to a Green Card. It was just too good to turn down.

So, Miguel accepted, and after a simple eight-week camp, he knocked John Thomas out in round three.

But Miguel wanted more, and he was impatient. Though he knew it would take a good three years to take on the big names and get paid well, he demanded big-name fights immediately after this first win, much to his promoter's chagrin; it was bad for business, he said, to rush into those fights without a reputation. No one would take him seriously.

Roma was wily. He had on his signature suit and a pencil cigar in his mouth when he met Miguel to talk about his next opponent. Taking a puff from his thin Havana, he said in his trademark Polish accent, "Friend, I can put you in with Crawford or Mayweather now, but they'll probably school you. A loss like that, and your record will have to be rebuilt. It's not advisable technically or financially."

Miguel didn't like it, but he understood. Like every other boxer, he knew how the game worked: you go slow, develop your skills for the pro game, and eventually reach a fight where someone's O has to go. It sells, and if you lose, at least you got paid; you'd only have one loss, and you can rebuild with easier fights and have a crack at big fights again.

As Roma put it: "If you go straight to the top too early and lose a few, no one knows that you aren't a bum. You get me, kid?"

"Yes, I understand, sir," said Miguel. But he was growing tired of working fifty hours a week and training late.

Other things were going on behind the scenes. One of the mechanics at work spun the clocks on cars in his spare time and got Miguel in on it. They were making five hundred dollars per car with only minutes of work — they could each manage to do five cars per month without getting tracked. Best of all, it was pure cash, straight into his pocket.

The police were only interested in the bigger players, if they were interested at all. Truthfully, the police were also involved in such ventures, but the criminal mechanics still had to be wary of the honest cops or the competitors in blue.

Despite the risks, he loved the thrills and the instant cash. Boxing wasn't giving him that adrenaline rush anymore, and even if he got to the top, a hit like this would only come along a few times a year. If he was built to be a champion, he would stick at it. But that notion was becoming more and more questionable. As good as he was, there were no guarantees he wouldn't be injured and forced to quit. It was a dicey game. Maybe it wasn't worth it.

There was a darkness in Miguel; he didn't care much if he used it for good or bad.

The discipline and art of boxing had kept him, by and large, on the straight and narrow until now. His coaches in Cuba referred to the Bible, laminated a particular passage on a card, and had him keep it in his wallet and read it everyday:
"No temptation has overtaken you except what is common to mankind. And God is faithful; he will not let you be tempted beyond what you can bear. But when you are tempted, he will also provide a way out so that you can endure it.
1 CORINTHIANS 10:13"

The day before he met Priscilla, Miguel had already thrown it in the bin, so she couldn't be wholly blamed for the direction Miguel took in his life.
He was going that way anyway.

Priscilla arrived at the garage one day wearing white hot pants and a pink top, her blond hair wrapped and pinned in the most alluring way. All the mechanics were struck by her beauty; they winked at each other when she wasn't looking.

Since everyone else was busy with urgent work, Miguel, the lowest-ranking employee, was appointed to take care of her. He was fully aware of how attractive she was, but Miguel was a cool customer. She was actually the one expending more effort to control her nerves.

But Miguel was used to that. Ladies had been known to lose the run of themselves around him, unable to resist his long, dark hair, high cheekbones, and deep-set brown eyes. The environment and uniform helped, too: the tank top he was wearing accented his muscles; the oil and grease covering his dark skin made him look tough and capable.

"What can I help you with?" Miguel asked with his Hispanic accent, smiling politely and cleaning his oiled hands with a used white cloth.
Priscilla turned to him, flicking her hair despite it already being in place, clearly impressed by the specimen in front of her. "I need to get my front left headlight fixed."

Miguel didn't reply; he just went straight to work. "Can you open the hood, please?"

"Oh, sure," said Priscilla, opening the driver's door and pulling the lever to pop the hood.

Miguel went about fixing it in silence. He finished it off and checked it by flicking the lights. It was good to go. He walked past Priscilla without a word, though it was clear by her expression that she was expecting some pleasantries or at least an acknowledgement.

Thirty seconds later, he returned with a clean white cloth. With an easy, relaxed flick, he threw it at her. She wasn't expecting it but managed to catch it. "Here," he said. "To clean your hand." Priscilla had a small splotch of dirt on her hand where she had tried to get at the bulb herself before making a stop at the nearest garage.

"Thank you," said Priscilla, wetting the cloth with some water from her handbag and wiping her hands clean. "How much do I owe you?"

"Nothing," Miguel said. "It's just a small job." Since rich customers might come back with a bigger job and an even bigger tip, it was best to treat them on the small things.

"Oh, thank you," replied Priscilla, rather astonished that this guy didn't try too hard to impress her as most men did; at the same time, he treated her with unexpected care.

Of course, there was also her deep and instant physical attraction for this young hunk.

But Miguel was now ignoring her. He was busy checking something on his phone when she approached him and gave him her card. "If you ever want to service me, just give me a call," she said. He took a drag of his cigarette, flicked the hair from his face in the Texan heat, and smiled as he took it.

As she was reversing and pulling away, he returned to his phone and his cigarette as if nothing had happened.

That weekend, Priscilla got the call she was looking for. A few hours later, the boxer rolled into the estate house on his motorbike, the engine's sound filling the air with excitement and adventure.

As Miguel dismounted his bike and removed his helmet, he ruffled his hair with his fingers and shook it back to life. He wore grey jeans, black leather boots, and a black leather jacket with a blue Ralph Lauren sweater underneath.

Brad was peeking out the front window, admiring Priscilla's latest conquest; he wouldn't be making any requests, though, since he was still on probation after his recent incident. Besides, he didn't think Miguel would welcome such advances anyway.

Priscilla was utterly enchanted by him; she loved that the only entertaining he required before bed was a cold beer and a flick through the sports channels.

Aside from that, to say she enjoyed sex with Miguel was a colossal understatement. With every encounter, he sent a sensual rush through her body like no other man could; he made every part of her quiver with excitement and ecstasy. It was easy for him to make her orgasm, and he was damn good at it — he could bring her to that blissful ecstasy multiple times a night for every night they spent together.

Miguel had a power over Priscilla that no one else — apart from a few evil families that ran the deep state — had.

That power came in very handy when he got caught clocking too many cars and landed himself in Cafford Jail. He rang Priscilla to tell her he wouldn't be able to see her this week; when she asked why, he'd been released on bail within thirty minutes. Charges were dropped the next day.

Now, realising the influence she wielded, Miguel became even more captivated by this attractive older woman.

He was back working in the garage the next day, but as part of the agreement for the charges to be dropped, he had lost his side-hustle of clocking cars. His colleague at the garage was none too pleased he had gotten greedy, going through twice as many cars as usual. However, the attention hadn't been brought to him, so he was still under the radar. Even if Miguel ignored Priscilla's request, they wouldn't bring business to a marked man.

Miguel was now without his side hustle, and without the thrill it provided, he was bored and broke — not a good combination for a man of his temperament.

Within a week, he had cracked. Miguel walked into a convenience store with a balaclava over his head and a gun in hand, shouting for everyone to get on the ground and the teller to give him all the takings for the day.

It gave him the nice twenty-five hundred dollars he was missing out on this month, and, like clocking cars, it only took five minutes. *That was easy*, he thought. Until he heard a siren and a police car pulling up outside his apartment block. Before he could get inside and count the cash, he was body slammed against a police car, cuffed, and thrown in the back.

Little did he know some of these new cash registers have a chip code on one of the notes to track a robbery.

He called Priscilla.

After a scolding over the phone and a police station coffee, Miguel was back in her bed within the hour. There was a bit more paperwork for the police to do with this one, but she had once again secured his freedom. Priscilla made it very clear that this was the last time — she wasn't going to bail him out again for his side hustles and silly adrenaline rushes. But because she knew he was an ambitious thrill seeker and, more importantly, because she didn't want to give up the sex, she presented a win-win situation.

She told him to continue his day job and work for her on the side. There would be no clocking cars, no robberies, or anything else — he was only to work in the garage and for her, and he would be very well compensated.

He agreed.

His first job was to intimidate friends of Lucas, the man Brad had murdered in cold blood. He began tailing them, finding where they lived, and throwing bricks through their windows. Eventually, he waited until they were walking alone in the dark, stuck a knife to their throats, and told them to keep their mouths shut.

As fearful as they were, Lucas' friend Marcus kept pressing on. So the next task Priscilla had for Miguel was to get all of Lucas' friends to back off entirely.

Priscilla placed a hit on the journalist so he could never publish his book. And she would get Miguel to do it.

Miguel followed him into a quiet parking lot and parked beside him. As the journalist got into his car, Miguel came up from behind and shoved a cloth doused in chloroform over his face to render him unconscious. He threw him in the back of an old Cortina from the garage with fake registration, brought him down a back road, and waited for him to come around. Miguel beat him for over seventy minutes before shooting him point-blank in the head.

He tortured this man to death.

The worst thing about Miguel was that he enjoyed hurting people. The thrill of doing something morally corrupt and getting paid very handsomely to do it was intoxicating to him. And he couldn't get enough of it.

Chapter 6

Geoff had time to stop for a coffee before making his way to Martha's place. Nowadays, even having a quiet coffee in town would mean him having to smile at many passers-by who recognised him — no such thing as a shitty day for politicians when they're out in public.

He made his way to Martha's home in the suburbs, arriving a few minutes early. It was a quaint, pale-red, detached house with steps up to the front door and a white picket fence all around its perimeter. The property was narrow, but it boasted a substantial garden out the front and back. All in all, it was a typical home in the American suburbs.

Martha's two boxers came running out from the backyard to greet him. Despite their energy and power, they were well trained and friendly; Martha had total control over them. After they said hello by sniffing and licking Geoff, they pulled back at Martha's command.

"Beautiful dogs," said Geoff.

"They are," replied Martha, "when they behave themselves." She laughed and reached out to hug him. "Come here, you!" Geoff appreciated her warm embrace, throwing his arms around her in return; her non-judgemental presence alone helped Geoff feel more at peace.

"Come inside," she said, ushering him into her home. The entrance hallway was narrow with a wooden floor and a knitted rug that wove red, green, and brown together.

She brought him into the medium-sized sitting room, and they sat on the grey couch adorned with a red throw that matched the cosy red carpet beneath their feet. A fluffy cream rug lay under the glass coffee table before them, and across the room, the old fireplace was accented with unique crystals and ornaments resting on its mantle.

"Now, tell me what's going on," Martha asked, fixing him with a loving, concerned face.

"How much do you know about The Free Masons?" asked Geoff.

"Enough to know they are Satanic," replied Martha.

"Good, this conversation will go a lot smoother then," said Geoff with a look of impending horror on his face. "They control the very fabric of society, Martha. All the top dogs are in it. It's a network of secrecy to have power over every facet of what we call the system: bankers, lawyers, judges, politicians, doctors, and executives from every industry at a high enough level... They're almost all involved. A vast majority of the powers that be are plain evil, and the remaining few are making the best of a horrific situation." He looked at Martha, hoping she would understand.

"I know what you're talking about, Geoff. I've been awake since I was sixteen years old. I can see this in the structures of society. What happened that forced you to see all this?"

"I saw paedophilia going on. They didn't even try to hide it from me," Geoff recalled with disgust and disbelief. "And they're obsessed with this drug, adrenochrome. They tried to get me to drink a child's blood."

"I've heard about all of that. They are Satanists — literally! It's all sacrifices and other sick practices. They get the adrenochrome from torturing a child. Just before they die, the adrenaline shoots into their body to create adrenochrome in the blood. When they extract this blood from a child, it gives them youth and a huge high. They are deeply addicted to it," said Martha.

"Jesus Christ..." Geoff exclaimed at the thought.

"This is what's being hidden from normal people," added Martha. And Geoff agreed.

"I had a meeting with Priscilla before I came here — the Mayor's wife who got me into this," he began. "They told me I'm no longer in the Free Masons because I wouldn't go along with it. They threatened me to stay quiet, that if anything came back to me, I'd end up in a shallow grave. I tried to counter that by adding some insurance, telling them I have a friend I've spoken to about this, and he could bring disclosure if anything happened to me… but they aren't afraid of that. They have access to the TV stations and newspapers as well — we all know that. Look at how they handled the media during this Coronavirus bullshit.

"I'm basically stuck until the end of my two-year term. I have to keep my head down and go through the motions, not rock any boats. What can you advise me on? What path do you think I should take?"

Martha looked at him earnestly and said, "Geoff, once you've woken up, there's really no going back. I'm not telling you to do this or that or not to finish your term. However, you will need to improve your understanding of yourself and your connection to the source because this is all a spiritual war. It's coming to a head in these times. So you must remove all fears, conditioning, and noise from your heart. Then you will know what to do. A connection to God and a lack of fear will protect you from the dark entities. You will be on a different level. That's what they really fear: those who don't fear them.

"When people say God-fearing, it's actually not a truthful statement. A person with a relationship with God respects Him but doesn't fear Him. They understand God is light and love and walks with Him. God is a metaphor — it's just easier for some to relate to thinking of it personified.

"I'm going to give you several things to study and practice to form the foundations of your daily routine going forward. And I want you to keep in touch with me every week; more often if you like. Ask me anything. I'm always here for you," Martha said lovingly.

"I'm going to do a session with you today — I'll do an auric clearing to get you started. They're great for facilitating healing and teaching people about energy in and around their bodies, even in areas they may not know. But at some point, these journeys have to be taken from one's own centre, from your own heart. That's the only way to truly know God — or the Universe, or whatever you want to call it — and your purpose here in this lifetime."

Martha asked Geoff to stand beside the couch as she proceeded to do a session of touching acupressure points and chakra centres. She told him to breathe deeply and imagine himself being enveloped in white-gold energy.

She did this for about ten minutes before they sat down again. "That will give you a flavour and a feeling for letting go of blockages and fear, to feel your level go higher," she told Geoff.

"There are many ways to do this, but you must tune into your heart and know where your energy and emotions are. You'll start to gain control of your focus then. You've had a huge amount to deal with in the last twenty-four hours, so I'm not going to give you any more today. Just go home, rest and come back in the morning; then, we'll have more to discuss."

Martha was truly gifted; Geoff had so much noise running through his head, but she had somehow set him free of his bigger fears, and he slept like a baby. The mental stress weighed on him, but his heightened awareness threatened to induce a tired and wired situation where he wouldn't sleep a wink.

Thanks to Martha, he got a good seven-hour sleep before he rose at 8 o'clock and went through his routine. Though still rattled, at least he had a wise mentor to lean on now — not one that would guide him into horrible places like Priscilla.

Geoff arrived back at Martha's by 10 o'clock in the morning, ready and willing to listen. He knew he was in the right place.

"Come in, Geoff," Martha said as she welcomed her favourite 'nephew' back into her home, bringing him into the sitting room. "So, how are you feeling?"

"I slept pretty well, but there's still a lot going on in my head," Geoff answered.

"Of course there is," said Martha, "but that's what I'm going to talk to you about today. There's a routine I learned from a Heyoka Wiseman named David Ian Rogers that I think will serve you well."

"Okay," replied Geoff, wondering what it might be.

"Simplicity is genius when you have it spot on. This man showed me simple questions that can illuminate how the mind actually works." Martha studied Geoff to be sure he was still following.

"You tune into the memories, thoughts, emotions, or traumas troubling you. The more of those things you bring into awareness, the quicker it will work; but if you only have the feeling, that's okay too.

"Then you simply ask, 'Is this interesting, yes or no?' and say 'no'. The mind won't hold onto something you have consciously declared isn't interesting. But for deeper matters, you also need to do a few more things to break it up.

"In that case, the next question is, 'Do I want to clear it, yes or no?' and say 'yes'.

"The last bit is to make some funny sounds," Martha finished, blowing a raspberry. Geoff laughed. "It's great that you're laughing," said Martha. "That will work even better."

"Now," she said, resuming her explanation of the technique, "think: did the sound I just made make any sense to you? And you say 'no.'

"As crazy as it seems, that is how the mind works. A lot of the monkey mind is crazy, and it's not even from us. It's from outside conditioning, often suggestions or ideas from formative years that we were too young to understand. So that's why we have to approach it on the same level.

"Now, the last part is to put your right hand on your belly and take five deep breaths through the nose, holding at the top of the inhale for a moment before exhaling. Just follow your breath."

Geoff was feeling a little embarrassed to be doing this kind of stuff, but he trusted Martha, so he went with it. First, Martha asked him what was bothering him the most at the moment, knowing the probable answer.

"I fear that those Free Masons and Priscilla want to ruin my reputation. Or even kill me."

"Okay," said Martha, "let's tune into that fear and all the thoughts that go with it." So she asked him the same questions from before, and Geoff dutifully answered each one. She then took him through the breathing exercise.

"How do you feel now?" Martha asked once they had finished.

"I feel a bit better, but there's still a lot of it there."

"Okay, no problem. Let's go through it again for what is still there."

When they had finished repeating the exercise, Martha asked, "And now?"

Geoff was visibly more relaxed. "I feel much better, but there's still a little bit there."

"Okay, let's go again," said Martha, starting the process over.

As soon as Geoff had finished the breathing exercise for the third time, he said, "I feel clear now. I don't have that fear. I know things will work out and I feel protected."

"Beautiful," said Martha. "Now you are discovering deeper truths and your own power.

"The power is with you. All you have to do is stay clear of noise and fear by clearing it, helping others, and striving to take steps towards your goals. The Source will protect you, and those in line with Source will protect you.

"By working on removing discordant energy and fear from your mind and soul, you will be able to clear your mind. But be aware of yourself and keep tuned into your thoughts to stay on track."

Geoff replied, "That's amazing. I feel so much calmer and clearer. It really works."

"Yes, it does," said Martha, proud that she had helped. "Now, the important thing is to stick with it. Avoid everything fear-based: no people or entities can attach to you unless you hold negative energy."

"I have a question."

"Shoot."

"Can you do this in your mind? Like when you're in public?"

"Yes, of course," said Martha. "Furthermore, for smaller thoughts and on the go, you can just ask, 'Is that interesting? And say 'No', and it works brilliantly. For deeper things with stronger emotions, do the full process."

"That's brilliant. And simple," added Geoff. "As you go and live your life, you will see things from new perspectives, from a position of truth and strength, no longer shackled by unhelpful fears like most people. Stay grounded in your truth, and you'll find good things and people will come to you simultaneously. It will give you faith that you are walking in the right direction. Remember to be compassionate to good people that are still asleep — they are stuck in fear."

"I will," said Geoff, hoping what he was being told was true. "I have to go back to work to catch my meetings. Thank you so much." He gave Martha a heartfelt hug and left her house feeling renewed.

He drove into work, already optimistic about his new direction in life.

As he went through his emails, he found messages from concerned constituents about the Coronavirus situation, but he was reading them in a new light. He felt the Covid-19 agenda had always been fraudulent — he'd been in the empty hospital wards at the height of the so-called pandemic in 2020, seen how the media had been arm-wrestled into repeatedly broadcasting what they were told to say and to repeat it every five minutes on every channel.

Most importantly, he'd seen how certain tech companies were running fact-checkers funded by people with huge stock in Big Pharma.

Geoff saw how many false positives there were — they ramped up testing, so anyone that died after testing positive was recorded as a Covid death. Watching all this from the inside, he knew it was probably just a bad flu, and the pandemic scare was really about covering another financial crash.

However, now that he was in a higher vibration, he noticed even more. Geoff was checking out links people were sending him, like ones outlining how data analysts had found that overall deaths of any cause were the same in 2020, but in 2021 were much higher, including large spikes in specific age groups after the vaccine rollouts. Other analysts were finding that the highest vaccination rates in the country were also the places with the highest new infection rates in the country. You couldn't make it up.

He rang three separate virologists and a couple of immunologists and they all said the same thing, "none of this really makes sense and we've yet to see verified isolated samples of covid-19, but if we speak out we could lose our jobs."

So he not only knew a lot of fishy stuff was going on, but he was also figuring out the exact details, going deep into rabbit holes as to why this was happening to ultimately find a firm conclusion about the way forward.

When he found information on the Great Reset and the New World Order, it suddenly made a lot of sense.

Geoff had also discovered that the Federal Reserve was privately owned by the Rothschild family; while he was in The Free Masons, he had been told they were near the top of the organisation.

The Federal Reserve had been printing money not backed by anything for over a hundred years and charging interest on its return. One didn't have to be a rocket scientist to work out what that meant: a debt slavery system with repeat crashes creating an ever-widening gap between rich and poor. The spiralling debt would continue until it was so out of control that the fiat currency system would completely collapse worldwide.

"*That's* what this is all about!" Geoff said out loud to himself in his office.

He called Martha immediately. When she answered the phone, he said, "I know what's going on with the worsening state of affairs in the world."
"The Great Reset," she replied without missing a beat.

"Yes, exactly," said Geoff, still reeling from his epiphany. "Can you tell me more about this?"

"Well, I could," Martha began. "But to be honest, there are people far more up-to-date on the details and better at explaining it than I am. I'm going to give you the phone number of a man called Michael Clarke. He's ex-CIA, a very sharp operator, and he's been studying this for a long time."

Michael Clarke was a person you definitely wanted in your corner.

He was born in 1950 and raised in Cafford, Texas. His father was a military man, and his mother a housewife. It was a strict home; from a young age, Michael was expected to do extra chores alongside his schoolwork. But later in life, he would appreciate it because it gave him a focused and disciplined attitude.

Michael was always a very straightforward person. He had three interests that had never really changed: sports (mainly soccer), military missions, and cars; watching his dad working as a soldier and fixing up cars in his spare time certainly influenced that.

If he wasn't practising his skills with a soccer ball, he was playing 'Vroom Vroom' or GI Joe from as young as two years of age. When he was doing these things, his father would set him tasks, though, in his young mind, Michael often disregarded these to focus on his creativity.

But around age five or six, his dad had him learn the makes and models of all his dinky cars and had him name the cars when driving to places. It was a game they really enjoyed together, and Michael was getting very sharp at it; when he was messing around with military pieces on a battlefield, his dad would show him how to draw the enemy and surround them.

Michael always had a ball with him and constantly practised against a wall. Then, as he got to eight or nine, his dad gave him drills to do. He got him a ball on a string with a video of exercises from the Ajax Academy in Holland, and he marked targets on a big wall beside the field in the nearby park so Michael could practise hitting the targets. Finally, he would come home and give a score out of a hundred after ten shots and ten crosses at each one.

His dad also gave him a ball on a long elastic string he could anchor in a field to practise passing the ball, controlling it, and passing it again while it would rebound back to him. So Michael would do that on either foot, sometimes taking a touch or just passing it the first time, over and over.

And it paid off.

Michael joined a local club and was immediately the best player. When he played with his friends at the park, he played against teams with nearly twice as many boys to bridge the gap in their skills.

His technique was so precise that he was a cut above. In every underage game he played, he would take the ball past four or five players and finish by picking the right pass or shooting and scoring himself.

When he wasn't kicking a ball around, he was at school or fixing cars with this dad. Michael's father was a big car buff and loved restoring old classic cars. He would show Michael all the parts and how to take things out and put them back in, demonstrating how and why they worked together.

It was an excellent education about something Michael loved.

This was the routine outside of schoolwork or soccer. Michael's mom would make them sandwiches for lunch and traditional meals for dinner.

When Michael turned fifteen, he began playing for the Texas state under 16s. Of course, he was the stand-out prospect. Word had even gotten as far as Europe. Two of the big English clubs had US scouts in the crowd for the game between Texas and Florida, but they were only there to see one player.

The first half was a scrappy, tight, and cagey affair where Florida put all their energy into the game. They were pressing very high and not allowing the Texas midfielders any time on the ball.

So although Michael was doing okay, he couldn't show off his usual game. His touch was assured, but it was difficult, and he was often playing the ball sideways or back to avoid losing possession. He was calling for the strikers to make better runs in behind so he could pick his head up and try to find them.

After forty minutes, the Manchester United scout got up and left. He felt he had seen enough to know that this boy would never be good enough for United. Texas were 2-0 down, and the star man was indistinguishable from any other player.

Unfortunately, he left prematurely, and a few elements in the second half brought Michael to life. First, the Florida team's constant pressure dropped off, giving him more time on the ball. Second, his team started making far better options for him. Third, his coach told him to take control of the game — if a pass forward didn't always work out, so be it, but make the right passes instead of being cautious.

In the second half, Michael played like a mixture between Andrea Pirlo and Carlos Valderama. He was sensational. Everything good Texas did came through him: he setup two goals and scored a screamer from outside the box to win the game 3-2.

When he was heading for the tunnel, Micky Villenovas, the Tottenham scout, was waiting for him.

"Hello, Michael," he said in a Floridian accent. "I'm with Tottenham Hotspur. Can I have a word?"

Michael was awestruck and said, "Yeah."

"You were brilliant out there, son. Can you come over next month for a trial with us in London?" asked Micky.

"I'm sure I can; I'll just have to talk to my parents," replied Michael.

"Of course. Tell them to give me a call at this number, and I'll answer all of their questions."

"Great," Michael said with a relaxed smile. He was a kid that didn't get too up or down; nothing really flustered him, so it was easy to keep his composure. In fact, his level-headedness was part of why he was such a good player.

Michael's parents arranged for him to fly to London in five weeks to spend a week on trial at Tottenham Hotspur. The flight and accommodation would all be paid for by the club.

After three weeks passed, Michael was still playing very well. He was a dominant force in the centre of the pitch.

Then he had a game against a team of New York City youths. The game was moving along and into the fourteenth minute when disaster struck. It was a 50-50 ball, and Michael and an opposition player were both going for it.

Michael planted his right leg on the turf beside the ball while simultaneously turning towards it for a kick. But his foot got stuck in the ground, his leg twisting and crunching with the movement, ligaments snapping. As the other player went for the ball, they collided, compounding the damage. It was hard to know if the tackle was deliberately dirty or just mistimed. However, that was not the biggest concern.

Michael had torn his anterior cruciate ligament so severely that everyone on the pitch heard it. An ACL injury in the seventies was often career-ending, as surgical repair wasn't as advanced back then. The prognosis looked bleak.

Michael was not one to writhe around or show pain, but he was in such agony it was difficult to hide it.

The medics hurried onto the pitch and carefully wrapped his leg, placing ice on his knee before carrying him off the field in a stretcher. The other players wished him well, knowing he was in a lot of trouble.

In the days that followed, the extent of the injury became apparent. X-rays showed that his anterior ligament had a horrific tear, and not only that, but the medial ligament was also badly torn. He would need an operation in the next week and would be on crutches for six months.

So much for his potential move to London.

The surgery went well, but even a good recovery would probably mean that Michael could never play soccer at the highest level. There's too much twisting and turning on a soccer field, and he wouldn't have the full capacity in that leg.

Despite those difficulties, he came back to playing eight months later. But Michael was a shadow of his former self. He was compromised. He could still play at the youth level and could likely hold his own at the collegiate level, but he wasn't going to Tottenham, that was for sure.

For a while, he was devastated. He grieved for weeks over the loss of his future soccer career; months ago, he was sure he would eventually play in huge matches in the English first division and European competition.

His dad helped him through it, talking some sense into him by explaining a million reasons young players don't make it to the top; he was full of talent and could focus in another direction. And Michael knew just where to look: he loved the idea of a career in the Armed Forces, hopefully in special ops, as he longed for the excitement of missions.

Almost overnight, he had his inspiration and way forward again. It wasn't long before he regained his inner confidence. With a couple of years left in high school, Michael resolved to work extra hard on his exams.

He aimed to earn a Navy scholarship to get into an undergraduate degree while completing Navy training, enter the CIA academy (which requires a degree) and complete his education with the advanced Navy SEAL course.

Having this multi-faceted repertoire would give him a significant advantage in getting into special operations.

In his final year of high school, he applied for the ROTC Navy Scholarship program to do the Bachelor of Science degree course at Texas A&M University.

He passed his high school exams with top-class honours and was awarded the scholarship in the course of his choice. He was delighted, as were his parents. It would be a challenging four years ahead combining college work and the midshipman regime; the volume and hours involved were arduous. However, Michael had an outstanding work ethic.

As part of the scholarship, the Navy would also pay for his accommodation and give him a stipend of $35 a month, which was a very decent amount in those days. To keep up their end of the bargain, students were expected to do well in school and training.

Michael duly did that. He even found time to captain the college soccer team, training twice a week and playing matches on weekends.

Although he wasn't as good a player as before, he was still a high-level collegiate player and helped his team compete for trophies. It also helped him keep fit, which was a prerequisite for advancement in the midshipman course.

In the end, he completed both the degree course and Navy program with top class results.

This would help him with the next part of the plan: applying for the CIA academy. After reviewing his record and conducting a successful interview, Michael was accepted into the Central Intelligence Agency training program.

First, he had to go to their headquarters in Fairfax County, Virginia for eighteen months of training. And he loved every minute of it. Of course, it was far more about gathering and disseminating information, strategic planning, and mission operations than field training, but he still got a good bit of that.

They learned a lot of wild stuff: body language training, like detecting patterns in behaviour and communication; data analysis and how to set desired events in motion; undercover training for stealth missions, various weapon training, how to torture a captive enemy for information, surviving torture and lessons in how to take out a target cleanly.

Michael was in his element, and the extra challenge of this type of training brought the best out of him. He emerged as one of the stand-out graduates after a year and a half.

After a three-month summer break, he was ready to apply for the final part of his formal education: Navy SEAL training. To get the interview, he'd first have to pass the physical examination, but he wasn't worried. Though it involved rigorous swimming, running, and demanding bodyweight exercises, he knew his consistent activity regiment from his college days would see him through it.

As expected, he passed the fitness test without issue before impressing recruiters again in the interview.

Finally, he was accepted, and in September, he moved to the Naval Amphibious Base in Coronado, California, for another year of gruelling development to reach the elite standards of this famous unit. The physical Navy training dovetailed nicely with the more cerebral development of intensive CIA education. However, this was more about carrying out team missions, specialised training for dangerous marine/naval operations and peak physical performance.

Things got quite tasty in the Navy SEAL academy, especially when it came to Michael's superior, Captain Moore. He was an imposing six-foot-plus man with a larger than average head and a strong personality.

"Clarke, CIA stuff is a different game. You are a waste of space around here until you prove yourself as valuable to your fellow SEALs. When they have a gun to their head and you're their only way out, we have to know they can rely on you, you hear me?" the captain bellowed, getting up in Michael's face.

This reminded Michael of a worse process: CIA desensitisation training. During that uncomfortable exercise, he had a hairdryer blowing right into his face just before getting his head dunked into an ice bath.

"Sir, yes, sir!" Michael shouted back.

"Glad we have that clear," Captain Moore said in his thick Texan drawl. Perhaps he wanted to make it crystal clear that the CIA agent from the same state as himself wasn't going to get any favouritism whatsoever in the Navy SEALs. He quickly moved on, ready to find his next victim.

He used to tell them, "You may hate me, but I don't hate you. That's why I'm a son of a bitch to you, because if you ain't tough when you get out in the real world, you'll be coming home to your momma in a body bag, and I'll feel like I let you both down. I don't want to feel that. I don't want to be that asshole at your funeral, so you little vagina cubs better get right in line and do exactly what I demand of you. I will turn you into real men or women with balls — you understand?'

"Sir, yes, sir!" the Navy officers shouted back in unison, trying not to laugh at the captain's witty sense of humour. It was the seventies, and politically correct speech wasn't even close to being on the agenda in places like this, nor is it now.

Captain Moore wasn't just a hard-ass taskmaster; he was also a profound thinker. Every so often, he would give the SEAL trainees a deliberately erudite, articulate speech on something important:

"Political correctness is a form of censorship. It engenders group identity bullshit and a lack of personal responsibility, and it isn't conducive to building tough individuals! Besides, context and intent also matter, which are difficult to quantify.

"People like myself in higher performance areas would be loath to anything other than freedom of speech; to express oneself is to give oneself the facility to refine one's perceptions. This means you will not be subject to outside bullshit narratives. If you don't have the license to think and say what you want, how can you make a mistake and get better? How can you challenge nonsense in media and government? And how on earth could I make my satire jokes!"

The SEAL trainees laughed, but Michael listened keenly to the captain's experience and wisdom. "How can we be so insulting to the listener that they cannot be allowed to have their discernment?

"Well, that's why they engage in such lunacy. It's all of the above. To keep and increase the tiering of society by dumbing down the participants and having them fight among themselves. Well, SEALs cannot be sheep. SEALs have to be leaders — sharp and united. It's your job to serve the people, set an example for our future society, and protect the freedoms we have in the hope that there are greater days ahead."

Michael felt inspired listening to this, and it was written on his facial expressions and body language. The Navy SEALs in the seventies certainly weren't involved in creating rudderless operatives.

The first thing they did was measure how long all the trainees could hold their breath. It was somewhere between two and two-and-a-half minutes for most. "Not good enough for the SEALs!" Captain Moore shouted as he went through the results.

Michael held his breath for two minutes and forty seconds. He wondered if that was good enough.

But he'd get his answer soon because the captain wasn't finished.

"To give yourself the best chance of survival in low or zero oxygen, you need to be able to hold your breath for at least four minutes!"

Michael and others tried to hide their surprise and disbelief, but their eyes couldn't lie.

"How do we get to that point as quickly as possible? Well, super fitness will usually get you to two-and-a-half minutes plus; most of you are already there. But to get up to four minutes quickly, you'll also need held breath training. The body responds to the temporary extra CO_2 build-up by expanding the carotid arteries and pumping blood around faster to get rid of the waste gases. This is how you can hold your breath longer."

The SEALs were now starting to see a way to the goal and had more confidence on their faces.

"And the most effective way to train that quickly is to engage the mammalian diving response. The carotid expansion happens more powerfully when underwater, as even more circulation is shunted into the internal organs, including the brain, than just with the CO_2 carotid artery expansion! So within three weeks of daily training, you should be hitting four minutes and have those carotids expanded permanently, bringing more oxygen and nutrients to where they are needed and clearing wastes quicker. It will help you in more ways than the obvious."

With an exact strategy in place, the recruits were excited. After all, that's why they were here. When the captain asked if that was clear, they responded with a forthright, "Sir, yes, sir!"

He also had them start a regime of calisthenics training, with a clear progression of bodyweight training, starting with a high volume of the usual compound movements: push-ups, pull-ups, bridges and squats. As they progressed, so would the difficulty of the exercises. For example, in twelve months, they would be expected to be able to do at least fifty one-arm push-ups.

He put it to them like this: "The Russians proved you get a higher hormone response from moving your own body through space, and that you're also building coordination, balance, proprioception, and functional strength with these exercises. Herschel Walker was a useless athlete as a kid. But he became obsessed with bodyweight training; he never touched a weight and became one of the greatest football players ever. We've tested everything. We aren't against free weights, but if you aren't doing bodyweight exercises, you won't make it through the SEAL obstacle courses and complete your missions out in the field."

Michael subtly nodded his head in agreement as he listened.

"We use kettlebells because you can throw them around and use them at different angles. They're more like objects in the real world and are useful for many things, including high-intensity cardio."

Captain Moore put them through a five-kilometre run. Their times were measured, and they would have to get up to decent county race-level at least. Michael was fit enough to breeze through the run in a decent time; however, he had some pain in his injured leg almost all the way.

After several weeks of these runs, their ten-kilometre times would also be taken — again, they would need to be competitive at the county race level.
"You have to have exceptional stamina to be a SEAL. You have to be the best of the best!" shouted the captain.

Then he took them to the 40-metre dash and recorded their times. "We will train you in explosive plyometric exercises for running and practise these dashes," he said. "Getting stronger will help you go even faster. We want to see max effort and improvement on this score. There are times when a good dash as a SEAL will save a life."

The SEALs had their hands on their knees, exhausted after repeated all-out sprints.

Captain Moore then measured them for reaction time, balance, eye tracking, coordination and ambidexterity. Based on the results, they were then given an individual practice regime of twenty minutes a day to hone these skills.

He told them, "Foundational physical brain wiring has been proven not just to be important for these skills, but it also extends to many aspects of brain function like learning, focus, and performance of specific tasks."

Even on the first day, they were already learning so much. Michael, in particular, was listening with a keen ear to the captain's wisdom and knowledge. He was very open-minded to the innovation and progression of himself and others.

Over the next several months, military operation training, fasting, extreme hot and cold training, breath work, and meditation were also added to the mix. They had to be tough, to be survivors, to be mentally strong and in control.

This type of training gave them all the foundational abilities and tools to be a Navy SEAL. In the final months of the course, the curriculum became more focused on field training and missions.

Michael excelled, and the fact that he already had CIA training made him an excellent asset to the secret services. As a result, he got great assignments right away.

Near the end of SEAL training, he met his future wife, Diana Duplant. She was a beautiful girl of French descent with wavy brown hair, blue eyes, and a soft temperament. Within a year, they were already married, much to the happiness of Michael's parents — they were conservative and delighted he had settled down early.

The young couple loved one another very much; they were a perfect match.

Diana was a hairdresser, and after they were married, she went from full-time to part-time to create a wonderful home for her and Michael. As she was from a more traditional family, she loved homemaking and caring for her husband.

Michael would work two weeks on and two weeks off, undertaking many short missions worldwide. He worked mainly for the CIA but would abscond with SEAL units at times. His unique dual qualifications meant he was generally left free for complex short missions rather than pigeonholing him into one team or a long-term operation.

That suited him fine. In fact, it was how he wanted to work.

When people asked him what he did, he told them he was a detective. It was much easier to explain and meant he didn't have to bat away questions surrounding subjects he couldn't discuss.

He was also trained and adept at remote viewing, so he was often consulted for this type of work. Intelligence agencies worldwide know about the power of the mind to do things beyond the normal scope, and remote viewing allowed practitioners to see into timelines outside of the present and obvious.

In his time off, Michael relaxed by doing what he used to do with his father: fix up old cars. In fact, he often invited his father to spend hours in the garage working away at some banged-up old Cadillac or Chevy, and they both took great pleasure in getting it back to its former glory. Of course, they regularly sold them on for a hefty profit too.

Michael and Diana wanted to have kids, but after trying with no success, they decided to get checked out medically. Unfortunately, Diana discovered she couldn't get pregnant due to a malformation of her ovaries.

They were devastated, but with time, they began to consider other options. In the end, they decided not to foster or adopt. Instead, they settled into the upside of a quieter life, figuring it just wasn't meant to be. So when an operation of global importance landed on Michael's lap, he felt it would be an excellent time to take it.

The mission was to go to Argentina to 'hunt Nazis,' as his work colleagues put it. But it was a lot more subtle than that: it was an intelligence mission that may lead to capturing war criminals and putting them behind bars.

The assignment would begin in six months. Michael was already fluent in German from previous missions, so he spent the downtime studying Spanish, utilising the same advanced learning programs and techniques he used to learn German.

It wasn't long before he was on a plane to Buenos Aires and renting a car to drive to Bariloche. When he arrived, he was struck by the European architecture and city structure. *You'd almost swear the Germans and Swiss built it*, he thought to himself sarcastically.

It was common knowledge that Argentina became a safe haven for Nazis after World War II. President Juan Peron was a known Nazi sympathiser with close ties to Mussolini and other dictators; Juan Peron had even arranged routes called ratlines for the Nazis.

Interestingly, the Vatican signed the papers to allow their extradition. The Patagonian city of Bariloche was one of the most popular places of refuge for these characters. Dr. Mengele, who contravened the Nuremberg code with Aryan race experiments, had been there before relocating to Brazil. Infamous Commander Preibke worked in the city as a school principal when he was arrested in the early nineties, along with another Third Reich officer, Reinhard Kopps.

There were rumours that Hitler and Eva Braun had made it to Argentina, but these were never verified.

Michael had already found all of this out on his three-year mission to Argentina in the seventies. It had all been documented, filed and repressed by the CIA. This was the first red flag Michael noticed; it made him believe there was a network of individuals behind the scenes acting separately to the service of the people.

Michael knew this to be the case because many of his findings originated from the Vatican, the CCP in China, and other communist states like Cuba. The Nazis and the communists were ultimately one and the same — a full circle of left and right, ending up in a similar place. However, what was incredulous to him was that they had infiltrated American agencies.

JFK had made his famous speech on secret societies, that he wanted to go to gold-backed currency and smash the CIA into a thousand pieces.

As Captain Moore put it to Michael in private: "It's almost certain that he lost his life for these reasons and not as a result of a rogue individual or a patsy being masqueraded as the killer of a great president. It was no coincidence that his brother Bobby was also shot." Michael noted years later that the less famous Bobby Jr. also said the same things about the deep state in 2022 and was labelled a 'conspiracy theorist'.

So why did they send Michael to Argentina? Who knows, but the CIA didn't like the truths he came back with.

That led Michael down many rabbit holes in search of deeper truths. He wondered why it seemed that there was a deep state funding both sides of the wars.

During his three years of intense undercover work running a cafe in Bariloche he couldn't go home that often. He had to look legitimate and have an easy way to network in that city. A cafe owner was an ideal cover. But it also meant he could only go home every six months for a couple of weeks. No one in Argentina that ran a cafe went on four holidays a year, no matter how well they did.

The mission led to problems in his marriage, though. He found a great distance now existed between him and Diana, when before they were so close and in love.

When Michael was away, Diana was suffering from childless loneliness. So maybe Michael shouldn't have been so floored when, upon his return, she admitted she had an affair.

Diana begged for his forgiveness and tried to explain herself: she missed him so much, she was depressed, and things got out of control. Michael didn't know what to think.

That was the night he got drunk and spent the night on Martha's couch. He had to sort his head out. So he went to Austin the next day and walked the city, perusing the parks, buildings, and nature.

He knew he had to go home and forgive his wife. Military business was very hard on marriages, and he had to zoom out and take a bigger view. Diana still loved him, and he still loved her; she just made a mistake.

However, that mission would never leave him. And because of it, he began to investigate all manner of things.

When a mysterious virus started in 2019 and the studies surrounding it were fraught with inconsistencies, it only confirmed his suspicions that those behind the scenes were up to no good again — that they were funding a situation and an agenda.

He saw a pattern of the deep state accelerating their ideas, now more overtly moving into the Nazi playbook to take over with fear, emergency policies, propaganda, socialism, medical experiments, biomedical passports, and eventually social credit score systems. They worked in conjunction with the CCP and other deep state players like the Vatican and Cabal politicians worldwide.

However, Michael was about to gain an ally in public office.

Chapter 7

Geoff's phone pinged: it was Michael. He called back immediately. After some short introductions, they arranged to meet at Michael's house in the afternoon, just after Geoff's obligatory meetings.

If these meetings with the local council weren't mundane enough on a routine basis, with Geoff's new appreciation of the situation, he found the rote bureaucracy of these proceedings to be pure monotony. *A chimp could do this job; it's all a setup anyway,* he thought.

He was really looking forward to meeting Michael Clarke.

When the meeting was over, he got straight into his SUV and headed for Michael's place. He lived in a lovely suburb called Antler Grove; the houses were well made, each featuring unique designs and tasteful architecture. Michael's home had a slant roof with one side of the top floor higher than the other. There were decent-sized rooms in this six-bedroom house, only occupied by himself and his wife.

Michael welcomed Geoff at the door and said, "Pleasure to meet you, Geoff."

Michael was a tall, athletic, handsome man with a face that said he'd experienced more in his lifetime than some would in ten. Geoff immediately got the impression that Michael was also a man who would say no more than what needed to be said.

"Likewise," Geoff replied. As they stepped inside, Geoff suddenly felt more purposeful than he had in his entire life; the only thing that came close to this conviction and focus was organising the charity events.

The interior was old school fifties-style; the hallway had a stand-alone wooden coat hanger inside the door, cream carpeted floors, and an impressive picture of John F. Kennedy on the wall.

It was a no-fuss, uncluttered, organised home.

However, they soon moved into a more cluttered room: Michael's office. Two large bookshelves faced each other on opposing walls, and between them hung a large board of drawings, clippings, and images, like a detective's investigation centre. A desk sat just in front of it.

"Welcome to my office," said Michael without apologising for the bestrewed nature of the room; he knew it was a workstation, and he was confident in his ability to do great work.

"Take a seat." Michael ushered Geoff to sit on the swivel chair before his desk while taking residence on the seat behind it.

"I appreciate you coming here," he continued; his warm tone suggested he'd been waiting for more visits of this nature that hadn't yet materialised.

"I'm told you can give me answers," said Geoff with an air of curiosity and intensity that masked his excitement to be stepping onto new frontiers.

"I'll do my best," said Michael.

"I don't know how much Martha has told you about my situation, but I got into politics, as I'm sure you've seen, and then into the Free Masons," Geoff began. "As things progressed, I knew I had to wake up and get out. I've been looking into the situation, and there are many things I need help to understand."
Geoff paused to consider his words, then asked, "This is all a financial situation, isn't it?"

"Mostly, yes... the whole world is bankrupt," replied Michael with a Clint Eastwood-like grimace. Geoff interjected, "Because they've been printing money backed by nothing for a hundred years."

"Spot on," Michael responded, his voice tough and husky; Geoff suspected it was a by-product of a rough life spent building his character. "But the rabbit hole goes a lot deeper... and I'm guessing that's why you're here."

"It is, sir," Geoff said, respectfully waiting for Michael to continue.

"Before we go any further, do you want to carry this conversation on playing a quick six holes? Martha told me you're a member up in Oak River. I play in Millers Garden over this side of the city. I'd love to take you out there."

"Sounds great." Of course, Geoff was all for that. He loved to play golf and get out in the fresh air; it was why he always kept his clubs in the back of his SUV. Besides, it was probably an excuse to talk to a knowledgeable man for longer than they would in the office.

Meadows Garden was one of two exclusive country clubs in Cafford — the other being Oak River. It was upmarket, had fantastic facilities, and an excellent golf course.

As Geoff drove in the driveway to the clubhouse, he was reminded why it was called Meadow Gardens. The trees, flowering and manicuring of the grass were beautiful.

Michael was an index 3 player even at his age, and Geoff was a handy 12. Michael's long history of sports training and building his athleticism made him a coordinated, strong-bodied player, giving him an advantage over Geoff.

Over eighteen holes competition, Michael would give Geoff nine shots, but since it was only six holes, he was only obliged to give three. They put a friendly wager of buying dinner afterwards on the game, and Geoff got his extra shots.

The course was quiet today and the timesheet reasonably empty, so it was just the two of them playing together. They had serious matters to discuss, so the arrangement was ideal.

Michael stepped up first and cracked a ball 270 yards down the middle.

"Impressive," said Geoff; Michael's low index of 3 wasn't just a stat on the screen.

Geoff teed up, lining his shot left of the fairway to accommodate his customary slice. He hit his shot, and it started left but curved into the fringe on the right-hand side.

"Not bad," said Michael. "You are fine there."

Despite it being a decent shot, Geoff was 50 yards behind thanks to that slice-spin.

Michael had already noted that Geoff's grip was causing that left-to-right curve but hadn't yet decided if Geoff would be receptive to a tip. Some players weren't fond of unsolicited advice, only wanting it from a significantly better player, if at all.

"So, you were going to bring me further down the rabbit hole," said Geoff inquisitively.

"Yes, indeed," replied Michael. "A system of printing money backed by nothing is basically a glorified Ponzi scheme.

"Every country is constantly racking up debt. Do people even know where their taxes go? Well, it's mostly diverted into Cabal accounts and the many civil servants in an ever-increasing government to keep their scheme going. It's the banks and the lobbies that really control the government. And the more people they have working for the government or reliant on grants, the easier it is to control."

"Look who you're talking to," admitted Geoff. "No shit Sherlock," Michael joked in his gravelly voice and they both chuckled.

They hit their second shots into the green. Geoff hit one up just short of the green, and Michael clipped a ball into the center.

They discussed how fantastic the course conditioning was on the way to their balls. There was hardly a blade of grass out of shape; when down grain, the perfectly mowed lawns glimmered in the sun.

With his next well-placed chip shot, Geoff was in a decent position. And with his extra shot, he ended up taking a surprise win on this hole.

As they moved to the next one, the conversation continued.

"But the current government system gets worse," Michael went on. "Take a look at your passport." He gestured towards Geoff's golf bag, where he had left his wallet. Geoff rooted out his card passport, handing it over to his partner.

"See this, all caps... your name is in all caps, which signifies a corporation. So you are not a human, a living soul under this system; you are a corporation. And what is the significance of that?"

Of course, Geoff immediately knew the answer.

"They can carry out policy and actions on you based on your corporation status and get around your constitutional rights," Geoff explained. The whole picture was coming together more and more.

"Exactly," Michael said. "And they can do that because they are also a corporation. They can't do that as a constitutional entity, and they also can't do anything to you — whether they're a corporation or not — if you don't consent. You must consent to a bullshit contract with them."

The game went on, but Michael and Geoff both missed their birdie putts and knocked in three and four-footers for pars. Geoff had no shot here, so they halved the hole, and he remained one up.

They moved on to the third hole and hit their tee shots.

"What was your life like growing up, Geoff? Did you play sports?" asked Michael.

"I played some basketball and some golf, but I was never really serious about either," Geoff answered. "I was more into computer games. And when I got older, I also liked socialising, partying, and working part-time jobs."

"No surprise you ended up in insurance and politics then," said Michael.

"No, not at all," responded Geoff, making them both laugh.

"Martha told me you are very focused and not averse to hard work. Those are great traits to have," Michael continued.

"Thank you," replied Geoff, taking it as a hefty compliment from a man with Michael's credentials.

"Where do you see things going for you now in the political sphere?" asked Michael.

"I don't know. It's all up in the air," said Geoff. "I'm not playing their sick games. I'm going to fight for what is right for the people."

Michael was learning more about Geoff, and he was impressed by his conviction and integrity.

They reached their golf balls, which were sitting okay for the second shots. There was a large body of water on their left but plenty of room to lay up for the third shot to the green.

Luckily, Geoff's left-to-right shot curve took him back into the centre of the fairway. Michael was coming from the left rough and aimed down the right side of the fairway, hitting it straight with a slight curl from right to left, bringing him closer to the green than Geoff.

"The CIA must have been fascinating to be involved with, going on missions and that," Geoff said to Michael as they began walking again.

"It was indeed," replied Michael, his tone and facial expression hinting at the vastness of such experiences.

"It's very specialised and exciting, but it's also difficult and quite lonely. You go into very intense situations, and then you can't talk to anyone about it.

"For example, I went on a solo mission to Argentina to uncover the Nazi trails in the seventies. That's all fine, and I'm built for it, but then the CIA buried everything I found. That was the big wake-up call for me, similar to what you are going through.

"Then I found real intellectual loneliness; not only could I not talk about missions, but even the very fabric of what I was seeing was completely disconnected from what people think of as the reality of life. You are walking around among a herd of sheep, and they haven't a clue about the deep state, how everything is controlled, propaganda, media narratives, and all that. The cognitive dissonance isn't easy, but you learn to live with it."

"I hear you," replied Geoff, honoured that Michael trusted him enough to disclose things he normally wouldn't talk about.

Michael continued, "Let me tell how bad it is: they are creating these shootings when they need a big distraction and to further their agenda to dismantle the Second Amendment. They fear a civilian army revolting against their corruption. I would advocate better background checks for purchasing guns, but you have plenty of other countries with one gun per two civilians without these shootings. The three letter agencies drug up vulnerable people, mess with their mind for months, and then get them to do it. I'm also not even sure these things always happen — they may simply design and contract actors to be there, relocate everyone involved with new names and a very handsome income, and stage the whole thing. I've seen crisis actors that were in Syria suddenly appearing at school shootings. The mockingbird media are part of this Truman show. You have to question every detail."

"Nothing would surprise me at this point," replied Geoff. And despite the incredulity of those statements, he meant it.

Geoff hit his third shot to the green and leaked it a bit right, primarily due to the fear of the water that continued up the left side and behind the putting surface. Having more control and confidence, Michael got his ball within 10 feet of the pin.

"Martha is helping me through this process, mentally and emotionally" added Geoff.

"Yes, she is a sage; she's brilliant," replied Michael.

"She is indeed," Geoff concurred.

Now, Geoff was in a bit of a pinch. He had a bunker to get over to hit to the pin, but the shot he needed to accomplish this task was risky. He'd shoot straight into the water if he didn't slide the club perfectly under the ball.

Geoff committed to the shot regardless. He opened the blade of his lob wedge and took a big swing at it, but the contact wasn't brilliant. The leading edge hit the bottom quarter of the ball, but that was still high enough to send the ball screaming across the green, taking one hop before plunging into the lake.

Geoff giggled, and so did Michael. At least Geoff took it in good spirits.

In the end, Geoff salvaged a double bogey, though Michael won the hole, levelling the match.

They headed for the fourth hole; beautiful white, yellow, red and pink flowers surrounded the tee box as they took their shots down the fairway. Michael's landed in a nasty sand trap that Geoff managed to avoid, though Michael's ball was still closer to the green.

As they strode off the tee, Michael got back to talking about the law.

"All these acts, policies, and mandates — they're all obligatory only if you consent. But you don't have to consent or abide by anything that isn't in the Constitution. Maritime law was invented to declare the real you as 'missing at sea' and put a corporation straw man version of you on your birth certificate; that allows them to offer you all these Ponzi scheme tax and medical contracts to control and steal your real worth."

Geoff was listening keenly.

"These countries bastardised their common law constitutions into corporations of their own, which is the crux of the issue. These country corporations are all going bankrupt; they need a huge excuse, a distraction, and a reason to explain the mother of all crashes and a reset into an even more suffocating technocratic system of biological passports and digital currencies. Hence the Coronavirus," Michael said with an air of authority.

"Bingo," said Geoff as the larger picture came together in front of him.

As they reached Geoff's ball, he wasted little time, clipping the ball nicely onto the green about 15 feet away from the pin. Unfortunately, Michael was not in such a good predicament. He could only chip it out sideways, which he duly did.

His next shot connected nicely, but it wasn't far enough, settling 30 feet short of the pin. Michael putted up an inch short of the hole and Geoff hit his ball back to him. Geoff now had two putts to win the hole and go one up. He lagged his ball up to the cup, it almost fell in but just tailed off at the end.

"I'll give you that," said Michael as Geoff grabbed his ball. Geoff wouldn't have felt confident about winning a hole against Michael with no shot; it just shows how the game shakes out at times. Geoff was now ahead with only two holes to play.

But on the fifth, Geoff lost the run of his swing, which always resulted in a bad slice for him. He hit it into the right-hand trees. Michael teed up and boomed one down the middle. The ball hardly moved in the air.

"Can I give you a tip?" Michael enquired.

"Please do," replied Geoff.

"Strengthen your grip by holding the club more in the fingers and having the crease between your thumbs and index fingers point between your right ear and shoulder," Michael explained while demonstrating the technique. Geoff grabbed his club again and correctly placed his hands.

"Very good," Michael said. "Now, also swing more to the right; having a better grip will allow you to do that without hitting it too far off course."

"I'll try that," said Geoff, excited to utilize this new technique.

They found Geoff's ball in the trees, but it wasn't an easy one to extricate himself from. While trying to navigate through a small gap, he hit a branch and ended up behind a tree. Even after another hack, Geoff was still deep in the woods. Finally, he picked up his ball and conceded the hole.

Making his way back, Geoff dropped a ball on the fairway, eager to try out the new advice. Though he got the feeling of swinging to the right, he was actually swinging straight, and his new grip kept the face from opening. The shot wasn't the greatest, but it flew straight.

"See, that's much better," said Michael. Geoff agreed.

As they walked to the green, Geoff asked, "How is retirement treating you?"

"You never really retire from intelligence," replied Michael, "not if it's your passion. You'll always be looking to figure something out and piece a puzzle together, especially in times like this."

Geoff nodded. "Saw that in the office," he said, and they both smiled.

They hit a couple of putts each and moved towards the next tee and their final hole. Once again, they were square.

The final hole was a medium length par 3 with bunkers guarding the left and front sides of the green. The flag was on the back left. Michael hit first and pushed his ball out a bit, ending up on the right side of the green 30 feet away.

Geoff walked in between the tee markers, teed up, and took a few practice swings with his new grip. He would normally play a five-iron, but he felt he'd only need a six-iron if he got his new technique right. It felt stronger.

He addressed the ball, making sure his grip was spot on, and went to repeat the feeling of the practice swing. The ball clipped off the clubface perfectly, sailing straight towards the pin with a small draw from right to left. It settled down 2 feet from the hole.

Geoff was ecstatic; he'd never hit a ball so pure.

"You have my address. I'll expect a check in the mail," said Michael joking.

"Yes, but you'll have to pay for dinner first," quipped Geoff.

They both had a good laugh. Michael was delighted to help him improve, and Geoff would take that shot home with him and remember it fondly for months. Golf could be a cruel but deeply rewarding endeavour in its own way.

When they reached the green, Michael crouched down behind his putt to read the slope. He had to make this putt to have any chance in the friendly game. Michael rolled it nicely, but it was a little speedy, running past the hole on the left before it could break in. He knocked the four-footer he had left back into the hole and immediately picked up Geoff's marker, giving him the birdie to win the match.

Geoff was chuffed.

Even then, he wanted to go at the birdie putt for his own satisfaction. So he quickly stuck the ball down and knocked it into the centre of the hole.

As the two men walked off the green, they agreed to have dinner in the clubhouse.

When their Irish stew dinner was served with non-alcoholic beers, they discussed all manner of subjects including who might win at Augusta that year, the price of oil increasing, and whether a man should marry or not.

Michael assured Geoff that it was a good thing if he found the right girl.

Michael picked up the bill as he lost the golf match; however, Geoff insisted on paying for the drinks.

When they exited the clubhouse to the parking lot, Geoff still had a question bugging him.

"Just while I still have you, quick question: who exactly controls the corporations?"

"The old guard," Michael answered. "It's still the Vatican, the Venetian families, the Royals; below them, you have the Rothschilds and the Rockefellers; further down are the prominent political and business names you see promoting mandatory vaccination programs, BLM, and the metaverse. These entities are also known as the Cabal, the Illuminati, the deep state — all Free Mason Satanists, by the way," Michael said with disdain.

"No doubt," Geoff said. "I've seen how it all works, how they get the chain of command to play ball. If the top of the tree are Satanists, then that's why the lower-ranking members act like they have to do it to get along. But there's a point where it becomes too much. They don't have to do it; they like it. If you have any decency or moral courage, you can't stay in that sphere."

"Yes, I agree," Michael said with a nod. "And what's more, this 'Build Back Better' system will be one of complete control; control over your money, social life, and privacy. It's all there in plain sight."

At least they were both in agreement. They concluded that matters were coming to a climax for humanity before deciding to part ways for the night.

As they said their goodbyes and shook hands, Michael assured Geoff that he would always be on the other end of the phone if he needed help or had more questions. Michael felt it was important that a man in office showed this kind of integrity and awareness; it was all too rare, although more were starting to stand up publicly.

Michael was a very honourable man and would always help people, especially with understanding this crucial information at a seminal time.

Geoff went home to rest and digest things. He had the feeling Michael, like Martha, would be a vital mentor for him in navigating the way forward.

He plonked himself belly up onto his bed and splayed his limbs out. Many things were bubbling up inside him, so he decided to take a twenty-minute cat nap before doing his Heyoka clearing and formulating his next moves.

He set the timer on his phone. Though only twenty minutes had passed before it went off, Geoff felt like he'd gotten hours of sleep. Refreshed, he sat up and easily cleared his mind of what bothered him.

If any negative thoughts came into his consciousness throughout the day, he repeated his training, asking himself the identifying questions and releasing his thoughts. As a result, he felt himself getting stronger, becoming more centred in truth and reality.

He knew the first thing he had to do was sell the properties he bought, put that money back into his offshore account, and have the bank send it back to wherever it came from.

Second, he had to publicise what he knew about the Coronavirus in a calculated attack plan against the fabricated narrative; he wanted to serve his constituents instead of the status quo elites.

Third, he had to find those children in the TACFA foundation who were abused and get them to safety.

He knew the biggest part of achieving these goals was to follow Martha's advice.

Something else was also becoming abundantly clear to Geoff: there was zero choice or cop-out in this. You had to be either for or against this evil, and there was no way of getting around it. If you knew what was going on, you knew that the resulting world would never be worth living in. Understanding this and doing nothing would be almost as bad as being one of the evildoers carrying out these atrocities.

He called Martha and said, "I'm going after these bastards, and I'm not going to stop until they're taken out. There's no other way. I would take a bullet in the head if I had to so the next generation could live in truth and freedom. There comes a point where you have to stand up and be a man."

Martha had never been so proud of him. He'd been jolted into life, and although she guided him to remove his shackles, it was Geoff that was doing the hard work. He was a new man.

"A person has to face the darkness within their soul to integrate themselves," Martha said in a sincere, supportive whisper. "To deny you also have a monster inside you is to deny life; to let it take over is to destroy yourself and others; to face it and control it is to recognise evil and use it against the same when you need it. The fact that you have control of it, that you have a code you live by and have removed your fear, makes you stronger than your enemy."

She paused before adding, "Keep yourself free of fear and walk forward. Keep going forward."

"I understand," said Geoff, and for the first time in his life, he really did.

After the phone call, Martha reflected that this shift must have been subconsciously building in Geoff for some time — he had found fortitude and conviction so quickly. The dark side had underestimated him the first time, but they may have underestimated him even more this time around.

When he was off the phone with Martha, Geoff immediately called his accountant and realtor to sort out selling the extra-curricular properties and closing his account. Given the sought-after nature of the items, that business would be concluded swiftly.

His next call was to the press secretary of the townhouse about a press conference he was going to hold in the morning. He told her the contents would be confidential until they went live, but all the town's press should be there in full force.

These short-notice press conferences happened now and then, so there was no alarm or late calls to Priscilla.

That was a mistake.

Geoff immediately went to work on his plans for the morning, compiling the list of things he would say and the backup files to prove his points.

The list was extensive, and each item was damning.

There was a new gunslinger in town — and he was about to announce himself to the world.

Chapter 8

The stage was set in the Cafford townhouse: the mics were ready, the lights were shining, and the cameras were recording. The press core was prepared for the county executive of Tohana to make his entrance.

Geoff trotted himself out to the podium in his finest black suit. "Welcome, everybody," he said in his friendly, smooth timbre. After a short pause to get his documents in order, he proceeded.

"I entered this line of work to serve the constituents that elected me. As such, I feel integrity is of the utmost importance, even when difficult conversations need to be had. This is one of those conversations. A volume of information has come across my desk that required investigation. When I did so, many pressing concerns for public well-being came to my attention.

"What I am referring to today is the Covid-19 situation and the way we, as a global community, nation, county, and city, are handling it."

Geoff could see the masked hack's eyes starting to widen already. They were unconsciously communicating, *Uh oh, here we go...*

"There is a whole list of matters that need examination and answering. I would also venture to suggest that there is a list of red flags that reveal a jigsaw puzzle, a larger unseen picture that also needs a level of scrutiny that is very rarely being put forward in the public eye."

The journalists in the crowd were already torn between the excitement of their long-repressed fundamental journalistic instincts re-emerging and the fear of dismissal from their agenda-pushing bosses.

"Let me begin with my list of red flags that I will ask the journalists in this room to investigate one by one:

Red flag number one: After coronavirus research was deemed illegal on US soil, Dr. Fauci used American taxpayer money to export research to the Wuhan Respiratory Virus Lab in China. We have the paper trail on this, and Dr. Fauci does not deny this fact. He also funded gain of function research, which in layman's terms is messing around with the natural viruses and altering them, potentially creating artificial versions. He tries to call this by another name now to cover his tracks, but he will be cornered soon on that one as well."

You could hear a pin drop in the room now.

"Red flag number two: Covid-19 has never been isolated and verified. There have been thousands of requests for an isolated sample from independent scientists with expertise in virology and immunology. All the scientists in question got was a rejection or a sample that they tested and only found influenza A & B. Of the 1500 tests they did by Koch's Postulates, they found no Covid-19. The samples have also gone to Stanford and Cornell with the same result. The CDC was then asked again for viable samples, and they replied that they did not have any.

"The four papers that do describe the genome extract were never successful in isolating and purifying the samples. They only describe a small bit of RNA 37 to 40 base pairs long, which all the virologists I have spoken to tell me is not a virus. A virus is typically 30,000 to 40,000 base pairs long.

"With as bad as Covid-19 is supposed to be, why has no one in the entire world isolated and purified it in its entirety, like every single other virus in history? And how can you have a PCR test or a vaccine that works properly without this? But we will get to that next.

"Perhaps they won't release a viable sample because if they did, it would be found to be man-made."

Geoff could feel the tension building in the room.

"Red flag number three: how they are recording Covid-19 cases and deaths. The PCR test is an umbrella test for many things. It has a very high rate of false positives, and if you ramp up the testing of something very prevalent every year anyway, you will get a lot of positives. Where it gets totally unscientific is where any person that has tested positive and then dies of anything is down as a Covid death. When you test people coming into hospital, they are there because they are sick from strokes, heart attacks, cancer, or other illnesses. And if you have a test for many things that have loads of false positives — in the region of one-in-three — then your Covid-19 death figures will be ludicrously skewed.

"Experts estimate they are at least 95% higher than they should be. The other 5% is from either a manmade Covid, the seasonal flu virus, or coronaviruses that are around every year. Five percent of the Covid death figures being touted would be around the regular amount of flu deaths we would expect to see in that time frame anyway, with the flu having mysteriously disappeared.

"We have asked the WHO for their guidelines, and this was confirmed as exactly how almost every country is recording cases and deaths from Covid-19."

As Geoff looked out into the crowd, some of the media were already looking away and phoning headquarters. However, on the other hand, some were becoming more glued to what he was saying.

"Red flag number four: Treatments. For some reason, there seems to be this ongoing idea that there are no anti-virals that are powerful enough to take out even an acute infection when they've even been proven to be very effective with chronic conditions.

"There are thousands and thousands of independent university studies on the anti-viral efficacy of herbal medicines and compounds like hydrogen peroxide at very low concentrations for internal use.

"There are also medicines such as hydroxychloroquine and ivermectin, which, when combined with zinc, open the pathway for zinc to kill the virus. We have testimonies of thousands of doctors that have used these medicines very effectively against Covid-19, getting early admission patients out of the hospital in as little as twenty-four hours. Dr. Kory even outlined this in the US Senate in late 2020.

"Not only have these treatments not been discussed, debated, tested, and rolled out for usage, they have been ignored, banned, and even called dangerous.

"They've been used for eighty years without a problem. Until now. It seems all too convenient."

Some of the journalists were already leaving. Geoff noted how many were dishonest, compromised, and lacking any journalistic integrity. Yet, he was becoming more resolute in continuing.

"Red flag number five: No information on strengthening your immune system. Instead of blasting people with fear and herding them like sheep, couldn't that time have been spent educating people that the overwhelming factor of how any person handles any virus, including Covid-19, is the state of their immune system? Avoiding processed food, increasing the uptake of powerful nutrients we all learned about in science class, exercising to increase oxygen levels and blood circulation, and keeping body fat levels in a healthy range are all known to have a significant effect on one's immune system strength. Yet how often did you hear that on mainstream news in fighting Covid-19?

"I would advocate freedom of choice and education, but if you were bringing in totalitarian mandates to save lives, wouldn't you surely close fast food places, processed food suppliers, and suppliers of alcohol and cigarettes before you would close gymnasiums and golf courses?

"And you would put the immune system education on blast every five minutes. If you want to brainwash people, surely it should be in a positive direction, not telling them there are no solutions other than isolation.

"Especially when it's been proven that one's immune system is the largest factor in reaction to this virus, and people can empower their immunity and supplement it with anti-virals that are cheap, safe, and very effective. One would think so if there was any logic to this."

Geoff got the impression the mask-wearers still in front of him were gasping for more than just oxygen at this point.

"Red flag number six: The official death statistics in 2020 showed no increase in mortality from all causes. However death statistics show increases of 10-15% worldwide in vaccinated nations, with particular spikes in deaths close to vaccine rollouts in specific age groups.

"It has also been observed that the highest vaccine take-up rates also correspond with the highest infection rates within specific regions. For example, the two highest vaccine uptakes globally are in Ireland: Waterford at 99% and Carlow at 97%. So guess which counties in Ireland lead first and second for current infection rates?

"This death and vaccination percentage to case numbers have been brought together by data analysts in many countries, and I am aware that a court case is pending in Ireland on these matters."

More journalists departed, unable to question the narrative they had been so fixated on for almost two years.

"Red flag number seven: The asymptomatic spreader lie. Every virologist and immunologist worth their salt will tell you that someone with no symptoms can't spread an infectious airborne viral load. They have to be ill and showing symptoms to have that infection in the respiratory system.

"Now, if you have a bogus PCR test with so many false positives, you can make anything appear infectious. That's what happened here.

"The people saying 'follow the science' are not following science at all. What they really want you to do is follow the authority verbiage and narrative."

Geoff was getting ready to wrap things up.

"For the files and proof of what was talked about here today, visit the references section of the paper handed out before the press conference."

"Before departing this stage, I'll leave you with one question. I ask the people of the public who think all this is all perfectly okay: have you heard of Stockholm Syndrome, and are you in love with your captors?"

He couldn't see their mouths, but he could tell the room was stunned. They were jolted to the point that they couldn't even ask a question, likely afraid the answer would put them in even more of a hole.

After dropping mega truth bombs left, right, and centre, Geoff departed the stage. The audience imagined a mic drop, such was the intensity, scope, and curt nature of his speech.

The journalists were scribbling away, but Geoff immediately wondered how much of this would make it to the papers and how it would be covered. No sooner had he left the stage and gone into his backroom than a short call arrived from Priscilla.

"We will be keeping an extremely close eye on you from here on out," she said. "I would draw a line if I were you, and don't expect to be treated favourably in the press tomorrow!"

Before he could even reply, the line went dead. She was fuming.

Priscilla immediately rang the prominent media editors in the city to walk them through how to handle this bombshell.

"You are to deal with this the same way Senator Rand Paul, Senator Ted Cruz, Governor De Santos, Governor Kristi Noem and Congresswoman Marjorie Green Taylor are handled. It should be twisted to suit our narrative that he's just a rogue politician and a conspiracy nut. Make him look like an idiot and place him in that box from now on.

"Listen, it's fine for now; as you know, we need a certain level of coverage of opposition to maintain plausibility that it's not only our narrative. Just make sure the audience watching it is still deathly afraid of Covid-19 and pro-vaccine, simple as that. You do that, and I'll keep Geoff Hurley's office responsibilities limited."

The next day, the papers painted Geoff as a man not 'following the science' and going against the doctors and medical boards worldwide. They described him as a dangerous man — a threat to democracy and the population's safety.

Jesus, if they only knew, Geoff thought to himself. He was slightly annoyed, but he knew this would happen; he knew the system and how it was rigged.

His new emotional centredness and lack of fear meant that he knew he did the right thing. The greater good was on his side, and he had started walking in the right direction.

At eleven o'clock in the morning, Geoff received a phone call from Michael Clarke. Michael, being a straight shooter, got right to the point.

"I admire the stand you took," he began.

"There are some people who can support and protect you through this, and they want to meet you. Can you come to Dallas with me tomorrow for an overnight trip? I'll book us an urgent flight."

Knowing that Michael was a serious, knowledgeable, connected man who wouldn't go on trips just for the sake of it, he immediately agreed.

"I'll come with you," Geoff said. "I'll have to clear a couple of things, but that's no problem."

Michael answered, "Great. I'll pick you up at nine o'clock in the morning; the flight is at half-past eleven."

"Wait, there's something else," Geoff began. "Call me crazy, but I have a hunch that before we meet these people, we could obtain valuable documents and hard proof of what you told me a couple of days ago."

"Shoot."

"Priscilla Stewart confided in me that she is the most powerful woman in America, albeit under the radar," Geoff said. "She has high-level access and clearance to the FED buildings in DC. I'm betting she keeps the clearance key cards in a safe in the townhouse, which I have access to. We would need to find the safe, get into it, and then get into the FED buildings. Maybe it's impossible, but I thought I'd put it past you."

"Wow, well, that would be a large undertaking, but it wouldn't be impossible if planned correctly," Michael answered. "Can you get into the townhouse without raising suspicion? Do you know where the safe is?"

"Yeah, we sometimes go there for extracurricular meetings, off-the-record stuff, or just to enjoy the games room," Geoff explained. "It's usually empty after 11pm. Of course, finding the safe is another matter."

"I have a small metal detector we used in the CIA for various things, including finding safes," Michael said. "It can be set to look for a metal object the shape of a box. We will find it. Cracking it will be the issue.

"Let's go tonight; if we get in and find the keys, I'll reschedule our flight in the morning for DC and postpone the Dallas meeting for late tomorrow."

"Sounds good!" said Geoff excitedly.

"Getting in to the classified parts of the FED buildings is a completely different kettle of fish, but one step at a time," Michael cautioned. "There is an obvious danger in getting caught in these scenarios. We have to plan and be very meticulous every step of the way."

"Understood," said Geoff.

Michael invited Geoff over to his house again, and they spent the day planning to get into the FED buildings. If they managed to get that far, the plan would have to be elaborate and on-point.

They felt they had worked out the perfect heist. This was right up Michael's alley; he had elite training in these aspects and had also seen the minutia of some of the most professional operations (legal and illegal) in recent decades.

Geoff marvelled at the exacting blueprint. Michael let the men in Dallas know about the rearrangements, and they were okay with that, provided they were kept informed.

As the hour approached, Geoff and Michael made their way into the townhouse in separate cars. Geoff entered the building first — using his key card — to see if the coast was clear. They were in luck, so he pinged Michael a message.

Geoff let Michael in the front door, and they headed for the main meeting room downstairs, the same room where Priscilla had first introduced Geoff to the political machine in Texas.

Michael carried a case full of tools, though it was indistinguishable from a regular leather business briefcase. Should anyone else arrive, that was their cover story: Geoff and Michael had just come here for a game of snooker and a business meeting.

Michael was simply known as a retired detective in Cafford, which had always been his front for the public. Many higher-up retired law enforcement officers owned commercial or residential properties and conducted business, so being here wouldn't look particularly out of place.

As Michael looked around, Geoff setup the snooker table and started taking shots, leaving two cues by the table, with chalk for the tips resting on the timber perimeter. Now it looked like a game was in progress.

The most likely room for the safe would be a smaller locked office off this main room, where Geoff held meetings with Priscilla and her assistant Sandra, who worked there most days.

After Michael had scanned the main room with his small audiofeedback machine and found nothing, they turned their attention to the office. It was locked.

However, this was an old building, and the only modern keying was at the front door. An old school lock wouldn't present great difficulty for a man of Michael's talents. He used a picking tool and had the door open in seconds.

Michael looked for a camera and didn't see one. The only camera in the place appeared to be a regular security cam at the front door.

He scanned behind the large picture, first thinking that might be the spot, but came up with nothing. He then moved to the back cupboards, and the detector started pinging like a jackhammer.

"Found it," he announced to Geoff, who was standing outside the office's shut door in case someone entered. Geoff popped the door ajar for a moment.

Michael nodded at the cupboards. "There's some kind of button to open this cupboard and access the safe. I've seen this before, under the bottom right of the skirting board. It took a while to find it. This may be done by the same company."

Michael was already getting down on his hands and knees, taking out a chisel to manoeuvre the skirting open. He found a little opening, apparently there by design. The piece of wood popped loose and was easily taken out. Shining his flashlight into the crevice, he saw a button. He pressed it, and the middle cupboard at head height started to open, revealing a safe.

Geoff peeked into the room again, flashing a smile at Michael. Both men were enjoying this, with spikes of adrenaline coursing through their systems.
But the tough part was coming.

Okay, what have we got here? Michael thought to himself.

Geoff made a quick enquiry: "How is it looking?"

"It's a biometric fingerprint key," Michael answered. "Is that painting on the wall Priscilla's?"

"Yes, it is," replied Geoff.

"There might be a fingerprint on there," Michael expanded as he rooted for some other items in his master toolbox. Finally, he fished out a bluelight.

He dusted the sides of the painting and shone the light, searching for prints. Luckily, it lit up like a Christmas tree, showing an extensive human trail.

Next, Michael put on a quick amino acid test on some less-defined prints to see if they were male or female.

"There are both male and female prints here, probably two people," he explained. "I'm guessing the female ones are Priscilla's. I just need a thumbprint." Diving back into his box of tricks, Michael used some transparent double-sided tape to extract the thumbprint carefully.

"That came off nicely," he told Geoff as he put a piece of paper matching the complexion of a Caucasian person onto the other side of the tape. Then, he wrapped it around his own thumb and pressed it into the safe sensor. The metal box clicked before popping open; Michael pulled the door the rest of the way to examine the contents, bringing out a few items of interest.

"Bingo, we have FED building keys!" he exclaimed, flashing the keys to Geoff.

"Magic!" said Geoff, making a victorious fist to keep himself from shouting.

Michael quickly put the card keys in his briefcase, closed the safe and the cupboard, put the skirting back and tissued off the white dust on the painting. He made his way out of the room, shut the door and picked the lock to shut it behind him.

It was like no one had been there.

"Now for the game of snooker," said Geoff as the two men exchanged smiles, knowing they'd only been in the building six minutes; if a regular security man were watching the front door, he'd expect them to be there at least a half an hour.

They were both so excited that the snooker wasn't really on their radar. Instead, their minds were on the massive day ahead. To kill time, they potted some balls but weren't interested in the score, and eventually, they had both cleared the table.

They left the townhouse with the keys in Michael's briefcase, each driving to their own places after arranging a nine o'clock morning start, the same as before.

When Michael got home, he made the necessary rearrangements for the following day without too much difficulty, including with the men in Dallas.

The heist was on; tomorrow would be a huge day. They needed to be in good shape and totally on the ball.

Michael advised Geoff to sit for a while to calm down and have some alcohol to take the edge off before bed. Then, back at his own home, Michael took his advice and got to sleep quickly.

Not being as used to such situations, it took Geoff an hour and a half, but he eventually got himself to doze off and got a good six hours of rest.

Michael arrived just before nine the following day in his shining new navy BMW 5 series with a cream leather interior. Geoff was already prepared with luggage in tow as he came out into the underground parking lot to see Michael waiting with the trunk open.

"Top man," said Michael, looking dapper in his understated but classy black knitted jacket and tweed hat. He was a punctual man who appreciated Geoff being bang on time. "We should be there by half-past nine, which will give us plenty of time."

"Yes — better to be early," Geoff agreed.

"What you did the last few days took balls," Michael declared once they had gotten into the car. He had a forthright look on his face as he added, "I knew you were going forward when you came to see me. Martha and I are always here to help you. The friends we're going to meet will give you information from the intel side."

"We have to stand up. When you know what we know, it's the case that enough is enough. As you said, we just have to be strategic and smart," said Geoff.

"Exactly," said Michael, his manner relaxed but matched with conviction.

Geoff was happy to have a man like Michael on his side. Although Michael was seventy-odd years old, he was fit as a fiddle and as sharp as they come.

Then Michael said something that really resonated with Geoff: "They are so arrogant because they've gotten away with it for so long. But they have no idea what is coming. Nothing can stop it. And that's what you are about to find out."

"Who are these people we're meeting later today?" asked Geoff.

"They are high-level operatives in the shadows. They've been planning what is about to happen back to JFK. Have you seen where Kennedy talked about smashing the CIA into a thousand pieces, where he talked about going to gold-backed currency?"

"Not really. It was before my time," Geoff admitted.

"Well, he did. That's what got him killed — he was about to expose the swamp. The team working with Kennedy knew they needed a much smarter, more long-term plan because the deep state was so powerful and deeply embedded in every facet of society. Many of those men are dead now, but the plan was passed on. You're going to meet some of them today."

Geoff was excited to find out more about this plan. He was filling in more and more parts of the jigsaw concerning the weird happenings in society, especially over the last two years.

It wasn't long before they arrived at Cafford Airport just outside the city.

As they made their way in, Michael said, "Let me do the talking when we go through security."

"No prob," said Geoff, eagerly anticipating those interactions.

Michael strode towards the check-in area. A security officer in a fluorescent yellow jacket came forward and said, "I'm sorry, gentlemen, but you will have to wear a mask in here."

"We won't," Michael replied firmly. The security man's eyes widened slightly, unaccustomed to hearing this response. Nevertheless, Michael continued without missing a beat and said, "We are both lawfully exempt."

The security officer was flustered and said, "Well, can you show me your exemption?"

"No, I can't, because that would breach my medical privacy and The Privacy Act. In fact, you have no business even asking me any of these questions. You are breaking the law. There is only a mandate or policy, which are recommendations — they are not law.

"If you want to ask the police officer over there to come over and show me the law, then be my guest — there is none, and he'll know that. It has to be by my consent or silence, which is a tacit consent to this bullshit policy with no science behind it and a lot of evidence against it. You have neither form of consent from us. If you want to stop us, we will take your name, and you will be served with liability. We will be on our way. Have a nice day."

The security officer was lucky he was in bright yellow to take attention away from the red accumulating on his embarrassed face. He gave them a tepid ushering as they departed, but they were already on the move.

"You see, Geoff, people don't know the law either, and that's another issue. When they know the truth and know the law, they will know they are not bound to this nonsense. Anyone with any knowledge of the science also knows a mask won't stop the virus from passing through; it's like a fly through soccer netting. Furthermore, you're creating a risk of infection from bacteria accumulating on the mask and increasing CO_2 within the mask to dangerous levels. It's ridiculous to have people doing this for hours at a time. At least in hospitals they pump the surgeries with oxygen and change the masks regularly, but even there the studies show it's a waste of time or worse."

"Absolutely," replied Geoff, organising his mental notes on common law, real laws, and how to deal with ridiculous maritime law.

"Sometimes, there wasn't even a mandate, just a press release, and I know this for a fact," said Geoff, knowing Michael would already have this information.

"Ain't that the picture worth a thousand words," Michael agreed.

Michael was a man that lived to get jobs done, knowing he had done right by the world, preferably with no acclaim. It was just something that gave him great peace and satisfaction when he was sipping his favourite beers, watching a ball game, or fixing up his classic cars.

At the moment, he had a lovely blue seventies Cadillac in his garage. He had got the engine ticking over well and was currently getting the paint job redone and sparkling. Those alone times in the garage working away were precious to him.

It also reminded him of his dad.

He took two things from his late military father: diligence and hard work. Over the years, Michael had added more defined core values and critical thinking to those solid foundations.

As they made their way to the departure gate, Michael once again schooled the clerks on the law, and after showing that the emperor had no clothes, the two gentlemen made their way onto the plane and took their seats.

Michael usually found that people don't care about much; they aren't thinking about more than getting home with their paycheck intact. When it came down to following orders or getting new ones to keep the machine running, they really didn't give a rat's ass which one it was.

Michael said to Geoff as they sat down, "You know, sometimes they even tell me they don't believe this crap either, but they ask to see some papers or some wording of the law so they can tell their supervisors they followed protocol."

They were in the air for almost three hours before they landed in DC. Everybody else on the flight wore a mask.

As they got off the plane and onto the runway, Geoff had a slight relapse into his old mindset. Still, he got away with it as his sarcastic humour hit the button: "Isn't it ironic that the great unwashed are so sanitised that their immune systems won't know what to do when a bug gets in? Maybe the new term for peasantry is 'the great washed'."

Michael laughed. "You don't know whether to laugh or cry. The farther they go in the education system, the worse they are, which is too ironic. On the other hand, blue-collar folk still have a lot of common sense."

Geoff concurred. "Yeah, the lobbies control the education, particularly in college. The concept of free-thinking institutes is just an empty platitude in modern times."

The two men made their way through the airport in DC.

It was still cold enough to wear hats and thin gloves, which suited them just fine. They also put on 'Covid masks' as that would actually be helpful from this point on.

They made their way out of the exits to the taxi rank and hopped into the first available cab.

"C Streets Northwest, please," Michael instructed the driver.

"You got it," replied the unmasked, gum chewing, bald Iranian driver.

"See, these guys don't bother with masks... street smart," Michael said under his breath, half-squinting an eye at Geoff.

Geoff always marvelled at the enormous freeways in bigger American cities; they were so massive you never knew which lane you wanted to be in.

Michael made a quick phone call, saying, "You can start now. We will be there shortly."

He was talking to a specialised team of mercenaries for hire that he exclusively and privately used when in the CIA. Michael had enlisted them on short notice to help carry out today's mission.

They continued making their way through the traffic, weaving in and out. After about twenty minutes they exited off the freeway and drove into the city. As they came up to the main streets, the driver pulled in and said, "This is as close as I can get you. It's just a one-minute walk straight up the avenue there."

"No problem," said Michael paying the cab driver as they both got out and began walking toward the FED buildings.

The team Michael called had gotten into the power grid for the street and, on his cue twenty minutes ago, cut the FED buildings out for thirty seconds.

Within minutes, the building management got a call from 'Electrics DC' saying someone was on the way to check all was okay.

Two members of the unit Michael had assembled were to arrive the same time as they would, heading in before them. One would be kitted out in Electrics DC gear, including a yellow helmet and mask, while the other was dressed normally to blend in while still being unidentifiable with his woolly hat and mask.

They had looked around earlier to find the internal power boxes and fire alarms. Michael had also cased the joint in full the previous day via open online layout sources; he knew where all the rooms were.

The plain-clothed operative went through the lobby and kept to an empty sitting area slightly further away from the front of the building. On his way out, he'd pass through a corridor with a fire alarm.

The one in uniform marched up to reception, folded step ladder in hand and showed a fake badge, which security barely looked at. They were happy for him to leave his mask on and directed him to the electric box.

One of the other unit members had hacked into the council's building blueprints earlier and had let them know that switch three would take out the cameras and ventilation system. The team only cared about the former.

Once the yellow helmeted agent was up on the ladder with the box open before him, he pinged Michael that they were good to go.

Michael and Geoff needed to get to the third floor. They came in the entrance, went across the lobby and got into the elevator. Michael texted the plain-clothed agent, 'go time' and pressed the keypad for level three. The agent shouted, "Fire!" and whacked the button under the glass on his way out of the building.

The alarm went off full pelt, the sprinklers came on, and everyone was in a massive panic. Security were shouting for people to get outside, doing their best to calm everyone down.

As people were streaming out the exits, the uniformed actor flicked off the camera system, closed the box, and quickly descended from the ladder to join the rest in leaving the building.

Michael and Geoff arrived in the elevator on the third floor, not far from the classified rooms, which were barely used. They already knew that the several occupied offices were on the other side, and they hopefully wouldn't run into anyone wondering why they weren't leaving. Even then, they had a plan: they would claim they had been on the way to look for Tom Ballard. Geoff knew from a government meeting that Tom worked here and was on sick leave.

But to be on the safe side, they remained in the elevator for a couple of minutes; as per fire drill instruction, everyone was leaving the building as quickly as possible via the stairwell.

After timing the wait, they exited the elevator. The coast was clear, and they headed for the classified rooms.

Michael opened up his briefcase, took out the main clearance card and pinged it into the key slot. The white door opened and shut behind them, and Michael flicked on the light. Luckily, there were no windows in this confidential room.

Now, they had to get what they came for and escape before security discovered the false alarm. "Over to you, Geoff," said Michael, knowing Geoff better understood government filing and could find the information faster.

"We need to get to international registrations," replied Geoff, repeating the plan. These were the most important registrations in the room because they pertained to corporations of governance.

"There," Geoff said, spotting a marked door on the far side of the room. They had two more keys, so they were betting the larger one was for interior spaces.

Michael flicked the key at the electronic pad, and the door opened. They made their way in.

There were filing cabinets for all manner of things: patents, land, energy, corporations, and many countries. Eventually, they came to U and US corporation files.

The cabinet had a keyhole shaped like a large USB port. Michael slotted the smaller key in, and a small screen underneath lit up with black text asking for a password.

"F&*k!" said Geoff, unsure of how to handle this setback.

However, Michael was calm.

"Don't worry, once the key is in above, I can pop this keypad open and cut a wire that will break the security circuit needed for a password," Michael explained, "It's just an additional authentication and not a sophisticated one."

He took out a penknife and manoeuvred it around the side of the screen, cutting at the perimeter to leave a minuscule gap. With a small blowtorch, he melted the glue around it, enabling him to pop the keypad out. When he sliced one of the wires, the cabinet opened.

"Nice," said Geoff as he quickly got to work on finding relevant documents. "Corporation Inc. Okay, let's see what's in this folder."

"United States of America registration as a corporation, United States of America dissolution of corporation! United States of America bankruptcy file! Bingo, we got it. Let's get out of here."

Geoff snatched the documents and stashed them in Michael's briefcase.

"I just want to put this keypad back in one piece," said Michael, knowing that leaving everything as if nothing had happened would be rather helpful; the longer it took for them to figure out things were missing, the better.

He pasted some glue around the back perimeter of the keypad and pushed it back in place, wiping away the earlier burn marks. Then, he removed the key and clicked the cabinet shut.

"Now we just have to navigate our way out of here," said Michael, focusing on completing the rest of the job.

They made their way out, quietly shutting the doors behind them as they left the classified area and passed the elevator, heading to the stairs connecting to the fire escape. They shuttled down the metal steps, merging with the people gathered outside just as the fire department arrived.

The area had been cornered off, with a closed gate 40 yards from the building that Michael and Geoff would have to go through. Unfortunately, it included security.

"Gentlemen, what took you so long?" asked one of the security personnel.

"We were stuck in an elevator. The power went out but came back several minutes later, and we were able to get out," replied Michael. "Any idea where the fire is?"

"We don't know yet," replied the officer. "Can I see some ID please, gentle..."

He hadn't even finished his sentence when an explosion shook the building.

Everybody at the scene ran. It was chaos; the civilians and security were all fleeing to safety. Nobody was interested in anything now apart from escape, which gave Michael and Geoff time to intermingle in the crowd and disappear down some side streets.

But they had planned how they would move through the roads, through shopping centres that had doors on one street and other exits around the block.

As soon as they had a chance, they replaced the hats with baseball caps of different colours they had brought in their pockets. They did the same with their masks, changing bright blue for brown for Geoff and black for Michael. Finally, they removed their jackets and put them in a large refuse container on a side street.

They were now different people. Even if spotted again, they would be written off as someone else.

A car was waiting for them on a side street. They hopped in.

"Well, that went nicely," said the last team member, the getaway driver, as they sped away.

"Like clockwork," replied Michael, removing his hat and mask. Geoff followed.

The driver was to bring them back to the airport for a flight to Dallas, taking off in two hours' time.

"Thank God that button in your pocket worked," Michael said to Geoff.

"Test one, and it fired," replied Geoff.

"I love it when a good plan comes together," Michael added half humorously with a coolness that only an experienced man could muster.

"That electric box and all the circuits are fried now, but it made far more noise than it did damage."

They also knew that no one was near enough to get hurt when they fired it, thanks to the false fire alarm.

"We can have a few drinks at the airport now," said Geoff, sounding like a man who certainly needed one.

"You got that right," replied Michael.

When they reached the airport, they checked in right away so they could sit down in the bar and decompress.

Geoff ordered a Guinness for himself and a scotch on the rocks for Michael. Geoff was half expecting him to request a martini, shaken, not stirred.

As they sat down, Geoff said, "How about that for a day? Do you think we can trust those mercenaries?"

"That team will never say anything, or they'll never work again," Michael assured him. "They live for that stuff. Plus, they think it was a CIA operation, so they'd fear for their lives if they said a word to anyone."

There was a growing realisation from both men of just how capable the other was. Michael's depth of knowledge and skills had been entirely on display in the last couple of days, and Geoff was showing remarkable aptitude, displaying his own substantial — if new — fortitude and talent to bridge this information to the public.

Of course, he first wanted to talk to the men in Dallas and see what they thought was best to do with the documents.

They enjoyed a few drinks, taking the edge off their nerves and allowing them to sleep most of the way on the flight. They arrived at half-past eight in the evening.

As soon as they got their luggage, they proceeded out of the airport and found an empty cab.
"The Army base on the eastern suburb, please," Michael said to the driver.

They reached their destination after twenty-five minutes. It had a gated entrance guarded by a soldier in full camouflage gear, a hat with a side slant, and a physique that said he was in the gym daily.

The driver rolled down the passenger window, and the soldier proceeded to tell them in a relaxed but firm manner that the taxi could go no further.

"No problem," said Michael. Geoff insisted on paying for this ride as they disembarked from the seven-seater cab.

The soldier was welcoming but at the same time wondered who they were and what they wanted.
"Code 483417," Michael declared to him.

"Ah, they are expecting you, Mr. Clarke," replied the soldier. "Just wait here a moment, and I'll hail a shuttle."

Around one minute later, a jeep arrived to pick them up, waited for the gates to open, and drove into the wider front area. Another soldier got out and met them at their vehicle. He was a little older and not as physically imposing as the one operating the gate, but he still looked wiry and robust with years of service and mental toughness displayed on his face.

"Hi Michael, how are you?" he asked.

"I'm good, sir," replied Michael.

Michael made the introductions and said, "Colonel Jeffers, County Executive Geoff Hurley," as the Colonel extended a firm hand to Geoff. As they shook hands, there was no mistaking this man's physical presence; such was the steeliness of his greeting.

"Thanks for coming, gentlemen. We have a meeting room setup for you further into the base," said Colonel Jeffers, inviting them into the jeep. He followed, stepping into the driver's seat before driving them back through the gates.

The base wasn't fancy, but it was functional with well-built facilities. There were houses on the periphery, but as they went further in, there were all kinds of warehouses, training obstacle courses, mechanic shops, storage facilities, fleets of vehicles, and even some helicopters and tanks.

"The men you will meet today aren't all based here, but they wanted to meet you, Geoff," said Colonel Jeffers. "They greatly admire that you have pieced together the general outline and were brave enough to already bring some of it to the public's attention."

A few minutes later, they came to the meeting centre of the base. It was the most polished property they had seen since the houses at the front. It was a sizeable cream-painted building that looked like a cross between a hotel and a golf clubhouse.

Colonel Jeffers opened the door and held it for Geoff and Michael to enter. Geoff was immediately struck by the spaciousness, cleanliness, imposing architecture, and tall beams of the lobby. They proceeded to the end of the entrance room and ascended the escalator to floor two. The conference room was the second door on the left.

They entered, and several well-dressed and high-ranking military men rose from their seats to greet them.

The officer's outfits in the conference room varied from suited uniforms to camouflage gear depending on their rank, field, and expertise. But as the names were reeled off from admirals to colonels to lieutenants to generals, Geoff knew he was extremely fortunate to have an intel meeting with such important individuals.

They all gave their robust military handshakes to Michael and Geoff and promptly sat back in their seats, inviting Michael and Geoff to sit one and two places away from the general at the top of the table: General Flint.

Geoff was to General Flint's left. He was in awe to be in such a position with a man who had gone through vilification from the deep state in fighting them all the way before eventually clearing his name and regaining his rightful place in the US Army.

General Flint spoke in his light, lilted, strong tone and said, "Thank you for coming, Geoff and Michael."

"It's a pleasure to be here," replied Geoff. Michael smiled and nodded in agreement.

The general got down to business, steepling his fingers as he said, "You're probably wondering why we invited you here, Geoff. The reason is simple: some critical things are happening behind the scenes, and your awareness and determination show us we can trust you with our intel. More importantly, it means we can help each other." He looked Geoff in the eye, earnest and sincere.

"We've been scrutinising all American officials, but when we saw what you did and learned that you left the Free Mason network as soon as you realised what it was about, we knew you were a man we needed to talk to. After getting your permission, Michael filled us in on the details of what you have seen and experienced."

Geoff felt more at ease now and wondered what else this group could reveal.

"Anyway, let's begin," said General Flint. "I'm just going to be blunt: you and every other elected official in this country were fraudulently elected, including the sitting president. The Dominion Voting Systems technology is so compromised it's unbelievable. Have you watched any of the official audit reviews?"

"A few nights ago, I watched a replay of the Arizona audit because Michael sent it to me," Geoff began. "I could scarcely believe what I was watching. First, they lied about the computers being connected to the internet — that was proven. Second, it was also proven that even a decent ten-year-old hacker could get into these machines and do whatever they wanted." Geoff scratched his temple as if he still couldn't believe it.

Colonel Jeffers interjected, "Yes, that's it, Geoff. Also, there are many duplicate votes, some with the same signatures, all that bullshit. You saw it. Absolute carnage. You also know that it didn't make the mainstream news. All they said was the audit shows votes counted came out almost the same. Well, they would if you counted all the same bullshit again, right? The root of the issue is that the system is plagued by dishonesty, especially in the media. It's rotten to the core."

"I agree," said Geoff, nodding gravely.

"We knew this was coming," the general continued, "and we put a sting operation in place. We are going to expose everything. We have records of everything and everyone involved; they're deep state players, as you already know. It goes back to the Vatican, the royal families, and Washington DC. They cause wars, division, poverty, enslavement, and more. We are going to bury them forever. But we have to bide our time and do it at the right moment."

"What's your time frame?" asked Geoff, liking what he heard.

"It's hard to know, and if we had one, that's not something we would divulge," General Flint replied. "It's more event-driven. Then, when our ducks are in a row, we can move on to the next steps.

"I don't mean to sound vague, but this is a sensitive operation. The main criteria are financial circumstances and child trafficking rings. I know Michael has told you about the corporation system and treating people as dead at sea to force consent to maritime laws without their knowledge. This is the system they built to gain full control and easy wealth."

"Yes," said Geoff, nodding his understanding.

"Michael, do you want to take the next part?" asked the general, cognisant that it was ideal for multiple voices to speak at different junctures.

"Child trafficking is bigger than the drugs trade nowadays, Geoff," Michael continued. "As you probably already know, the governments worldwide have always made a fortune from narcotics. Well, child trafficking and paedophile rings among elites are even bigger money. Look at the number of children that go missing every year — Google it. Even if most of those are family member abductions, the number left over would still be staggering. These are mostly orphans and children who won't be looked for. Besides, these traffickers mainly use underground tunnels to transport them."

Geoff said, "I know about the Free Masons, so that wouldn't surprise me, but I've not heard of these underground tunnels."

"They're called DUMBS: deep underground military bases. Some were built hundreds of years ago. Back then, they were used for military purposes but were taken over and expanded upon by the Cabal for their satanic crimes with children," the general explained.

Michael took the baton again. "If you thought the paedophilia was bad, wait till you hear this. The adrenochrome part of the child trafficking trade is even bigger. It involves sacrificing children and taking their blood just after being tortured to death. This blood is full of child adrenaline —adrenochrome. It gives those who drink it an intense high and anti-ageing benefits. These people are sick."

"That's what they wanted me to drink that night," said Geoff, going white in the face.

"Yes," Michael affirmed.

It was collectively understood that the group — Geoff in particular — needed a breather.

The hardened military men were looking downward, and Geoff shook his head. Michael faced forward, but he was grimacing.

Geoff was struggling. The truth was hitting him hard. He did his Heyoka sentence in his head to let it go, remain calm, and re-centre.

After the break, Colonel Jeffers took the helm.

"People think it's just Jimmy Saville, Prince Andrew, Harvey Weinstein, Kevin Spacey, Rolf Harris, the Cuomo brothers, Jeffrey Epstein... but they're not facing the fact that these were institutional faces protected by those very pillars of society. This is part of that system. You know this, Geoff, but we're laying it all out on the table to show how deep it goes. You want to know more, and we can help you with this.

"Have a look at that Netflix drama, *Sons of Sam,* about the serial killers in New York to see how the institutional link was covered up. Notice the circle over the eye in the intro — connect that to pictures of modern celebrities using the same symbol. It's a satanic Cabal sign for seeing all, and it's also connected to a child sexual abuse symptom called panda eyes that results from the pain of penetration. It's sickening when you piece it together. And we have all the dirt proving who they are and what they do."

Geoff got up and hurried to the bathroom, where he started puking vigorously. He remembered the bruised eyes of the children he saw in the Lodge.

The men in the meeting didn't judge him. They had a similar disgust, and they'd seen some of the toughest bastards they'd ever met reduced to vomiting. Unfathomable evil was difficult to stomach.

Geoff did a full Heyoka routine, running through it three times until he felt much better. Then, he returned to the conference room with a clear head, ready to proceed. He apologised as he pulled out his chair and sat back down.

Speaking for the rest at the table, the general said, "We understand — it's horrific. Many of us had the same reaction. We all have sons and daughters, grandchildren, or nieces and nephews. It hits hard. That's why this has to stop."

Geoff tightened his jaw in agreement, nodding for them to continue.

Colonel Jeffers took the reins. "This is all linked to the Free Masons. The heads of that organisation are the three pillars discussed earlier. Why do people think Saville was very good friends with Prince Phillip and Prince Charles? Why do people think Prince Andrew was a frequent visitor to Epstein's island?"

Looking Geoff in the eye, he continued, "I know this is rough, but you are ready to hear it, and we'll help you. That offering you were about to get in the Lodge was adrenochrome."

"Yes, I worked that out previously," replied Geoff with a look of horror on his face.

"This is how they work," Colonel Jeffers continued. "Subtle manipulation and gradual exposure to see who will move into their circle. They even gather dirt on you before and after for blackmail. With some, they go so far as to force them to do things to kids — even murder — and film it all. It's so twisted, and this evil is so embedded in our institutions that we had to stop it. And that's what we have been working towards."

Geoff was a little puzzled and asked what he meant because things just seemed to be getting worse. "It's a very complicated chessboard," the general answered, "because the roots were so deep, and the brainwashing was so strong. We have to do it gradually, exposing governments, lobbies, medical institutions, voting systems, the Vatican, the Royal Family, the Venetian families, and the mainstream media. It's a huge undertaking with a clear plan of a long, drawn-out war in the background while people think there is a pandemic. We have to let this play out and steer it in certain ways to wake up the masses. Unfortunately, there have to be casualties; there is no other way to wake up from a mass psychosis. They have to be shaken to the core."

"I think I understand," Geoff said. "You have to let them see what would have happened and have them change their own minds." The general smiled.

"Exactly," he said. "In the end, we will probably also need to put out an emergency broadcast exposing the truth about these elites and exactly what they have done. It depends on how we judge the smoothest path to a transition. Still, some may not believe it.

"What people find very hard to understand is that many of these elites have already been tried in military tribunals. We have their confessions, and those people are in jail or dead. We have been using body doubles and CGI extensively. What do you think about Joe Biden now and five years ago? Is he the same person?" The general took out a side-by-side picture on his phone and leaned over to show it to Geoff.

Geoff raised an eyebrow and said, "He does look very different when you examine it; more like his brother!"

Michael added, "He's not even in the White House. People in Washington DC will tell you the White House has been empty, with no lights on since the 2020 election. He ain't there; he's filming from a studio."

"We have to let it play out," Colonel Jeffers said. "Let the corporation collapse and have mandates go out under his watch while the people rise against it. Then when the time is right, we can release the truth. It looks like a coup or a psyop if we go too early. But, even though it is a psyop, it is a good one, intending to gradually reveal the truth before using the emergency broadcast for those that still don't get it."

"Wow, that's interesting," said Geoff. "But so many are still asleep. They don't get that the vaccinated population is getting sick now, having strokes and dying in much higher numbers. 2020 was no different from normal; it was just reclassified and painted differently. How do you plan to destroy the media? Aren't they the major issue still left?"

"Good question," the general said.

"It's true. Six individuals under the three Cabal pillars own the mainstream media channels worldwide. Government grants fund the local radios, and big tech is owned by Cabal players. It's been very challenging, but the censorship and agenda-driven media has shown itself for what it is. I accept many still don't get it; the white-collar middle class are the worst offenders because they are the most indoctrinated and invested in the system. They are fearfully content in their slavery bubble. So we will need more to show them what is really going on and where they let humanity go off a cliff.

"That's where ultimatums and warrants will go into the media to stop the lying and let real journalism flourish again. We have them on huge blatant, deliberate lies, and we can do them for treason. The middle class will then get a harsh wake-up call, but they deserve compassion."

"Yes, that would be nice," said Geoff, thinking he sounded more like a teenager discussing a video game than a man discussing issues of grave world importance.

"With all the people calling out big-name politicians, Hollywood stars, and talk show hosts as child traffickers, adrenochrome consumers, and paedophiles, why have they never sued anyone?" Michael asked; a poignant question. "I'll tell you why. It's because they don't want it to go to court and be investigated. That's why."

"Indeed," replied Colonel Jeffers.

"On the vaccine issue, though," Geoff cut in, "I find it hard to fathom why you would let that go. Even children have been vaccinated. Why is that allowed to happen? Couldn't you have released the truth earlier to prevent this?"

The general answered, "It's a valid question, Geoff, but we are military strategists. We look at every conceivable outcome and weigh the results. If you go too early, you don't have a full picture of all the players involved, and you can't catch them in the act to bring it to the public. This is war, and as we said, there will be casualties. But if you don't do it this way, there would be even more casualties from a nasty civil war. If any doubt is left after the reveal, it could fester and rebuild into the same rotten structures. So we want it all gone as smoothly as possible to minimise the loss of life."

He paused before saying, "I know it's difficult. It troubles us too, but we have to plan it strategically."

And then he dropped the bomb: "Here's the next part. Our commander-in-chief and legal president, Donard Trapp, is bothered by this too. Still, he knows he has to go this route for optics with the sheeple for now. He has always been very clear that he is for freedom of choice on the matter — that people should be allowed to refuse and refuse on behalf of their children."

Geoff smiled, trying not to appear too sceptical, and he asked, "He's still president?"

"The Corporation of America is bankrupt and dissolved, and Biden isn't even Biden — he's a double. The election was fraudulent. We have it all on the quantum voting system, so the military was privy to this. They still answer to President Trapp," explained the general.

As he finished his point, Michael slid some documents across the table to General Flint: the US Corp registration, dissolution, and bankruptcy in the City of London records for businesses.

"Geoff knows all about the corporation status. That was why we were held up today as we took a detour to DC."

"Holy shit, that was you guys?" said Colonel Jeffers, having seen the explosion all over the news.

"Yes, and I'm pleased to say that it was a very clean job," Michael answered. "We obtained these important documents. Geoff works with one of the few people who has access: Priscilla Stewart. We 'borrowed' her keys after we worked out where she kept them."

"Wow, these are incredible," said General Flint as he leafed through the papers Michael had passed him. "We needed to get these documents, but we knew the job would be nearly impossible." He looked both men in the eye and said, "Thank you."
Michael and Geoff smiled humbly, knowing they had done something to help humanity.

"That's brilliant work," added the other officers.

After a pause, the general continued, "Okay, let's move on with the rest of the meeting.

"I accept that the vaccine matter will be the hardest one for the president to explain, but he will have to when the time is right. He was hamstrung and had to publically support it because the media and lobbies have too much power. The general public wouldn't understand until they could see the horror for themselves. And he will state that he never said people should be forced and supported choice. He also gave all the real cures in his speeches through 2020. Those who were ready and able heard what he was saying."

"That's true," replied Geoff.

"There are a lot of complexities with this war, but it is about the financial reset and the children," said Michael. "You have the New World Order reset and Nesara/Gesara, two totally different concepts. And the former will enslave people and abuse children horribly. The latter will set humanity free, heal and empower our children and future." Michael was making a fork in the road with his index fingers, and the officers agreed.

"This is a moment in history," he continued. "JFK was shot because he was about to go to gold-backed currency and return power to the people. We had a chance to take out Bush and his cronies back in 2001, but they did the inside job on 9/11 to turn the world on its head. So we have to play 5D chess this time and make sure everything is done right. The whole network of those f*#kers has to be cut off at the head with the rest ready to be indicted before we sign off on any new system."

"I understand," Geoff said, finally appreciating the significance of the job.

"There's something else going on here," the general explained. "Not many people want to hear or talk about this much, but it is relevant. Have you heard of Area 52 in Arizona?"

"That's the famous base where they researched and recovered a UFO, right?"

"Yes, but it's deeper than that. We've known about extraterrestrials for a long time," General Flint continued. "We are hardly alone in the galaxy. It's not just Area 52, but I wanted to use that as a reference because there was a lot of activity there, they had ships there that they studied, and they reverse-engineered the tech into stealth planes and helicopters.

"The point I'm trying to get to is that there are many civilisations out there, and they communicate with us at times. They have a huge concern over the direction our civilisation has been taking. Some elementals — entities or energies — also come up from the earth; the good ones are helping us.

"Extraterrestrials of an evil nature have visited earth and kept to the shadows to help the Cabal. That's part of the fight. If you come across them, you will feel it. Let's leave it at that — most people are uncomfortable with the subject unless they have really taken on board the rest of the matters first. But I want you to know that it exists."

"There is no doubt this is between good and evil," Geoff replied. "And when I look at scripture, it describes an end game, a potential apocalypse or a second coming, and it feels like this is that moment."

"Absolutely right," Colonel Jeffers replied.

"What we're talking about are entities and energies out there," Geoff said. "I believe everything is energy, including us, and there is a source energy of God and connectedness beneath everything. We will always return to that. Fears and things of that nature are the opposite of that. So I work hard on removing my fears because they cloud my judgement and keep me from connection and protection from Source energy." As he said this sentence, he was surprised it came out, but he had developed from his inner work, meditations, and Martha's guidance.

General Flint was impressed and said, "Geoff, you're getting right to the root of the matter now. The world is ascending, but we have a job to do. It also hasn't and won't happen all on its own. We have to be leaders and fight the good fight.

"However, we are being guided by powerful beings and the Source itself. We feel protected. Too often, things have fallen in our favour when we could have had another disaster on our hands, but it never happened. Taking down the Cabal appeared nearly impossible, but it's happening because God or the Source is involved.

"Truth always wins. Lies eventually fall like a house of cards. And there is nothing more in ultimate truth than the Creator."

This was a deep war. They were still in the middle of it, but they believed it could be won.
It had to be won.

Chapter 9

What an amazing experience, Geoff thought to himself as they arrived back in Cafford the next morning. The great knowledge of these officers had entranced him. Before he left, and after Michael had fully debriefed the officers on what happened with the operation to retrieve the documents, Geoff asked how he could go about helping the two children from the lodge and if they could assist him with it.

Their response was heartfelt and genuine but always cognizant of the bigger picture. Colonel Jeffers explained: "Worldwide operations are going on to clear these DUMBS and save the children from them, but we are only dealing with what is underground at the moment.

"Now and again, there will be reports of children being recovered on the surface with no reference to underground tunnels, even though that's where they're coming from. There are also DUMBS we don't know about but are working on them as we go."

"The bottom line is this: it is all covert," the general said. "Blowing our cover now would lead to mayhem and civil war. So we have a strategic and exacting plan. If you want to go and search for these kids to help them out legally, please do, and we will keep a watchful eye. You know who they are, so you can identify them — once you have, we will get the paperwork done to bring them to a safe location."

That was fine by Geoff. He understood and even preferred this approach because he wanted to feel he was the one that set it right. He felt guilty even though he shouldn't, plagued by the belief that he had somehow brought them into the clutches of the TACFA foundation.

But with Michael helping him, he could fix this.

When Geoff arrived back at his apartment, he sat down on the sofa and looked around his lovely open living room. He glanced over at the stainless steel pots and kitchen utensils hanging from the navy tiles above the stove, reflecting on what the officers had told him.

He was still in a reverie, like his connection to the Source had deepened, and he was linked to universal consciousness. It was a profound feeling.

However, he also felt trepidation and fear for what he was about to do to save these children because he knew Priscilla would find out about this sooner or later. This was going past the line of no return.

Would it be smarter to stay out of it? No — Geoff immediately shook off his doubts. He had to do something to stop their suffering; knowing the complete animals he was dealing with, Geoff feared they would meet a worse fate if he chose not to act now.

The more conscious and developed he became, the more he knew it was down to aware individuals to take action. All hands on deck were needed to speed up this process or ensure that it happened.

He thought to himself about something Michael said on the way home: "We can't sit back and wait for everything to happen. We have to be the change too, like we were yesterday. All this talk of the White Hats and the Black Hats — well, guess what? The ones consciously doing good are the White Hats, and those consciously doing bad are the Black Hats. Look how much we have already helped in the last few days!"

Once they arrived back home, Geoff and Michael worked out a plan to find the children and were sure to tell Martha everything. Michael briefed the military on their plan as well. The two men would start in the morning at Geoff's apartment.

Geoff began a full Heyoka process to conquer his fears; he needed to remain in a good state for what was to come. After fifteen minutes of this, he went to bed for a nap to regain his energy. Then, he relaxed to prepare for another potentially big day tomorrow.

Michael arrived bright and early, just as planned. They went into Geoff's office: a converted bedroom with a large desk, a new iMac, and a filing cabinet. He pulled the swivel chair from beneath his desk and slid it across the floor to Michael, grabbing a less glamorous folding chair for himself.

Geoff booted up the computer, and they began.

"It's amazing the things we accept as normal after a while," Michael said, gesturing to Geoff's new computer as it completed the start-up process and settled quickly on the desktop screen full of applications.

"In 1970, if someone said that you could switch on a machine where you could access billions of pieces of information at the touch of a button, use applications to make life easier, and contact someone face to face on the other side of the world, they would have looked at you like you just mentioned adrenochrome in Hollywood in 2018."

He sighed and said, "These things are wonderful when you think about it."

"They are, but they're a double-edged sword," Geoff answered. "The internet can be used to send propaganda to the masses."

"That's true, but it's also connected the globe and allowed people to talk, get the real intel out there and connect the dots. Ultimately, bringing light to things raises the awareness. The propaganda and control side is being exposed," said Michael with his head slightly tilted to the side.

Geoff had to agree. He was impressed how this tough, traditional man was also very profound and gentle when required.

They went to the TACFA Foundation login page. During his time as an organiser, Geoff had accessed it hundreds of times. But this time was different.

ACCESS DENIED

"Well, would you look at that," said Geoff with a hint of irony.

"They've banned you already," Michael quipped.

They paused for a moment, and Geoff wondered what to do, lightly tapping his fingers on the keyboard. Then, he remembered he had a second account — one he had setup and bungled a few settings before understanding how the website worked.

"Priscilla won't have spotted this account," he said, typing his new credentials into the page. "I didn't even put my name on it. It just has a username, GLuke, a combo of my first initial and middle name."

This time, he got in right away. Michael smiled, knowing that may have saved them quite a few hours of hassle finding a suitable hacker.

Luckily, Geoff also had this account in the admin role, giving him full access to all parts of the site, including details of all the children that had been 'helped'.

He went into the funding section, Cafford community centres, and the list of children who had free membership to the associated activities.

There were thousands of children. Their initial despondency with the size of the list was quickly replaced with determination, buoyed by the fact that every child had a profile and a picture. It was just a matter of Geoff sifting through it until he found the children he was looking for.

This was Geoff's task, and Michael told him to give him a call when he had the children's profiles. Michael would spend that time (at least a few hours) with the mint blue Cadillac sitting in his garage that still needed a few touch-ups.

Michael sent a text to Colonel Jeffers updating him on the situation.

Geoff loaded up on coffee and got to work.

After a while, he had worked out the process, and it was nearly automatic: press the name, view the picture, click back, repeat. It was tedious and time-consuming, but he was steadfast in his desire to find these children.

Boom — he had child one, the little girl: Sarah Kensington, a beautiful petit Latina girl with curly hair. He was 161 profiles into the list.

Finding her energised Geoff. He worked at an even quicker pace, his brain whirring as he sifted through the data. Eventually, he found child number two: Lawrence Survette, profile number 593, an African-American boy with platted hair.

Geoff was sure these were the right children. In fact, he recognised them immediately, unable to wipe the memory of their presence at the Lodge from his mind. It was almost déjà vu, like he was supposed to help them.

He called Martha immediately and said, "I found them!"

Martha clenched her fist on the other side of the phone and did a little punch of the air as she said, "Yes!" She paused to take a calming breath, then said, "Well done. Move forward with courage and don't look back."

"I will," replied Geoff with conviction in his voice.

His next call was to Michael, who made his way back just as soon as he had washed the oil off his hands and unrolled his sleeves.

"Great stuff, Geoff!" Michael said, glad they now had concrete details and ID to work with. Not only could Geoff see the big picture clearly, but he was also diligent and focused when he had to be. Michael thought to himself, *Sure, he would have had to possess these skills to make it to the top of the insurance company. Those businesses are all about carrying out tasks and hitting clerical targets.*

Geoff and Michael didn't know that Priscilla and her tech team were keeping tabs on numerous TACFA matters to do with Geoff, including the two children, knowing they might be identified.

No sooner had he landed on Sarah's profile than a flag went out. Soon after, the team checked the user's IP address accessing the information — after cross-checking that with the list of previous user IPs, they knew who had been looking at the list. Priscilla was alerted within minutes, and she quickly took action.

But Michael already had a bad feeling about this. *What if they had earmarked those children as something Geoff would possibly look into?*

He warned Geoff that they needed to move quickly on this information, hoping they could move speedily enough to get away with it. Since Michael still had his CIA badges, he had the authority to bring a child to safety if he thought they were in danger.

The children's residences were listed as a foster home and an orphanage, but they were also reportedly attending the same school: St. Margaret's Primary. It was Friday afternoon, just after the lunch break, so they were likely to be there now.

Michael and Geoff hopped in the BMW and made their way directly to the school, about ten minutes away. Because of Michael's thirty-year background as an agent, he could navigate the streets with incredible speed and accuracy.

However, they were in for a surprise as they approached the school: Miguel was putting eleven-year-old Lawrence into the back of a black SUV with blacked-out windows.

Geoff and Michael were stuck behind cars at a red light with vehicles steaming towards them in the oncoming lane. There was no way to get there. Geoff opened the car door and started to run towards the SUV.

He was far from fit. He was running out of gas before he got there, and the SUV was already pulling out. Geoff stood in the parking lot as they drove off, breathing heavily, unable to do more than watch as Miguel drove away.

He swore to himself but had no time to rest. No sooner had he blurted out his frustration when Michael had wrangled out of traffic, screeched to a halt beside him, and flung the passenger door open, ushering him to get in. Geoff climbed into the car quickly.

Michael was in beast mode. His eyes were narrow, adrenaline up, but his heart rate was calm. He was in uber focus. He was taking in every minutia of information, his eyeballs darting here, there, and everywhere as he sped after the SUV.

He had Miguel's dark vehicle still in his sights, copying his every move down sidestreets and through intersections.

Miguel ran a red light, and Geoff looked on in horror as they missed another vehicle by inches. Traffic screeched to a halt around them, allowing Michael to fly through the melee and keep pace with Miguel.

He was getting closer. But he couldn't get too close because there were kids in the car, and he couldn't put them in danger.

Michael's plan was for Miguel to get boxed in somewhere, take him out of the vehicle and demobilise him.

It wasn't long before they were out of the city and flying through the suburbs. The traffic was less chaotic at this point, but the chase was no less violent. As they rampaged through the Eastside suburb, they reached the countryside.

"I think he's heading for the Lodge!" Geoff exclaimed. "Why would he go there when he knows I know where it is?"

"Well, he might be using it as a diversion. Or maybe it's connected to an underground tunnel — a lot of those places are."

"Holy shit, you might be right!"

The beamer's suspension was being pushed to the limit, but it was still smoothly traversing the country roads at a breakneck speed. But there was a train crossing ahead.

"You've got to be kidding me!" Michael said in frustration. Miguel had just gone over the tracks, blowing through the wooden gate like it was nothing, but the oncoming train would surely block them in.

As they approached the crossing, the long train roared past before they could make it through. Michael slammed on the brakes.

He thumped the steering wheel with the butt of both his palms exclaiming, "God damn it!"

Geoff sighed in frustration alongside him. All they could do was wait. Michael texted Colonel Jeffers a further update.

When the train had finished crossing a few minutes later, Michael threw the car back into gear, hopping over the rail even before it started uncoupling.

He followed Geoff's directions to the Lodge, hoping Miguel would be there.

"He has to go somewhere, and I'm betting it'll be there," Michael mused, "because he wants to get to the underground. He thinks no one can get him there."

"Can they?" asked Geoff.

"Well, he doesn't know the military gave me a master key for the DUMB entrances," Michael said with a smile.

"Brilliant!" said Geoff, his hope and enthusiasm returning.

"Some of the deep underground military bases are still being used for nefarious activities," Michael continued. "They haven't all been found, cleared, and excavated yet. If he's down there, chances are it's one of those."

They sped along the country roads with minimal traffic. When they met a car, Michael was adept at overtaking it with the effortless acceleration of the BMW.

Finally, they arrived at the gates of the lodge.

Unfortunately, the entrance was so far away from the clubhouse that you couldn't see any signs of life until you were well into the property.

Geoff punched in his code, but the machine read 'incorrect pin.'

"They changed it," said Geoff. But Michael was already springing into action.

Within seconds, Michael grabbed his bag of tools from the trunk and dismantled the key code unit. He cut two wires and placed them together, and the gate was opening.

"You can have all the encryption and difficult pins you want, but if someone can open your box, you only have to cut the wires and put them together," Michael quipped.

"Nice," said Geoff, becoming more used to his partner's wide skillset.

With the gate open, they flew up the access road.

"There's the bastard!" Geoff called out as they saw the black SUV. But he couldn't see Miguel — he may have already made it to the lodge and escaped underground.

Michael skidded the car to a halt in the gravel parking lot. Both of them stepped out and approached the SUV. Cupping both hands on the glass, they were unsuccessful in seeing inside the blacked-out windows, but they assumed he had taken the children inside. They made their way to the entrance, which was closed.

Geoff had no doubt Michael would find a way through the door, but every barrier was more time lost. Michael took out a revolver and shot the handle. "Sometimes subtlety is overrated," said Michael, almost sounding like a particular famous secret agent who loves Aston Martins, attractive women and witty one-liners. With how calm and composed Michael had been, Geoff was beginning to wonder.

Nah, he thought to himself, *that's the movies... but maybe they based the character on Michael Clarke!*

Michael directed Geoff to the right side of the door, and as he opened it towards himself, he slid himself around so the door sat between him and the wall. He took out another revolver and threw it at Geoff.

"You know how to use that?" he asked quietly.

"Sure, my dad was a gun-totin' Republican," Geoff whispered.

"Good," said Michael, "but only use it if you really need to. Follow my lead."

Geoff nodded and loaded the gun.

Michael pivoted out to the middle of the door with his gun cocked and ready. He entered and scanned the area, firearm extended in front of him. Geoff followed in the same way.

After they had cleared the hallway, Michael pushed against the left sidewall. Michael directed Geoff with hand signals to clear the front left room as he checked out the back left room.

They silently cleared each room and found nothing.

"Most likely, he's taken them underground," Michael said as he met back up with Geoff. "Any idea where there are hidden rooms or elevators?"

"If there are any, it's most likely in the Masonic room," Geoff answered. "It's the circular one off the room you cleared."

They made their way into the room decorated with elaborate thrones and robes hanging from the walls.

The room contained an altar with a central step leading to three middle chairs. Geoff had never ventured to the back left of the room, which looked like a priest's cloakroom. He wondered if there might be something back there.

They made their way past a black curtain into a little back room. A red curtain covered what looked like another door.

Geoff pulled the curtain.

"Bingo," said Michael with relish as an elevator door was revealed.

Military security was a different grade, and this time, there was no getting into the elevator by breaking open the box or shooting it. Luckily, Michael had his master key.

He hovered the card over the keypad, and the lock clicked open. They heard the elevator starting to come up. Just in case, the two men drew their guns and peeled off to either side. But when the doors opened, the cabin was empty.

They proceeded into the heavy box and pressed the button for the basement. They knew this was probably more than a regular underground, given how they entered.

They were entering a small DUMB, a facility devoid of people but still operational. It connected to a vast network that had been cleared, but offshoots like this were still accessible, even if they weren't manned. They used to be monitored and used by scientists and technicians coming from the main bases to oversee the offshoots.

The only ones to use it now were Cabal figures from overground.

"I hope your stomach is feeling sturdy," said Michael, concerned with what they might find down there.

The elevator was fast, but they were going deep. Really deep. Geoff could only imagine how far underground they were going with how long it took.

When the elevator stopped, two men closed up against the walls as the doors opened.

Michael snuck a peek at what awaited them: a clean, white, empty corridor. He stepped forward and out, and as he did so, he gestured with his head for Geoff to do the same.

They crept forward, slowly and quietly traversing the hall so as not to alert Miguel or anyone else to their presence. Various dimly lit rooms containing mechanical whirring broke off from the long corridor, but they didn't have time to investigate.

Near the end of the hallway, they heard a Latin man's voice. It was Miguel. They carefully and quietly made their way up to the door, both against the same side of the wall, with Michael leading. They had to be on the near side wall to be invisible to anyone in the next room.

Michael made a rapid sneak peek around the corner, and he saw Miguel and the two children. He had a gun in his hand, and the children were near his side, obeying for fear of what he might do.

But Michael didn't realise there was a glass pane angled between them and Miguel, and the light was shining in such a way to make a somewhat decent mirror.

The image of Michael caught Miguel's eye, and he immediately sprung into action. He grabbed Lawrence, using him as a human shield and fired at the open door. The bullet whizzed by Michael and Geoff, hitting the opposite wall.

"Come out and put your gun on the floor, *mi amigo*," Miguel called out in his thick accent.

Michael realised that Miguel may not have spotted Geoff and waved him around to circle back from the other side. Geoff nodded and carefully slipped away.

There was a side corridor not far from where they were, and Michael guessed there was at least one more door in the large room Miguel occupied.
Now it was about buying enough time for Geoff to sneak around.

Michael edged his head and gun around the corner to see Miguel pointing a pistol directly at him, still using Lawrence as a shield, while Sarah had run to the far corner. He pointed his gun at Miguel's head, but it was too exacting a shot.

Miguel was pensive. He had to work out the moral code of the man in front of him, so he kept his gun aimed at Michael's head.

Since Michael wasn't shooting, he got his answer.

He put the gun to Lawrence's temple. The poor child was grimacing, hoping there was some way to get out of this situation. But he knew there was little he could do as Miguel overpowered him.

"Come out!" Miguel called out again. "Put the gun to the floor and step away with your hands behind your head."

"Okay... okay," said Michael, stepping out into full view. "Don't shoot the kid, and I'll do as you say." Out of the corner of his eye, he glanced at the side door and thought, *Where the hell is Geoff?*
As slowly as he could, Michael began to lower his revolver to the floor. He still had his hand on it when Geoff kicked through the side door.

"Drop the gun!" Geoff yelled. Miguel immediately drew his aim at Geoff, but Michael had drawn his weapon on Miguel too.

Miguel went to aim at Michael, then back to Geoff; it was dawning on him that he had no way to win this gunfight. Trying to find a solution, he pointed at Geoff, a drop of sweat forming on his forehead beneath his medium-length jet black hair that matched his leather jacket and jeans.

There was a back door only six feet away. He aimed the gun back at the child's head and crouched down to Lawrence's height, retreating towards the door.

Michael and Geoff knew they couldn't safely shoot. Miguel also knew he had to act before one of them felt confident enough to send a bullet in his direction. The door was ajar enough that he could slip out, and as he did, he pushed the child forward.
Once he was through, Miguel locked the door immediately. He heard a bullet hit it from Michael's angle, but it couldn't get through.

He sprinted down the corridor. Michael shot the door lock twice, the second one doing the trick.
He burst through the door and ran after Miguel.
Geoff crouched down near the kids and asked them if they were okay. He gave them both a hug. They were still in shock, unsure if Geoff could be trusted, but they gradually realised he was there to help.

It wasn't long before Michael returned. He had hit a dead-end — Miguel knew some way out of the side doors that Michael couldn't find. He was sure Miguel was gone, either back overground or into some other underground network.

After settling Lawrence and Sarah, Michael and Geoff each took one by the hand and agreed to take a quick glance around the facilities before getting to the surface to call for help.

Geoff was careful not to hold Sarah's little hand too tight as they proceeded down the corridor.
Opening the rooms as they went, most of them looked like unused chambers filled with seats. Geoff couldn't work out what they were for. However, one of the rooms was different: it had strobing red lights and machines buzzing with electricity.

They entered to see exactly what was in there.

Geoff looked over at Michael. They both wore the same expression, one that said *what on earth is this?* Even Michael was chilled to the core — and he had seen it all.

They were looking at cloned humans in tubes and organ harvesting ovens. Torture cubicles sat next to them, old blood seeping from their entrances in the underground darkness.

Now Geoff also knew what those other chambers with the seats and straps were for. He took out his phone to capture this incredulous scene on video.

The bodies in the tubes were sometimes half-formed, some fully formed at different ages. He didn't even want to look at the organ ovens or the torture seats.

They knew they had to take the children away from this horror show immediately. So Geoff and Michael sped up to the surface, checking at every turn in case Miguel had returned with friends. But he was nowhere to be seen.

When they got up to the ground floor, Michael immediately called the military, and they were on hand, having been briefed yesterday that quick attention may be required.

"Colonel Jeffers himself is in the area in a high-speed chopper," Michael said, updating Geoff once he got off the call. "He was waiting for the right moment to step in. I had to keep it to myself, as they are only cleared to be back up, and mission intel can only be shared between officers and agents, particularly while it is happening. As you know, they can't get overtly involved, and going in with a chopper when Miguel had two hostages wasn't going to be subtle or very successful either."

"Fair enough," said Geoff, knowing his friend was correct.

"If we had lost Miguel when he had the children, I'd have called the colonel to try to locate and track him for us," Michael continued. "We had the best chance with that strategy, and we succeeded."

"We did," said Geoff with genuine satisfaction.

The chopper landed down. Lawrence cracked the first smile Geoff had ever seen. While he brought the children towards the helicopter, Michael hurried over to brief the military men.

"We'll take you back to our base in Dallas," Colonel Jeffers said to Geoff.

But Sarah wasn't willingly going anywhere without Geoff. No one had ever stood up for her, let alone risked their own safety to defend her. She wasn't about to let him leave and grabbed him by the waist.

"It's okay; you can come, Sarah," Geoff said. "And you too, Lawrence."

Geoff helped them both into the chopper before Michael gave his farewells and headed off to drive his BMW home. Geoff and the colonel gave him a thumbs-up as he reached his car; Michael thrust a happy fist into the air before he got in.

"What a job you did, Geoff," Colonel Jeffers said with a smile.

"Thanks, colonel," Geoff said. "I just followed Michael's lead, but we pulled it off. However, Miguel got away."

"Don't worry about him. You made the right decision. His day will come," replied the colonel.
The pilot got the helicopter airborne, and it climbed quickly. Geoff rubbed the back of his neck, trying to ease the discomfort of a question he wanted to ask.

"What was that down there?"

"What did you see?" asked the colonel, though he probably knew the answer.

Geoff brought his mouth closer to the colonel's ear so the children wouldn't hear, but they were distracted anyway, marvelling at the world getting smaller and smaller below them.

"Bodies being grown in tubes, ovens with organs in them, small torture chairs," Geoff explained.

"They've been cloning humans," the colonel whispered into Geoff's ear. "You don't think it stopped in 1993 with Dolly the Sheep, do ya?"

Geoff's eyes went wide.

The colonel continued, "They reckon there are millions of clones in the world and that they're different from normal humans — soulless. Their eyes are empty."

"Have you met some?" asked Geoff.

"Yes, I have," the colonel admitted. "The freaky thing is the memories carry with the DNA, so they act like the person, have their memories, and don't even know they are a clone."

"Wow," replied Geoff.

"The organ harvesting is a similar process, but it is for individual organs," the colonel continued.

"The torture chambers are for industrial production of adrenochrome. The adrenochrome from clones is different, so they want real children. Horrific stuff."

Geoff shook his head and grimaced.

"Now, we'll go in, block out, or blow up that DUMB. We don't prioritise the small ones until someone from overground goes below. On a larger scale, we've basically done the job," the colonel said with pride on his face.

"Brilliant," replied Geoff switching to an optimistic hope for what they were doing.

"Lucky you didn't hang around down there — there was a convoy of black vehicles headed out to meet you," the colonel said. "I don't think they were bringing flasks and sandwiches. As soon as they saw us, they turned around and headed back to the city."

Geoff nodded, appreciating how balanced that whole situation was. He was relieved that they emerged unscathed.

"We strongly recommend you go into protective custody for awhile. Is that okay?" asked Colonel Jeffers. "We will do the same with the children." He paused, giving Geoff breathing space to think.

"It will give me time to reflect and work out how to move forward," Geoff said.

"Absolutely, it will," said the colonel, knowing that they also had a plan for Geoff that he didn't even know about yet.

"First things first, you will be taken to a place in Canada," the colonel began. "You will be declared missing for a while. After your speech, that will raise huge alarm bells and wake more people up."

Geoff smiled, liking the idea of faking his death for the greater good, adding, "I can go with that."

Time passed by in the helicopter with both men sitting back and relaxing. Geoff was deep in thought. About twenty minutes later, he leaned forward to say something to the colonel.

"I'd like to take care of these kids and foster them while in protective custody. Would that be possible?" he asked.

"I don't see why not," Colonel Jeffers replied with a smile, appreciating Geoff's loving gesture towards the children.

"And Banff looks incredible; if we can go there, that'd be great," added Geoff hopefully.

"I'll talk to the guys and see what can be done," replied Colonel Jeffers.

Soon after, they landed in the Dallas base. Despite their understandable mistrust of people, the children still had their innocence and felt something was different about these adults.

They were in awe of the uniformed men and women and giant machines that dotted the base. They had never been on a helicopter before, and they were about to board a plane!

Colonel Jeffers made some calls, and the military organised a private plane to take them to Banff in Alberta, Canada.

"Don't say we don't take care of you, Geoff!"

Colonel Jeffers shook Geoff's hand before giving him a strong embrace.

He then bent over and gently shook the hands of the two children, smiling as he assured them they would be well taken care of. He ruffled the top of their woolly hats and wished them all the best.

"Thank you for everything," said Geoff as he and the children climbed the steps to board the plane. After quick introductions to the pilots, the soldier accompanying them and the children getting a grand tour of the cockpit, which Lawrence thought was the coolest thing he had ever seen, they took their seats on the spacious plane.

The children could choose between a large screen to watch a movie or play board games. They said they would start with a movie, and they flicked through Netflix, searching for something they both liked. They eventually settled on *Boss Baby*.

Geoff loved seeing these kids content and protected after all they had been through.

He sipped an Irish coffee (which he liked from time to time) and started reading Kane and Abel by Jeffrey Archer. He had bought it in a shop at the military base when they had a few minutes before the flight. He was already well into the novel at home with another paperback of a slightly different cover. But it had the same contents, so he took up where he had left off.

Archer was Geoff's favourite writer because he kept everything flowing and engaging yet simple, and he wrote captivating plots with many thought-provoking segues and commentaries.

They arrived at the airport in Alberta and were driven up to Banff in a rented car by the soldier accompanying them. The scenery in this part of the world was extraordinary; Geoff and the kids marvelled at the forests, rivers, and snow-topped mountains.

Private Caniff was a quiet six-footer that followed the protocol to the letter.

He brought them to a lovely cabin up by the mountains and got them settled in. He was to stay a few days before departing.

The wooden bungalow cabin was wonderfully insulated and cosy, with a wood stove in the kitchen, fireplace in the living room, and radiators in the bedrooms. Everything inside was wood apart from some large fluffy rugs on the floors and tools hanging on the walls.

There were three bedrooms, so the private insisted on sleeping on the couch while he was there.

Geoff was setup with a credit card and a vehicle before Private Caniff wished them well and was on his way. Banff was close, so Geoff could get supplies when he needed them.

He was allowed to call his parents, siblings, and a few friends. He got in touch with his mom, dad, and only brother, telling them he was fine but wouldn't be in contact for a while.

He did the same thing with Syed and only told him that he was hiding from the Cabal. He wanted to tell his friend more, but he knew he couldn't. Syed had told him about the Free Masons, so he knew there was more to this than met the eye. But he also knew that he wouldn't find out anytime soon.

The last two calls he made were to Martha and Michael. Geoff was able to call them as often as he liked because they were an essential part of the process — both in the past and future.

Geoff didn't know the full extent of what the alliance wanted from him; he understood that he would come back to speak out more and that he was being more insularly protected and supported in the meantime.

He had no idea how much of a figurehead they wanted him to be.

Geoff thought Michael was the man, but Michael knew he was assisting a person that could take more people with him than he ever realised. Geoff had leadership qualities, intellect, and a position that could make a huge difference.

The intellect part took Geoff by surprise because he never considered himself to be remarkably intelligent. However, he had always been street smart. This past year though, he had been questioning so many things, reading a lot, writing his thoughts, and recently began clearing his heart and mind of noise — it was having a drastic effect on his mind.

He noticed he was a very adept writer now, his speeches were on point, and he could hold an audience with more than just trite charm — now they were listening intently. He was also able to gather details quickly and clearly see the bigger picture.

Any mediocrity he had in certain areas was disappearing. Geoff realised this was more about the individual than the collective.

People allowed all this nonsense to happen because they couldn't disseminate truth from fiction, science from scientism, and didn't have a strong enough claim on their rights. They were not aware, not developed enough.

The education system treated people like blank slates, pouring information onto them and, generally speaking, churning out rote memorisation parrots — the farther people went in that system, the worse they were.

Geoff knew this was the main root of the problem; it was why most people were so easy to control. So he knew he had to look into learning.

Geoff wanted to help Sarah and Lawrence, which was a significant part of it. What he had done with himself was pretty remarkable, and it could be replicated. He wanted to transform their pain into joy and help them shine. It was how he would give them the best chance in life.

The Heyoka process was excellent at healing traumas and fixing negative beliefs, but he wanted to know more about homeschooling and accelerated learning. He studied everything he could on it.

He also applied to foster the kids through General Flint, and it was granted. This made him and the children very happy — when he told them the good news, they hugged him so hard he thought they would never let go.

Their happiness confirmed it was the right decision and made him more determined to help them.

What Geoff discovered about learning knocked his socks off. Ancient Greece and the Renaissance had schools based on drawing out the student's perceptions, and they produced more geniuses in those periods than all of world history combined!

He learned that there were eight intelligences, and the education system only really catered to two: verbal and mathematical. Combined with the rote memorisation system, they were producing people that could memorise the authority narrative and generally avoided errors with grammar, spelling and sums.

Hardly inspiring. It was actually dangerous. So he created a plan for the kids that developed all their intelligences and their whole brain (which is sensory-based) while drawing them out of their perceptions to gain trust in their own minds.

When he spoke to Martha, she said, "That's absolutely right, Geoff. We are sensory beings of movement, and our brains are almost entirely sensory-based, so we learn through things that engage our natural instincts."

Sarah and Lawrence were kids that now photoread books, flicking through the pages and then going back and reading them normally. So their memory, comprehension and understanding of the materials went way up.

They were really enjoying it. Sarah said at one point, "I don't even have to read some books normally. I can just recall details when I need them." Geoff marvelled at their adaptability.

He asked them questions, and there were no right or wrong answers on their current thoughts or perceptions, as it was a self-correcting feedback loop. They freenoted their thoughts on things as well. They could link subjects to seemingly unrelated, but in reality, connected matters. They also described the 'random' images and video streams playing in their mind in sensory terms for several minutes a day.

Lawrence told Geoff, "It's like being able to think in pictures. I love that."

In addition to training their brains, they exercised their bodies for cardiovascular health and coordination, balance, eye tracking, and proprioception. They did those for at least twenty minutes a day to improve the plumbing and wiring that underpinned all of their visual, auditory, and kinaesthetic perceptions. As Geoff was learning, these concepts were the foundation for all human perceptive abilities!

They both loved this physical development as they were sporty and enjoyed being active. It was also helping their basketball, a sport they loved to play together out in the backyard.

Geoff would often hear them exclaim with excitement when one of them demonstrated a skill or made a difficult shot. This was, of course, also helping their development process in many ways.

When they made notes on materials, they would not just freenote on it, but also mind map it in a visual picture form. One bubble would be connected to another, forming a web of thoughts. This would also engage the artistic right side of the brain.

Sarah, in particular, enjoyed this practice. Depending on the subject, she would put her head right down on the page and use her pencils to draw out her maps in creative cartoons, bubbles, and storyboards.

Their perceptive ability and trust in their minds went through the roof.

They also entered the scouts, martial arts classes, and basketball as their extra circular activities to socialise with other children.

Last but not least, Geoff worked with them daily for twenty minutes on releasing trauma, noise, unhelpful beliefs, and worries. He could see the light coming back into their eyes day by day. Over a few months, they went through tremendous growth — they were becoming sovereign persons with independent, critical thinking abilities and extraordinary competence for their age.

This healing, development, and releasing of the potential of these children was by far the most rewarding experience of Geoff's life. He smiled inwardly every time he thought about it.

The bond developing between them was beautiful as well. There was nothing better than this.

Chapter 10

After a few weeks in Canada, Geoff had released his mental blocks to exercising and had joined a local running club. He became friendly with some of the other runners over the months there, and they invited him to a night out at the recently reopened Aurora nightclub.

The headline act was Maceo Plex, a famous DJ from Flower Mound, Texas, whom Geoff was a big fan of. He hadn't had a night out in a long time, so he wanted to let his hair down. Geoff also needed some new clothing since his physique had changed.

He headed into town for an afternoon shopping spree.

He was given an average enough Ford Mondeo car that was several years old to not draw too much attention to himself. He liked it, though; it had effortless power, a luxury interior and a satisfying purr to its engine.

Once he'd parked near the main shopping streets, Geoff went into a clothes shop called 'Born'. When he pushed the door open, a young lady greeted him.

He told her he would like to try a new style, something more slim-fitting since he'd been losing weight. For colours, he preferred browns, greys, blacks and navy in particular. He would like shirts, t-shirts, tops and pants.

Geoff was nicely dressed in brown cords, Ecco shoes, a dark green sweater and a brown-grey suede overcoat with a grey scarf. Though he had always been pretty well-dressed, he was a different man now. He was in good shape, and he had an inner confidence and self-assurance that he never had before. And it showed.

The girl, probably ten years younger than Geoff, told him she needed to check and went back to the counter to see what was in stock. Her middle-aged supervisor commented that Geoff was 'quite yummy', making the younger one giggle.

"Back in one minute," she shouted over at Geoff before she retreated into the storeroom to grab some items.

Geoff had lost nearly fifty pounds and suddenly possessed a handsomely chiselled face. However, the main change was how he carried himself. All aspects of Geoff were congruent, making for a magnetic man.

When the young lady returned with the clothes, she said, "You might want to try these on. The changing rooms are down the corridor behind you."

"Thank you, some of these look really good," said Geoff.

He had some stylish Ralph Lauren, Oscar Jacobsen, and Tommy Hilfiger gear draped over his arms as he headed to the fitting room.

He tried them all on, sometimes just looking in the changing room mirror and sometimes coming out to the hallway for a better view. In the end, of the sweaters, he liked the black Ralph Lauren one with red seam lines the most and just wanted a second opinion. The girl serving him said, "Oh, that fits lovely, and it's a nice colour on you!"

That was all he needed to decide he would wear it tonight. It would go well with the slim-fit black jeans he had also picked out.

Geoff bought three outfits and left the shop in a good mood. *Tonight will be fun*, he told himself.
When he returned home, he asked Sarah and Lawrence for their opinion on the clothing, laying them out on the clean kitchen table for their perusal.
Lawrence felt the fabrics and was clearly impressed.
"I like your style, Dad!" It was the first time he'd called Geoff 'Dad'. Geoff didn't say anything but put his arm around to hug him. Lawrence was a tough boy but a very good-hearted one. Geoff always felt he would make it past anything and eventually come out a winner.

Lawrence had been an orphan all his life and couldn't put into words just how grateful he was to have someone who cared about him. And it wasn't just that — through all the work they did together, the confidence he was building from succeeding at tasks and releasing his traumas made him feel deserving of good things in life.

It was a big moment for Lawrence and Geoff, one that Sarah had with Geoff two months previously. Sarah was an indigo child, and despite all the abuse, she still had a close connection to the Source or ultimate truth.

She clearly saw Geoff's intentions right away, and it took her less time to open her heart. She had as many issues to work through as Lawrence, but it showed more in emotional instability for her. At times she threw tantrums, screamed, shouted, and banged doors.

But her dad would come and hug her. Just like Lawrence, her self-confidence increased, and through the healing practises, the traumas started to feel like they happened to someone else. The problems were disappearing.

Geoff and Lawrence had come to love her dearly. She was the Yin to their Yang and brought an earthliness and nurturing to the home. She was an old soul and idealistic for a child, always wanting the best and fighting for what she saw as right.

She went through her dad's new clothing with a far more scrutinising eye, wanting no less than excellence for her father on his first night out in months.

"These are nice, Papa. But which ones are you wearing tonight? I want to see if they match."

"The black Ralph Lauren top, the slim fit black jeans, and the red polo shirt," Geoff replied, wondering if she would approve.

"They will go well together, and the red collar will look great with the black," Sarah said with a maturity well beyond her years.

"Okay, sounds good," Geoff said, thankful to have such a beautiful little soul wanting the best for him. "Thank you."

Geoff kissed her on the forehead before gathering up his clothes and heading for the shower.

After a thorough wash and application of Dolce and Gabbana cologne, Geoff was ready to put on his smart new outfit.

He put it on and fixed it up. It stretched out nicely and easily into a good fit, which was always important with the new slim designs. His black Ralph Lauren belt with a steel buckle and slightly pointed polished black shoes completed the outfit. Finally, he emerged into the living room, where Sarah and Lawrence watched Netflix.

"I like it," said Lawrence, smiling.

"You look great, Dad," Sarah said and gave him a thumbs-up, her curls, dress, and white socks making her all the more adorable.

The eighteen-year-old babysitter from next door arrived as Geoff was phoning a cab. She was a kind-hearted, responsible girl, and Geoff trusted her. Within five minutes, the driver was outside, and he whisked him into town in less than ten minutes.

Geoff got out at the Aurora nightclub venue.

As he entered the club, his friends spotted him and let out a big cheer. They were in a party mood and had never seen him outside the running track before.

Maceo Plex was in the DJ booth; he gave it all his energy and was even busting out moves himself. He was also a good dancer and played his own song *When the Lights Go Out*. His enthusiasm was infectious, and everyone in the room loved the music. People on the dancefloor were in a trance, moving their whole being with the rhythm.

Geoff's main two buddies in the running club were Colin and John. He discussed the English Premier League with them — Geoff and Colin followed Man Utd, and John followed Arsenal.

They said that both clubs had struggled to replace such pivotal and inspirational figures at their clubs, Alex Ferguson and Arsene Wenger, respectively.

As interesting as this discussion was for soccer fans, something else had caught Geoff's eye: a thin but curved, straight-haired brunet sipping a drink and dancing stylishly with the music. It was Denise! Geoff had been wondering if he'd bump into her at some point.

She was on her own, waiting for a female friend that had just gone to the bathroom. She wore a v-necked black top that showed off her arms and chest. It was smartly matched with a black skirt and high heels.

Geoff couldn't keep his eyes off her, but he wanted to pretend to be paying attention to the conversation with his friends so she wouldn't spot him looking. He already thought he had to talk to her, but he wanted it to be organic — or at least look that way. More importantly, he didn't want some other mongrel to get in there first.

There was only one solution. Without a word to his friends, he purposefully grabbed his drink and marched up to her. The guys all looked on in admiration.

As he approached, she spotted him. She hid how impressed she was, but she didn't want to be unfriendly, either. She just wanted to play it that way and see how he did, hoping he wasn't drunk or a bonehead.

"Hi, I'm Geoff," he said coolly, holding his hand for her to shake.

She shook it and said, "I'm Denise," and smiled. Then, she looked at him again with a flash of recognition in her eyes. "No way!"

"Yes, way," replied Geoff.

"I didn't even recognise you," said Denise.

"I've been exercising, mainly running a lot."

"I can see that. But people can look different on Zoom too."

However, it was more than appearance; Geoff's energy was also different.

They began to catch up on various things and talked about the DJ, Banff, and whatever else. Denise was very curious about why he had ended up in this town three months ago. She wanted to find out more, but Geoff just told her it was because he needed a break somewhere quiet, and the photos she showed him of Banff really struck him, which was all true.

After ten minutes or so, Geoff's drink was nearly finished, and he noticed Denise's glass was also low. So he said he would get a drink and offered to get her one too.

"Yes, I'd like a vodka and tropical fruit juice with a slice of orange, please," she said.

Geoff looked at her with a smile wondering why it didn't have a more exotic name. Almost reading his mind, Denise said, "I haven't given it a name yet."

She gave him an extra-long look as he headed for the bar.

The friend she had been waiting for came back over to have a chat and said, "Who's he?"

"Geoff Hurley from Texas," Denise replied with a flirtatious eyebrow raise.

"He's hot," her friend said with a teasing laugh. "Be careful of those Texan lads, though. They're only after one thing. And if it were me, he could have it." They both giggled like a pair of naughty schoolgirls.

"I'll leave you to it, honey," said her friend as she headed for the dance floor.

Denise had already decided that she wouldn't be sleeping with Geoff tonight — one-night stands were very rare for her. Besides, she liked him and wanted to see where it could go this time.

Geoff returned with the drinks, feeling inspired as he always did when good house music was playing. Now, they had put their drinks on the circular counter beside them to stand closer together.

They were having a deeper conversation about life, agreeing that what was going on in the world was totally upside down, based on lies, and would fall apart when the real truth emerged.

By this stage, Geoff had naturally placed his hand on Denise's hip. She wanted to get her phone from her side pocket to check the time. As she moved, her fingers brushed his, and when she put the phone back in her bag, their fingers interlocked.

Geoff knew this was the right time to kiss her. He looked her in her brown eyes and moved in slowly, first giving her a little kiss, moving a few millimetres back, lingering there, before kissing her again for a little longer.

If things weren't clicking before, they were now.

Back at the table, John, a single man, commented, "That's what happens when you invite a foreigner out," and they all laughed.

Geoff brought Denise over to the table and introduced her.

"Can't bring him anywhere," Colin said with a grin.

"Oh really?" Denise asked, wondering if she was just one in a long line of conquests.

"Well, seems like it," continued Colin, just throwing meaningless volleys out for a laugh.

"Don't mind these fellas," Geoff said, defusing the shenanigans. "This is the first time I've been out with them."

Geoff and Denise were still holding hands; it felt like they had known each other a lot longer than a few Zoom calls and the thirty minutes they had spent together.

The night continued with music, alcohol, and good company. When it was time to leave, Geoff offered to drop Denise home in a cab. Arriving at her house on the other side of town, Denise gave him a kiss and her number before they said their goodnights.

Geoff was delighted to have her number; he wanted to see her again, but he had a babysitter at home that he needed to relieve.

Denise Buthyran was born in Banff, Alberta, Canada, in 1994. Her father was a farmer and a local storyteller, and her mother was a herbalist.

She grew up in an environment where herbs, good food, and fresh air were the order of the day. This kind of upbringing was the envy of many in the years to come.

Denise had two brothers: one older and one younger. Because of them, she could hold her own in any rough and tumble. Growing up, she may have even been described as a bit of a tomboy, but she was also quite feminine. She liked to dress up, try her mom's hairstyles, and put on makeup.

People from Banff were generally outdoor types since they lived in such natural splendour. However, with the advent of the internet, that wasn't always the case with the newer generations.

But Denise was a real outdoor girl. She got an incredible thrill from mountain climbing and canoeing, but the thing she loved most was the fresh air and adrenaline rush.

Her day job was in a local health food shop, where she put all the knowledge she acquired from her parents into practice — Denise could tell you about every herbal remedy for any ailment despite having never trained in the craft.

Thanks to her father, who was big on eating unprocessed and whole foods, she knew the effect food had on the body. "Everything from the land," he would say. She had also studied nutrition to support her sporting and adventure goals.

One of Denise's biggest and most recent passions was being an Awakened Spirit coordinator, representing a wonderful organisation dedicated to truth, love, and spirituality.

In the last two years, things had heated up in that line of work. Awakened Spirit had a massive influx of members and created new groups worldwide. A mass awakening was underway, which led to a clamour for more meaning, connection, and spirituality in people's lives.

The organisation didn't impose any particular dogma or beliefs on anyone; they only presented a way to connect with like-minded souls searching for a better life free from Cabal nonsense, supporting the search for ultimate truths and love among man, nature, and the cosmos.

She held Zoom calls every Tuesday for Alberta, Canada. She looked forward to those calls immensely since it was what she regarded as an hour and a half with connected souls and away from the bullshit going on in the world.

This was the reason she and Geoff connected so quickly. Though they were on the same wavelength, Denise hadn't told him about her position in Awakened Spirit, and Geoff certainly hadn't told her about his protective custody and two recently fostered children — it wasn't something he would divulge right away, because he had to be sure he could trust her. As much as he liked Denise, he was only just getting to know her.

Geoff called Denise the next day to make sure she had safely gotten in the front door — a gentlemanly excuse to speak to her again and arrange another date.

Since Denise was from the area, Geoff asked about what adventure they could have together and what day would suit. She revealed her love of rock climbing in the mountains and challenged Geoff to a trek.

Geoff reluctantly agreed, knowing he would be out of his depth but that he would have to suck it up and power forward.

A couple of days later, their second date was in full swing. Geoff and Denise were harnessed, helmeted, and geared up to climb a cliff face not too far from the centre of town.

Geoff put his complete faith in Denise's expertise to keep this adventure fun and safe. They had already hiked the footpath to the top of the cliff and anchored a harness and rope securely into the ground above before throwing the end down to the bottom.

Once they hiked back down, Denise attached the rope to her gear and began to climb.

She had told Geoff to watch her closely to learn how to approach it. On one stretch where she couldn't get a grip to move up further, she took out a metal hook with a sharp point and slammed it into a softer area above her, using it for leverage.

"When you do this, you have to move quickly because it's not as stable as grabbing something by hand," she shouted down to him.

"Got it," said Geoff, getting nervous about what lay ahead.

It wasn't long before Denise had climbed all the way to the top. She got to her feet and stood triumphantly, raising her hands in the air to celebrate her victory.

"Now it's your turn!" she exclaimed with great enthusiasm.

This would be more of a triumph for Geoff than she realised. Or it would be quite an embarrassing second date.

Geoff had a fear of heights. In the past, he wouldn't have even entertained this, never mind putting himself in the position to face it. However, he had cleared so much fear from his mind recently.

Though his fear of heights was acute (more of a phobia), the cleansing practices gave him a reference point. All the previous day and this morning, he had done his mental processes to clear his fear of heights.

It gave him enough power to go for it, but he still didn't know how he'd react once he began. He knew that before he'd have looked down, froze, and quit early. But today, he was committed to clearing any negative thoughts as they came. So he started doing it before he even left the ground.

"Okay, let's do this!" he shouted. "Take it easy with me. I'm about to conquer my fear of heights." The way he phrased the last sentence demonstrated his excellent mindset, but it was easy enough to sound in control with his feet firmly on the ground.

Denise put her hands to her face in a moment of surprise before quickly switching to encouragement. "You can do this!"

"Let's go!" he shouted as he placed his right hand onto a rock and found quick footing for his left boot.

Before he knew it, he was on the cliff face!

"Now, stay calm, take your left hand, and do the same," Denise said. "Keep breathing."

With a solid anchoring on his right side, he created the same platform on the left, but a bit higher.
He established another few feet, now using his left side for grip. Sweat was already beading down his forehead.

"Don't look down," Denise reassured him.

In the past, Geoff would have quit by now. Instead, he had to have that moment where he would look down for a second, taste the fear, get past it, and move to a point where looking down was pointless and unproductive.

He had a quick peek downward, and the fear came rushing. He wanted to quit. However, unlike before, the fear wasn't all-encompassing and totally freezing him. He still had control of his emotions.

Is this interesting, yes or no? he asked of the feeling of fear and answered, *No*.

He took a deep breath and moved forward.

I can do this, he thought to himself, forcing his mind to focus on the job at hand: climbing.

And on he went. After successfully negotiating three steps, he was starting to feel a small level of competency. It would have been far too soon to say he was feeling confident, but this was much better — now, he had some momentum.

Before long, he was halfway there. Denise had picked a decent but short climb for a beginner.
As Geoff continued, he resolved not to look down from here on out. He powered upward. He wasn't far from the top now.

He was starting to feel confident, but right before the top, he had another challenge. He had to pull himself over the edge, something else he had never done before. It daunted him.

Thoughts of going flying off the cliff edge gnawed at him, and the safety rope only added a layer of comfort. What if the rope was not secured? What if the anchor came flying out or the rope broke?
Stop it! He gathered his thoughts, repeating his mental processes: *Is this interesting, yes or no? No!*

Geoff was back. He grabbed the ground above with his right hand as Denise watched, knowing his satisfaction would be greater if he accomplished it on his own.

He used all his strength to pull himself half a foot more — just enough to get his left hand onto the edge. Scrambling to find his footing, Geoff swung out his left foot until he gained a solid hold and gave him just enough of a push to heave his whole body over the finish line.

Geoff flipped onto his back, looking up at the sky as he cried out in triumph.

"I can't believe I just did that!" he said, incredulous.

"Well done!" said Denise, over the moon for him and clapping her hands in short bursts of celebration.

To an experienced climber, the climb was short and basic, but to a beginner with a fear of heights, it was exhilarating. With Denise's help, Geoff clambered to his feet, and they celebrated the moment with a kiss.

They wanted to drink it in, looking out over the snow-tipped mountains, tall pointed evergreens, and winding rivers, basking in the stunning beauty of the Rocky Mountains.

"Okay, that's enough climbing for today," Geoff said, relieved and satisfied with what he had done.

"Fair enough. But you do know we have to go back down," said Denise with a laugh. "Don't worry, that's the easy bit."

"Oh Lord," replied Geoff. If he could climb it, the descent shouldn't be much of an issue.

He still had to go through all his processes when he felt uneasy, but it was better than before. He made lighter work of the descent, and Denise followed expertly.

"Well done," said Geoff as she hit the ground. When they were both off the cliff, he gave her a quick peck on the lips.

He knew he could conquer this fear completely with more time on the Banff verticals.

They hiked to the top, huffing and puffing as they went along, enjoying their achievements. They quickly gathered all the gear together into two neatly compacted large backpacks.

On the walk back down to the ground level, they continued to chat about all manner of things. Neither of them ever had such a good time. Already, they were starting to feel comfortable, and the idea of a future together was beginning to take shape.

As they approached the bottom of the winding path, they decided to go for lunch. They went to Helen's Garden, a quaint little restaurant with a lovely outdoor area.

On the way there, Denise pointed out the Green Health Food store where she worked.

While they were enjoying the food and each other's company, they told each other all kinds of stories from their lives: things they had done, places they had been, and plans for the future.

They were in a bubble where only the two of them existed. And they were falling for one another.
Geoff was itching to tell her all about the protective custody and the children, but he couldn't. They were still in the early stages, and he felt they needed to have a certain level of familiarity that only came with time.

At one point, he went to the bathroom, and 'Lawrie' showed up ringing his phone. Denise didn't think much of it, only mentioning to Geoff that he'd missed a call.

They finished up, and Geoff took Denise home. Her dad had taught her to drive when she was eighteen, but seeing as she lived in a small town and was close to everything, she never saw the need for the added expense of buying a car. So she usually walked, cycled, or took a bus.

In the following weeks, they went climbing on a slightly longer cliff face, and Geoff became more comfortable. They went to another house music gig, this time to Canadian DJ Moovry, which they enjoyed. Geoff also took Denise out to dinner a few times in expensive places in town, even eating squid on one occasion.

They spoke on the phone almost everyday, and their feelings were becoming more and more real.

Even though Denise had told him about Awakened Spirits and had deep conversations about their beliefs, Geoff still hadn't told her his entire situation, even though he really wanted to. Finally, he resolved to do it that week; he knew their relationship had reached a point where honesty was necessary, and he had to put it out there and let Denise decide if she wanted to continue.

However, Denise was intuitive, and she already felt there were things Geoff wasn't telling her. She was growing suspicious; even though she was in love with him and adored their time together, something about it was too good to be true.

Geoff had never brought her to his house. In fact, she had never even seen his house. Plus, he kept getting phone calls from two people named Sarah and Lawrie, which he said were work calls, but that felt odd to her. He avoided questions about his home, saying it was messy and needed to be cleaned.

Before anything went further, she had to know. After Geoff had visited her briefly at work, she decided that she would get a taxi and tail him home. It was half-past seven on a Friday, and the store was closing at eight o'clock. Her colleague was fine to close up in half an hour. She hailed a cab, and they waited for the Mondeo to emerge from the parking lot.

She followed Geoff as he drove the roads out of town to his house ten minutes away. When he arrived, Denise instructed the cab driver to drive on for a few minutes, then turn around to come back to the house and wait outside as she went to the door.

She was shaking with nerves as he approached the front porch. There was more than one person in the house — she could hear them.

When Geoff answered the door, he looked shifty and nervous.

"Have you got something to tell me?" Denise asked angrily, one hand on her hip, her face looking hurt yet fierce.

Geoff pulled the door out as he didn't want to make a scene in front of the kids. But Denise didn't know that.

"What are you hiding?" she asked. "Are you married? God, I'm such an idiot!" she said, pulling at her hair and starting to cry. Through the glass, she glanced a woman grabbing some clothing in the sitting room.

Her eyes lit up, and she exploded. "Is that your wife?" she asked while pointing at the window.
"Oh my God, I'm out of here!" she said, taking off towards the gate before Geoff could explain.

But Geoff ran after her and grabbed her by the arm.

"Get off me, get off me!" she screamed.

"Listen to me, Denise — she's not my wife. She's our babysitter!" Geoff began. "I have two kids, Sarah and Lawrie, and we're in protective custody! I was going to tell you. I just couldn't, but I was going to this week because…" Denise was captivated by his explanation, no longer struggling to get away as she listened intently. "Because I love you."

Denise stared back at him, her watery eyes locked on his, searching to see if he was telling the truth. She hoped he was being honest.

"It's true," said Geoff, still lightly holding her shoulders as he met her probing gaze with sincerity.

"Come in, and let's talk. I'll pay the cab driver," Geoff said, handing him enough to cover the trip. He didn't wait on the change, thanked the driver, and headed back.

He gently ushered an emotional and confused Denise inside.

Having gathered her things, the eighteen-year-old babysitter was just leaving.

"This is Kate, our babysitter,' said Geoff.

"Hi," said Kate shyly. Denise raised her hand in greeting, smiling sheepishly, embarrassed at calling her Geoff's wife half a minute earlier.

"Have a nice night, Kate," Denise said, recognising the girl as her friend's daughter.

"Thanks, you too," said Kate, being very good about the whole thing.

Geoff and Denise made their way into the sitting room as she left. Denise was looking at him, and he could feel she had softened, but he still had to talk about it.

"Darling, I wanted to tell you this when we met, and ever since, but I couldn't," Geoff began. "I did work in insurance, but I became a politician. I got caught up with the Free Masons, but I didn't stick around. Instead, I spoke out against Covid in my city, got blackballed and called an idiot. Then I investigated TACFA and two kids I witnessed being abused, and it ended up in a shootout with the Cabal. After that, I had to be taken into protective custody."

"Who is protecting you?" asked Denise — sharp as she was, she knew you couldn't trust the standard three-letter agencies.

"I think it's what you Awakened Spirits would call the Q-team," he replied.

"Wow," said Denise. "And your kids?"

"They are the kids I saw being abused. So I went to find them, rescued them, and fell in love. Then General Flint helped me to foster them. And I want to adopt them," said Geoff, his bottom lip quivering as he tried to hold in his emotions.

Denise grabbed his hands. "I love you," she said, tears filling her eyes.

She slid around the table and embraced him as they both began to cry — especially Geoff. He had been through so much, and he was so happy he could tell her. She seemed to be accepting it and proud of him.

"I'm sorry I didn't tell you," he said.

"Don't worry, I understand," she replied. The two of them were forehead to forehead, smiling and laughing with relief through the tears.

"I think it's time you met two very special people," said Geoff. He pointed to the door knowing the two kids were peeking in and trying to listen, even though they couldn't hear much over the fire crackling.

"Hi Denise," said Sarah, opening the door and coming into the kitchen in her pyjamas.

"Hi," said Lawrence just after, also in his bedclothes.

"Hi, Sarah. Hi, Lawrie," said Denise, greeting both of them warmly.

"We've heard a lot about you. I always helped him with his clothes and stuff when he was meeting you," said Sarah. "And he told us about the dates."

"Oh, that's lovely," Denise said, smiling. "Well, your dad thinks the world of you two, and I want to get to know you guys too."

Chapter 11

Four or five weeks later, Geoff and Denise had grown closer, and the kids always looked forward to seeing her. On successive weekends the whole gang went to the movies, arcades, and the skating rink. They were having a blast.

Denise quickly became a fixture in their home, coming by almost every day after work and staying a few nights a week. With her knowledge of food and medicine, she had observed a few things in their lifestyle that she wanted to improve. So one night, she asked Geoff if she could cook for them and let the kids pitch in.

"Sure," said Geoff with all the opposition one would expect from a man with fish sticks and beans as his kid's staple meal.

In fairness, Geoff would also do a mean spaghetti bolognese or chilli con carne twice a week, usually when Denise was staying over. But on other nights, it was usually burgers and fries, fish sticks with beans, or chicken tenders and wedges. So Denise was more than ready to add her considerable culinary skills and maternal touch to proceedings.

She arrived one evening with two grocery bags, and Geoff knew she meant business.

"Okay, guys, can you help me put out all this food on the cutting boards, please?" Denise said to Sarah and Lawrence.

They got right to it and laid out fruits, vegetables, sirloin steaks, virgin olive oil, honey, Himalayan salt, red and black pepper, and baby potatoes.

"All of this is whole organic food, most from local farms," she told them.

"Whole foods are better because they are not processed, and organic means they aren't sprayed with pesticides and other things not ideal for health," added Geoff.

"Exactly right," said Denise, impressed that Geoff had gotten right on board.

The kids were so happy to help out; they had never cooked things properly before — mixing Heinz baked beans in a pot didn't count.

Lawrence filled the big pot with water, brought it to a boil, chopped the vegetables, and put them in to cook. When they were boiled Sarah masterfully smeared honey and sprinkled the herbs on them. She also put olive oil and salt on the baby potatoes. The spuds and vegetables were ready for the oven.

"You should be very proud of these two, Geoff. I certainly am," said Denise.

"So proud," replied Geoff firmly.

Geoff got up from reading *Breakfast of Champions* by Kurt Vonnegut and helped them put the trays in the oven. Denise got to work frying the meat, and it wasn't long before everything was done. She showed Lawrence how to pepper the meat, and he did so with style.

"One last step," she said as she squeezed fresh lemon juice onto the vegetables that now had a honey crust from the oven, handing the job over to Sarah halfway through.

"Now you're going to taste the fruits of your labours," Denise said to the eager children.
Sarah and Lawrence set the table and, with the help of their father and Denise, served the plates with the potatoes, vegetables, and meat.

They said a prayer of gratitude for having wonderful food and a good place to live. Then they dug in.

Lawrence gave a perfect sign with his fingers, his mouth too full to speak.

"Delicious," said Sarah.

"This is the nicest meal I've ever tasted," said Geoff, much to the delight of the other three. The herbs and lemon sprinkled with the right sauces on each item made it truly delicious.

"And entirely made with whole organic foods that will nourish your body well," added Denise.

After another month, Denise was staying over every night, and the evening meals of whole delicious food were the norm, with Geoff taking two nights a week to do his style of cooking.

On the weekend, they were going to go canoeing as a family.

They were all looking forward to it. The night before, Denise said to Geoff, "Sarah is such a spiritual soul, but she's strong as well. She's a bit afraid of going out on the water tomorrow, but she'll do it. Lawrie is tough, a good kid. He's hands-on, especially with physical stuff."

"Yes, that's exactly how they are," said Geoff. "And they are very close now. They both love basketball, which gives them something in common." The kids played out in the yard every day, competing with other teams from the area; the two little twelve-year-olds practised so much they could shoot scores from all different positions and angles.

Saturday morning arrived, and they were ready to head for the river. The local River Deep Mountain High shop was beside the water, and they rented four canoes, four helmets, and four lifejackets for the day.

The water was calm, and the weather was mild. It was a perfect day. They kitted Sarah and Lawrence up and got into the canoes.

"This is so cool," shouted Lawrence. Sarah was still apprehensive, but she paddled carefully and got to grips with it.

Geoff and Denise were now out on the water as well.

"Okay, take it easy, guys," said Geoff to the kids.

Denise had been out on the river hundreds of times from a young age. She had the ease and technical proficiency that Geoff was trying to attain. But each of them moved along at a decent clip.

After an hour and a half, they had gone about five kilometres down the river and had seen so much beautiful wildlife and scenery along the way.

They came to a piece of ground with an enclave.

"Let's stop here," said Geoff as he started to move over to the side to get out on land. So they all moved over and stopped as Geoff got out of his canoe before pulling his mini boat up after him and making room for Denise. She did the same, and they both helped Sarah and Lawrence onto the ground after that.

"Oh, look, someone left a picnic for us," said Geoff, smiling.

There was road access to this area, and you could walk from that point to get here. So he came this morning and left everything as a little surprise. He had packed chicken and tomato sandwiches with mayonnaise and flasks of tea in the tweed basket. It was welcome; they were hungry and wanted a break.

Geoff offered to put on a little fire. He said, "Just help me gather a bit of wood here, and then you can relax and have something to eat."

"Okay, Dad," they said, slightly exasperated.

So the children left to look for wood, but what Geoff was really looking for was to get Denise near a specific green nephrite rock. He was over near the picnic, pretending to be busy with a few sticks there, but he was watching her. As she got closer to the rock, he said, "Babe, could you get that stick over there? That brown one looks nice and dry."

She headed over, and just as she got there, she spotted the fluorescent emerald rock, a rare and beautiful sight.

"Wow, look at this rock. It's a beautiful green gemstone," she said as she picked it up.

Underneath was a little box.

"What is this!" she exclaimed.

"Which rock are you interested in now?" said Geoff as he made his way over to take the box from her.

He dropped to one knee as Denise started to get emotional. She was thrilled, her nerves high with anticipation.

Geoff got right to it: "I love you so much. And there are two people over there just as excited as I am."

They looked over at the kids, and the two were hugging each other and giving thumbs up.

"Denise Buthryan, will you marry me?"

"Yes!" Denise exclaimed. Geoff sprung to his feet, and they kissed. Even though the kids were a bit averse to seeing two adults lock lips, they couldn't contain their happiness.

For the rest of the picnic, Denise and Geoff held hands when they weren't eating, and Sarah and Lawrence joined in by cuddling up to them. Body heat was the warmth, as the whole fire thing was a ruse. Geoff didn't even know how to make a fire.

Geoff had learned so much about himself, the world, and everything else in the last year. However, he was now ready for the next phase.
Michael was starting to understand that too. In their last phone conversation, he began to drop some significant information.

"There are a lot of complexities to this war, and it comes down to the financial system and the children,"

Michael explained. "We are in a war between two different resets. The New World Order version consists of repeated lockdowns, repeated boosters, taking away more and more civil rights, censorship, 'fact checking' run by lobbies with agendas, engineered racism and division, genocide, and depopulation.

"It's where they cancel culture, tell you what you can say and think, propose that gender is a social construct, and families are deliberately made dysfunctional. It's where ordinary people would be part of the second tier; they would have a biological passport, no privacy, and their money would be controlled and taken away for non-compliant behaviour.

"It's a social credit technocracy, a modern form of totalitarian communism where AI begins displacing humans. Elites with an addiction to adrenochrome and proclivities towards paedophilia would be in control of you and your children as you live more in the unnatural metaverse or virtual reality. People would become depressed zombies." Michael's tense voice showed the gravity of the situation.

But he quickly moved to the other fork in the road: "The other side is Nesara-Gesara, the Golden Age reset. Everybody has their constitutional rights, development of the individual is paramount, 6000 suppressed patents are released for free energy and amazing health devices. All money and digital currency are asset-backed, so they cannot be funnelled into a fraudulent banking cartel system. All the gold and money that has been stolen from you from birth is returned. It goes to your ledger accounts and is released slowly unless requested.

"There will be so much reclaimed money that all legitimate humanitarian projects will be backed. The working week will be reduced to sixteen hours. Everyone will be affluent, and crime will be almost non-existent as a result. People will be connected to the quantum system for their money, privacy, passport, education, and voting. The Q-phones will be a link to this. People will vote through their unhackable phones for policy and not people at a community, regional, and national level.

"Business and life will go back to community living and not be controlled by big corporate chains. Schooling will develop the person and their perceptions instead of treating them like a blank slate into which information is poured. Essentially, all the satanic structures will be replaced by good structures for the people. And it can't be fooled because it is connected to gold-backed money and your consciousness. It is a freedom system, but it is also honest under natural, common law."

"It sounds utopian, but it's not. It's just how things should be, isn't it?" asked Geoff.

"Yes, that's right," affirmed Michael. "All that rat race stuff — two parents having to work very long hours to survive, the division, blatant censorship, exorbitant taxes, widening the wealth gap, the false paper money — it's all distractions and a setup."

"I agree," said Geoff.

"This is the war that is going on in the background. And we are winning. However, there is still danger and work to be done. The general has a special mission for you now. He will fly over in a few days to see you about this in person. Is that okay?" asked Michael.

"Yes, no problem," replied Geoff, wondering what the special mission would be. However, he was in a place now where he felt very able and ready for whatever he had to do. He knew this was a moment in history where you couldn't shy away, you had to stand up for what was right, or there was no hope for the future.

A few days passed, and a white SUV turned up outside the bungalow; out stepped General Flint, Colonel Jeffers, and Michael Clarke. They were all plain-clothed.

Geoff had just finished chopping some wood out back for the stove. He greeted the men and brought them into the sitting room, the fire crackling away and beginning to warm them.

Geoff thought to himself, *important people are in Banff, just to meet me!*

General Flint got down to business, steepling his fingers the way he always did when he had something serious to say. "Geoff, things are going very well in the war in the background. However, the other side is waking the population, and we need to speed that up. With everything we've dropped on the public, we're surprised we haven't been able to do it. The Cabal and their controlled media have done a number on the masses."

Michael took over and said, "There's a huge truther movement going on. Guys and gals like Chuck Nolan, Sim Parlour, Sal J, Christie Q, and Mick Venesius are doing an amazing job as citizen journalists and getting the information out there."

Colonel Jeffers chimed in and said, "However, we feel that someone like you going out there as an ex-politician that had to go 'underground' would get things moving even faster."

"Sounds good," said Geoff, feeling this was right up his alley.

But he had one request: "Before that, I want to adopt Sarah and Lawrie. They're great kids."

The general smiled and said, "You've done such a good job with them. I'm sure we can make that happen; just leave it to me."

Denise arrived after the meeting, Geoff had called her as he knew she would love to meet these men, look them in the eye and shake their hands.

And they were only too happy to meet Geoff's wife to be and an Awakened Spirits coordinator.

They were well aware of the very important role this ground up worldwide organisation had played through the tumultuous times of the last few years.

General Flint and the rest of the Q team were as grateful to people like her as she was to them – for engaging an important change in the world, that would hopefully come to fruition.

She had worked out a few weeks ago that these men were going to arrive at some point to talk to Geoff. The license plate they gave him on the mondeo was alphabetically-numerically coded:
CIQ 3917

Chapter 12

It wasn't long before the papers came through for Geoff to adopt the children, and after the marriage, Denise would become their mother. Geoff and Denise had talked about it, and it felt right to her too.

Geoff, Denise, Lawrence and Sarah were overjoyed and spent the day playing board games and basketball, watching a movie at the cinema, and then enjoying dinner at a lovely restaurant.

Sarah and Lawrence sat at the restaurant table, no longer orphans, feeling very special and loved by their parents. And Geoff knew they were a gift from heaven, filling his life with great meaning. He loved them dearly, and Denise felt exactly the same way.

But in the backdrop of Geoff's mind, he knew his broader mission was about to begin again.

General Flint assigned a technical and social media expert to setup Geoff's Telegram group, Bitchute, and Rumble accounts. They felt there was no point in doing Youtube because they were censoring and removing all channels asking relevant questions.

You couldn't even say 'vaccine' or 'Covid' or 'audits' without being removed — that was just how fascist and totalitarian things had gotten.

The general asked Geoff to start watching other Truther channels to pick up what was being said, get the gist of what was going on, and run things by him to assess their validity. Then, every week he would call him to discuss new intel and take any of Geoff's questions.

On the down low, General Flint discussed certain topics with Geoff that they could not yet release to the public, but that Geoff should know to understand what was truly going on and inspire confidence in his listeners. It was also essential to calm the impatient ones.

Geoff prepared a little office in his spacious bedroom for the podcast and Zoom calls. In the background, a painting of Leonardo Da Vinci hung on the wooden walls alongside a green glass candle holder.

It was an enchanting environment and an ideal representation of where he lived. His location was to remain secret, and of course, wooden cabins were also very common in various regions of the world.

The Truther movement was like this anyway: citizen journalists researching and releasing information genuinely and authentically. There were no airs and graces; only the information mattered. To see someone in a suit before a perfect screen only aroused suspicion at the moment.

A new slimmed-down Geoff started making videos on what was going on, adding his bits of intel. His channel immediately started to catch on, given who he was and the perspective he could bring.

He interviewed various interesting people, including collaborations with other famous Truthers like Chuck Nolan, Sim Parlour, and Mick Venesius.

On one particular Sunday, he had an interview setup with Chuck Nolan to discuss current developments.

He logged into his Zoom link, and they started the call.

"Hello, Geoff!" exclaimed Chuck with a big smile and cheeky English accent.

"Hello, Chuck! How are you?" replied Geoff.

"I'm good... I'm very, very good," said Chuck in his usual upbeat manner; he had a way of taking the listeners to peace and tranquillity in a time of utter chaos.

But he was leading by example, demonstrating that life was about perspective and individual connection to Source for objective truth, despite whatever was happening around you. The bravery people would need to win this war would ultimately come from faith in truth and light.

He was always dropping pearls of wisdom like, "God is not in the sky, he is in your heart," to show it with words too.

"It's a pleasure to be on your show, Chuck. You've done so much amazing work in the last two years; you've been a beacon of light to many people, a symbol of hope," said Geoff sincerely.

"Aw, thanks so much, mate… I was just lucky to have heard conversations in my line of work with diplomats, so I knew what was happening, even right at the start," replied Chuck in his customary humble manner.

They got down to business. These calls were informal and not entirely planned, often taking on a conversational manner like the *Joe Rogan Show*.

However, there were specific things they wanted to discuss, and they would come to it soon enough.

"Many of my listeners are new to delving into the world of Gesara, the Quantum Financial System, and things coming down the pipe. Can we talk about that?" asked Geoff.

"Of course we can; that's my specialty, if you like, as I've been part of the team working on the QFS," said Chuck.

"Great stuff. I'm doing well with many of the core ideas, like going to a gold-backed system, abolishing income tax, reorganising into small governments, only taxing non-essential items, and all that," Geoff prefaced. "However, one thing is hard for me to get my head around. I'm being told there was sixty-four quadrillion in gold recovered from under the Vatican, London, and various other places where the elites hoarded such ghastly sums of money away from the people."

Chuck raised his brows, his eyes widening a touch.

"Yes, it's true," he answered. "And it shows just how evil they were. All the poverty, starving people, and homelessness, and they were hoarding that unnecessary amount of wealth. Nobody needs that much, obviously," he finished with palpable disdain.

"Yeah, it's hard to stomach. Truly evil," Geoff agreed. "And the Gesara system will not be communist because it's just returning the money already owed to the people. Everyone should be abundant — that's how you can create a wonderful world. It's not that everyone gets the same reward; everyone has a full opportunity. That's what I love about this. And it makes sense when you think about it. Why does there have to be poverty? It's a setup."

Chuck nodded and said, "You're absolutely right, Geoff. It's a system where people were wrongly enslaved, declared dead at sea and then traded as a commodity. You know your birth certificate? The corporation one they made for you? If you get the true original, that certificate will have all sorts of stamps on the back where they have traded you as a commodity because that's all we are to them. How much will this person pay into our system to get us rich? So they traded you on that speculation, just like a stock or a coin."

Geoff moved closer to the screen, becoming totally engrossed in the conversation.

"It's amazing, isn't it? And we had no idea about any of this until the last couple of years," replied Geoff with wonder at all the important recent discoveries.

Before Chuck carried on, he rubbed his face, almost to shake his brain up, as he was already on his fourth call of the day.

"We had no idea. But that's what the Q-team did by dripping out military code on the Q-boards. It wasn't even telling people; it left breadcrumbs and clues to get people to ask questions. *Those* people put it together — not from dogma, but by asking questions and seeking answers. Trapp also put things out there because he knew what was happening and was part of the solution. This great awakening has been building for a while, and it ramped up more and more in the last few years," expanded Chuck, loving that they were delving deep into the subject and not just skimming the surface.

Geoff grinned, thinking about what was to come.

"An essential part of that is revaluating currencies and returning resources and assets that were stolen from developing countries to get their currency up to par. Then everyone will be on the same footing instead of the big, rich countries setting up a system where they rape and pillage poorer African, South American and Asian countries," added Geoff.

"That's critically important. And the Iraqi dinar is the first. The old dinar is worth at least 3 US dollars now, just while the change happens. It's only within Iraq at the moment, but the people have a lot more money already," said Chuck with glee.

"It's great, isn't it," said Geoff. "Can you talk about how debt forgiveness works, Chuck?"

"Sure. The old money-printing system would loan you money not backed by anything and charge you interest to pay it back. But it was a fraudulent system, so all of those loans will be null and void because the banks and financial institutions entered into the contract under false pretences," explained Chuck.

"That's exactly my understanding of it, too," replied Geoff.

He moved on to another important topic.

"The whole income tax fiasco is another one. I can speak to this because the government could cut down to a tenth of its workforce and have good people to run things smoothly. The wages for politicians are also ridiculous. Besides, a hell of a lot of that money that comes in through taxation doesn't go back to the communities — it's funnelled into making the rich even richer using schemes that amount to money laundering.

"Under Gesara, that will be abolished and replaced with a non-essential items tax at the point of purchase. And that will be more than enough to cover public expenditure if things are being run the right way."

"I couldn't agree more," replied Chuck.

"Another thing to mention is humanitarian projects. Gigantic funds are being made available to rebuild society. People can submit their projects, and if approved, they will be awarded funding to benefit their community. We want to create a world that evil bastards don't control!" said Chuck with East London fervour.

"The Cabal and the governments are the biggest drug dealers and human traffickers on the planet. Without going into details that I won't disclose just yet, I've seen that first hand," said Geoff earnestly.

"I appreciate that, Geoff. And it's hard to believe, but unfortunately, you're right."

Geoff wanted to make a point to the listeners. He said, "The whole Cabal structure is all-encompassing: it's in education, politics, police enforcement, the law and the military — though the army has been largely cleaned out now. You have mostly good people in these areas, but aside from the military, they're still controlled by the Cabal, and the workers just follow orders. I mean, how do people think the Nazis could do what they did? It's the same principle — you create fear and make it plausible.

"But that's what we have to undo. We have landed in Normandy, but we are not in Berlin yet. Things can go wrong — as they did with Kennedy and 9/11 — where they did things to stop everything from changing. That's why we have to be careful this time, awakening humanity as we go. It has to come from the people too."

"That's right," said Chuck. He could see Geoff had another point to make, so he left the floor open to him.

"The head is off the beast, but they still have factions everywhere because the tentacles were so many and so embedded, and those factions don't want to end up in jail. They want their system to continue and move into the New World Order. So we're still fighting on every front. It's an untraditional war; it's more about people living their truth to take power from the Cabal. We are not the resistance; we are the future, and by being that, we take their power away and bring it back to the people."

"I couldn't say it better than that," Chuck said with a warm smile, adding, "And Donard Trapp was also the bravest man on earth — he went right at it and took them all on without dividing races or genders. Apparently, not getting into group politics made him a racist and a misogynist.

"He wanted to build a wall to stop the drug cartels and their child trafficking, calling the gang criminals murders and rapists, and apparently, that was calling Mexicans murders and rapists. This is the logic the media was using, and no one questioned it. This is the power of the press and their brainwashing. But that's going to end very soon."

"He was brave," Geoff agreed. "He had no reason to run for office only to gain a lesser wage; he was losing money during that time, and his businesses suffered due to politics. The other political leaders, 95% of them, get filthy rich while in office!" Geoff explained.

"If you analyse the bills he signed and the speeches he gave, he was always for the people. All types of people. And this is coming from a Democrat, but it's not about that. I believe in Kennedy, and I believe in Trapp. It's not left or right; it's about good or evil. But as you say, most don't look at the facts. They look at the narrative they are being fed by the media. But not for much longer. The truth is coming. Nothing can stop what is coming."

They had been on the air for quite some time, and they both felt it had been a very productive interview. It was Chuck's show, so he was the one to wrap things up.

"Well, it's been an absolute pleasure talking to you, Geoff. You're a great guy to have on board."

"My pleasure Chuck. Lovely to speak to you."

Geoff felt great satisfaction with these interviews because each one was another ripple going out and vibrating with the masses. The future of humanity rested on several things, including this information getting out, which Geoff was reminded of when he saw the papers the next day:

Back from the Dead! Geoff wasn't murdered; he just likes telling lies. The whole article was a hit piece, no doubt engineered by Priscilla and her minions.

It detailed how he had received a substantial bonus when he first got into office and bought properties in Cafford and the Bahamas. However, nowhere did it say who gave him the money or that he had sold the properties, returned the money, and closed the account.

Of course, this was all to discredit him. But he said to himself: They can say what they like. The truth will come out. Their day is coming.

In fact, he doubled down. He had a show with Sim Parlour in the evening, and he was going to reveal more explosive revelations about the Cabal.

Priscilla began plotting to find Geoff and make him pay for his actions. She bet that one man may know where he was: his old friend Syed.

Syed lived a little bit outside the city in a rural area. Miguel was assigned to trail him, disable him, and take him back to Priscilla.

Miguel waited for Syed to leave work, get into his car, and drive home. He quietly began to follow in a dark blue Ford pickup truck he had 'borrowed' from the garage and put a fake registration on. There were a couple of cars in front, but Miguel didn't mind that. He knew where Syed lived, and they'd soon be on a quiet back road with no other vehicles.

When they reached a narrow farm road surrounded by fields, Miguel sped up to get close. He knew it was the time to strike, as Syed was still a good 12 kilometres from home. So Miguel drove quickly to the left side and rammed into the rear side door of the black Mercedes.

Syed hit the brake quickly and collided with the chest-high free stone farm wall on his right, going through the wall but disabling the car. He was dazed but still alive.

Miguel exited his vehicle. There was barely a bump on the side of the pickup truck thanks to its massive steel bumper. He went to Syed's door and dragged him out of the banged-up Mercedes, half-conscious with a cut on the side of his head.

Miguel taped Syed's hands and feet and dragged him into the backseat of the pickup truck. He called Priscilla to tell her the job had been done. She immediately called the on alert and nearby clean-up 'council' crew with a tow truck out to the scene before Miguel took Syed to a remote house on that side of the city.

It was another Free Mason-owned house with tunnels underneath. Although the military had blocked up the tunnels under the Lodge, they didn't have the time yet to investigate further tentacles out to other areas.

Miguel brought Syed to the kitchen and tied him to one of the chairs. After fifteen minutes, Syed started to come around.

"Who the hell are you, and what am I doing here?" asked Syed, mustering just enough energy to speak.

"Don't worry, chico, we just have a few questions for you," replied Miguel.

"Questions about what?"

"You'll see."

Within thirty minutes, Priscilla had arrived. She strode in wearing white trainers with pink laces, slim-fitting green gym bottoms and a dark green golf top with quarter zip.

Syed's eyes widened, but he had half expected she was involved. He raised his head to meet her gaze.

"Where is Geoff Hurley?" she said, getting straight to the point.

"No idea," Syed answered through the taste of blood in his mouth. "And if I did, I wouldn't tell you paedo scum anyway."

Priscilla slapped him across the face. Syed smiled all the while.

"Take out the electrics," said Priscilla ominously. And Miguel went to get a box under the counter, pulling out a wire and attaching it to Syed's left index finger.

He pressed a button, and Syed recoiled, clenching his hands on the arm rests and throwing his head back. It only lasted four seconds, but it was hell on earth, temporarily paralyzing him with excruciating pain. It reminded Syed of when he had a sensitive tooth, and the dentist drilled into its centre and accidentally hit a nerve. It was just as unbearable, but at least that only lasted a second.

"Are you ready to talk now?" asked Priscilla, her face stone cold and determined.

Syed looked at her, paused, and then spat in her face, clearly hitting her with some spray.

Priscilla went to the sink, washed her face and wiped it down with a kitchen towel. Syed knew things would get worse anyway; he wanted to get his shot in.

She came back fierce but perturbingly calm and commanded Miguel, "Turn up the dial."

He did as she asked, nearly sending Syed into an epileptic fit. His whole body was jolting, and even though it was only four seconds, it would take weeks to fully recover. Another notch higher, and he'd be dead.

"Talk, or things will get even worse," said Priscilla.

Syed's nervous system was fried, and he lacked control of his muscles. He couldn't even raise his head to look her in the eye now.

"I hear you have a wife and a lovely daughter," said Priscilla in a matter-of-fact way that veiled a heinous threat. Syed was further agonised, his face contorting in pain and worry.

"What part of 'I don't know' don't you understand?" he muttered in a gravelly voice.

Priscilla was evil, but she wasn't stupid. She knew he didn't know, and going after a successful man's whole family would have brought a level of scrutiny she didn't want.

"Take him underground. We might need him for leverage later."

Syed had no idea what was in store for him, but it appeared he would survive.

At least for now.

Chapter 13

Geoff was back on Zoom with another champion of truth, their conversation soon to be beaming out to hundreds of thousands of people.

"Hey Geoff, how are you?" said Sim in his gentlemanly English voice.

"Hi, Sim. I'm good. How are you?" replied Geoff with his slight Texan drawl.

"Good, I'm just enjoying a cuppa," said Sim. He was sporting a nicely threaded sweater (as he often did) in this office loaded with files, shelves, and documents. But this was a man with a singular purpose in a war coming to its most crucial period.

"Great to have a man like you on — one that's been in the system and seen what goes on," said Sim frankly; his glasses, cultured British accent and measured way of speaking adding gravitas to his words.

"It's an honour to be on your show, Sim. I want to speak on the Free Masons, if I may."

"Go right ahead," replied Sim. "It's a critical topic."

Geoff took a breath. He was calm, perfectly prepared to strike back hard at the heart of these satanic elitists.

"There was an article about me yesterday. It went out to the major networks worldwide, twisting everything untruthfully against me. Essentially, they are trying to blacken my name and ruin my credibility.

"Well, I'm here to set the record straight. The viewing figures for the Truther channels are larger than the major outlets, anyway. People want the truth."

Sim smiled and nodded his head, allowing Geoff space to continue.

"First off, I got embroiled in their system because that's what they do; they compromise you, blackmail you, and make it seem like you have no choice. I mean, look at where I am now. I am in a protection program where no one knows where I am. That's not by accident.

"Second, they gave me the money. I purchased those two properties in a moment of weakness, but I've since sold them. I even returned every cent before closing the account.

"Third, they keep attacking me because they are deathly afraid of the information I'm putting out there to wake up the masses. Well, I'm not going to stop. I am going to double down and reveal something big today."

He had already spoken to Sim before the public call and told him what he would say. Sim was perfectly okay with it.

"They tried to get me to join the Free Masons. I was in it for a few months because I was so politically ambitious; I had done what I was told already, and I was good at charity fundraising, so they saw me as valuable and malleable. They wanted to move me up the ranks, but they had to compromise me further.

"To cut a long story short, they wanted me to drink adrenochrome, the adrenaline-charged blood of a sacrificed child," Geoff stopped short with a look of horror on his face. This was not new to Sim, but his brow furrowed none the less. It wasn't anything any sane person could ever get used to hearing.

Geoff continued, "Before it happened, I realised something was very wrong. I saw two children with black eyes on the way in. They were clearly suffering at the hands of these mongrels. They didn't know it at the time, but those two saved my life — if I never saw them, I wouldn't have been nearly as suspicious. So after that, I got those kids out of that Hellhole and adopted them myself.

"So, who is in these Free Mason groups? Well, half of them are just ordinary people that think it's a gentleman's club and a networking facility, maybe a slightly or very corrupt one, depending on their position. That's all they think it is.

"But the next rung are paedophiles, and the rung above that are also into satanic rituals and human sacrifice. That's how bad it is."

"Yes," said Sim, again giving Geoff breathing room to continue his incredible revelations.

"They tie people into this. Though some are happy to play that game and enjoy it, some are stuck in it, controlled by blackmail. You have politicians, police, judges, solicitors, barristers, doctors, business people; you name it. The Free Masons have infested every organisation and union out there," said Geoff, pausing for a breather. The conversation was intense, and he knew the audience would need time to take it all in. Sim remained calm and listened intently.

"There are still many good people in these areas of life that have nothing to do with the Free Masons," Geoff continued. "There are also networkers in the Free Masons that don't know what it is about at the higher levels. That's how insidious and clever they are about all of it — it's called a secret society for a reason.

Sim concurred, "Yes, it's quite layered, and without wanting to compliment them, it is clever."

"Yes, nearly all the politicians are Free Masons; many are compromised or deep in the organisation," Geoff explained.

Simon interjected, "You know I was once a politician for Labour in my local jurisdiction?"

"Oh really?" replied Geoff, wanting to know more.

"I served two terms, but I reached a certain point of influence where it was hard to go any further without being part of the Cabal. In my case, they simply sent me a contract where I would be heavily rewarded for being part of their system, but I had to sign the contract to toe the line with their agenda. I never signed it, and soon after, I left the post. I guess that was like your experience when you first got into office — the same principle, but they wanted me to do it legally. Perhaps the English Cabal is more civilised in negotiation," Sim said with a chuckle.

Geoff couldn't help but grin before Sim spoke again. "But they are no less ruthless and disgusting!" Geoff was serious now, too; he knew more than anyone how decrepit the Cabal was.

The call ended happily, and both parties were satisfied with the discussion. Geoff thanked Sim for having him, and Sim was effusive with his praise for Geoff's bravery.

Of course, Priscilla was watching his every move, and she was equally confident that her side would win out, as they had done for millennia. In fact, with modern communication systems, a screen in every hand and the power of censorship, she was even more confident. The masses were easier to manipulate than ever before.

When she saw this most recent interview, she was fuming, vowing to do everything in her power to finish Geoff. Priscilla was arrogant, and she thought she could make him disappear for good, then control the media narrative that he had just run away from protective custody.

During this time, Martha got special permission to fly up to Banff to see Geoff and his family. She was thrilled to see how happy they were.

After the joyous reunion where Martha showered everyone in hugs and kisses, she said to Geoff, "I've something private to tell you. Can we have some time alone?"

"Sure," replied Geoff.

Martha wore a nervous expression, so Geoff asked Denise if she would take the kids for a walk for a while.

"No problem," Denise answered. After the two kids were suitably dressed up in their Chicago Bulls and Lakers winter garb, they took off into the cold but sunny day.

Geoff made Martha her favourite brew — an Americano — and they sat down for another famous fireside chat in his sitting room. However, Geoff had no idea what was coming.

Martha's hands shook as she held her cup. "I've something to tell you," she said again. Geoff was getting worried and began to think the worst.

"I'm your mother," Martha blurted out.

Geoff's eyes widened. He didn't know what to think.

Martha screened his face, trying to read how he was taking it. She could see he was just baffled and couldn't process it. Geoff needed more information.

"I hope you won't hate me, but I had to give you up. So I found an excellent home for you," she said with sadness as the pain of the loss rolled back for her.

"During your birth, there were complications resulting in a stroke. I wasn't right for about three years. I had a lot of rehab to do, and I wouldn't have been able to take care of a child. I also couldn't tell the father, or he would have lost his marriage," Martha revealed.

"Jesus, I'm sorry that happened to you."

A tear rolled down Martha's face as she said, "Never in a million years would I have given you up unless I had to. But it would have been too difficult. I always looked out for you."

"I know you did," Geoff said, remembering how good she had always been to him and beginning to understand the deeper reasons why. At this point, they hugged, as Geoff felt Martha needed one.

"I don't hate you. How could I?" said Geoff.

"That's a relief," said Martha, wiping away her tears.

Geoff put his hands to his face. "So my mom isn't my biological mom, and my dad isn't my biological dad."

"No," replied Martha, "but they were good parents."

"They were," Geoff agreed. "They are."

Despite becoming a bit distant from them as an adult, Geoff still loved his parents. His life was just so far removed from theirs.

"Who is my biological father?" asked Geoff. Martha took a deep breath and said, "Michael Clarke," realising this was an equally significant bombshell.

"*Wow*," Geoff said as he rose from his seat, putting his hands on his head and taking a deep breath. "Does he know?"

"Yes, but he only found out after you were eighteen," Martha said. "And then we had to find the right time to tell you. You were so busy, and doing well, so we let you be. I intuitively felt that when you became very conscious, it would be the right time to reveal the truth to you."

Martha continued, "It's crazy how things worked out; you didn't fall far from the tree in terms of your biological parents. You are just like us, and we played a big role in your recent journey, which we were more than happy to do."

"Yeah, it's crazy," replied Geoff. "And yet with my kids, it's the opposite — we are so bonded, I couldn't love them more than I do, even if they were blood... and I think they feel the same way."

"They do," Martha said. "They adore their papa. Everything happens for a reason."

Geoff sat back down again, feeling calmer.

"I never told you this, but Michael was the one that took me off the streets. He and his wife Diana took me in and gave me a chance to get a job and my own home."

"Oh, that's amazing," said Geoff, seeing how things had come together.

"They had trouble in their marriage because they couldn't have children despite wanting to, and Michael sometimes went on very long missions. On one of these occasions, Diana was suffering from depression and loneliness and cheated on Michael. He was devastated. He ended up at my house drunk one night. It should have never happened, but I loved him, and he was my hero. I knew he loved Diana.

"For many years, we spoke only sporadically because we were embarrassed about what happened. I owed him and Diana my life; they gave me everything. I couldn't tell him about you, or it would have destroyed their marriage."

Geoff was staring forward, just trying to take it all in. "Okay, I can see," he said in a near whisper.
That evening, Geoff got permission to call his adopted parents. He updated them on his situation and revealed the news he had gotten earlier from Martha. They told him they knew this day would come and didn't tell him earlier to protect him while he was younger. He said he completely understood, told them how much he loved them and appreciated how good they had been to him as parents.

They were relieved he was taking it so well.

His next call was to Michael. After the greetings, he got right into it.

"Martha came here today. She told me everything."

"When you say everything..." said Michael, swallowing hard.

"Yes, I know you are my biological father," said Geoff.

"I didn't know until you were past eighteen," Michael said sincerely. He was a very honourable man, and Geoff knew he would have helped him more if he had the chance.

"I know. It was a shock! Martha had her reasons for how she did things, and I understand them," said Geoff with empathy and maturity.

"Well, I'm pleased about that, and I'm very proud of the man you are," replied Michael in a rare, revealing moment.

"Thank you," said Geoff, not knowing whether to even say 'Michael' back to such a statement from his recently unveiled biological father. They resolved to chat again soon, as they did regularly anyway.

Martha stayed overnight and left the following evening. She wanted to spend more time with them, but she felt that there would be plenty of time for that later. Besides, Geoff needed time and space to process everything.

Priscilla contacted the media to tell them once again to spin Geoff as a madman. It was easy with the mainstream media as the government and the lobbies controlled them, and the Cabal owned the lobbies. The number of victims on Truther channels exposing household names made no difference to her; it was still buried in the eyes of most of the herd because it wasn't aired on CNN, NBC or the BBC.

Even though most people were tired or distrustful of mainstream news outlets, they still thought that it would have to end up there if anything were real.

Next, she went to her technical experts again to pinpoint Geoff's location. The tech team of high-end hackers and cyber security experts went to work to find one crumb to get them past the advanced military encryption protecting Geoff.

After several hours, their efforts proved fruitless. So they changed tactics. One suggested hacking all the CCTV systems in North and South America and Europe, using facial recognition to find him.

The team used recent images of Geoff's face from interviews to scan through millions of video captures from ATMs, shops, garages, and more. They checked millions of files worldwide. It took over two days, but then they got a hit.

Priscilla was alerted, and after the hackers successfully tracked Geoff to his home via phone GPS, she had a cabal unit within the FBI immediately sent out from Seattle to Banff. In less than two hours, their black SUV sped up the back roads towards Geoff's cabin.

"Come out with your hands up!" shouted the FBI agents.

Geoff was startled. *Shit*, he thought to himself. But before he could formulate a plan, three FBI agents busted through the front door.

They told Geoff to get on his knees and put his hands behind his head. He did so, and they cuffed his hands behind his back.

They had also rounded up Denise and the two children and put them with Geoff. The kids hugged him for dear life, scared out of their wits. Geoff told them it would be okay, but he really didn't know if it would be. Things were not looking good.

"I'm just taking a sabbatical," Geoff calmly explained.

"What the hell are you talking about?" said one of the officers as he picked him up and took him out to the car with Sarah still clinging to him. Denise and Lawrence were playing along as the agents bundled all of them into the back of the vehicle.

Geoff knew it was probably standard procedure to take a victim away from a more obvious scene.

They travelled further up the mountains and into areas without houses for miles.

The SUV pulled off the road, and the two agents got out of the car. Pushing the rest of his family aside, they dragged Geoff out of the vehicle.
The kids made a fuss, but he told them to do as they were told, and everything would be okay. But Geoff could only hope. He flashed his eyes at Denise and made a kiss with his lips. She feared the worst, her eyes brimming with tears, but she tried to stay calm for the kids.

The doors slammed shut, leaving Denise and the kids locked inside the car anxiously watching as the agents pushed Geoff to his knees. One of the agents loaded his gun and put it to the side of Geoff's head.

Denise covered the children's eyes and shut her own in pure terror.

"Priscilla told you to shut up. Why didn't you listen? You could have had an easy life. Any last words?" the would-be killer said to Geoff.

"Yeah…" Geoff said before cracking a wry smile. "Sabbatical was a code word set for my watch alert, you dumb bastard. You didn't think they would leave us out here completely on our own, did you?'

The agent pulled the gun from Geoff's head and spun around in a panic.

Geoff was buying time, hoping the rescue crew was already on the way. The military had a twenty-four-hour team ready for all eventualities on this protective custody, knowing that Geoff and his family were live targets.

And just after he repeated the code word, a chopper roared over the mountain top and headed straight for them. Some of the most highly trained sniper shooters in the world were on board. They had silenced sniper rifles with laser sights to focus on the exact targets.

It happened so fast the agents couldn't even react.

The silencer zip could be heard as the bullets soared through the air at lightning speed. Geoff could feel how close those bullets were to him as they lodged in the skull of the two agents, collapsing them to the ground. They died in an instant.

Geoff was emotional, taking deep, measured breaths to calm himself; he had come so close to leaving Denise and his kids in terrible peril.

The chopper landed on a patch of grass next to the road across from the SUV and the agent's bodies.

Lieutenant Covington, the lead officer on this mission, ran from the chopper and uncuffed Geoff immediately with a master key taken from his belt. The other soldiers took hammers and tools to the car doors to break the lock and get the family out of the SUV.

Denise and the kids ran to Geoff, and they hugged one another with all they had. They realised how close they had come to losing their lives.

Lieutenant Covington winked at his team for a job well done. Geoff shook their hands and thanked them.

"Just doing our job and protecting a good man," replied Lieutenant Covington. "Let's get you back to the base in Dallas. Two of the boys will clean this mess up and take your things back to base later."

After Syed didn't come home and his wife Isabella couldn't contact him, she was worried sick. When she awoke at six in the morning with no sign of him, she contacted the police.

They came immediately, asked her questions, and filed a report. After forty-eight hours had passed and Syed was officially declared missing, Isabella got another call out, this time from a pair of FBI agents. It appeared odd to her for a missing person's case to escalate that quickly.

They informed her that there were strong rumours in the city that Syed owed a million dollars to criminals in gambling debts. They speculated he was either dealing with this or that he'd been kidnapped — or worse — by these people.

Isabella didn't believe a word of it. She knew that Syed wasn't into gambling, and in the privacy of her marriage, she was privy to the fact that Geoff Hurley was missing because he was in protective custody in threat of his life from Priscilla and the Cabal.

Now she knew what was happening. It was Priscilla, but she was smart enough to play dumb with the agents. They weren't to be trusted and she had a child to protect.

However, none of this eased her worries; all she could do was hope and pray he was still alive and would return home safe and sound.

Chapter 14

Geoff, Denise, and the children arrived safely at the Dallas base and were put up in a lovely apartment near its centre. Surrounded by one of the most well-trained and competent militaries in the world, they felt a high degree of comfort.

Geoff was still running his podcast and talking about current affairs. Somebody had to do it; the mainstream media certainly weren't. In fact, they had collectively lost their minds. They could barely keep their own plan straight, and even their most ardent defenders were starting to question them.

After Priscilla's latest stunt, Geoff was hell-bent on proving that he was telling the truth about the Cabal. He had another large ace up his sleeve that he decided to unleash: the video footage he recorded in the underground. It showed everything he saw down there, including the child torture chambers with blood seeping onto the floor.

It was conclusive proof of the wicked depravity perpetrated by the Cabal and vindication of Geoff. The fact that they lied so much before he took out this trump card worked to his advantage and carried much more weight than if he had just released the footage earlier.

It was received with widespread shock and horror, and even though it didn't make it to mainstream news, it was going viral.

In the meantime, Geoff had also done some extra digging on Covid that struck him as very odd, discovering more evidence that helped him piece the puzzle together.

Little did he know his findings would also tighten the noose on the Cabal.

A few matters started popping out at him. First of all, the treatments the health authorities were admonishing; ivermection, hydroxychloroquine, and zinc were all treatments that reputable doctors found were working very well for early admission patients.

However, there was another one they were shunning called monoclonal antibodies or anti-venom. Geoff found that very strange. Why would they be preoccupied with that? What's that got to do with coronaviruses?

He searched for snake venom and Covid, noting that fact-checkers were feverishly trying to direct people away from any connection between the two. Instead, they were working on steering everyone to the bat link. Given that sweaty fact-checkers corrupted by vested interests were a propaganda tool to be very sceptical of, it piqued Geoff's interest further — maybe there was something to this?

He continued searching and came across a science journal stating the initial Covid sufferers in Wuhan had spike proteins similar to snake venom in their bodies. That was quickly followed by another research study in France saying Sars Covid-19 spike proteins were identical to krait or cobra venom.

Geoff soon became engrossed in these studies. He then found a story about a doctor at the University of Pittsburgh called Dr. Bing Lui, who was about to release all the data he had collected on the sequencing of Covid-19 spike proteins – and the day before he was scheduled to do so, he was murdered!

Every time Dr. Bing's boss was interviewed, he said they were going to publish his findings, but a year and a half later, they still hadn't.

Geoff was staggered already, but his jaw was about to hit the floor. He had another look at the recommended hospital protocols. In the US, Remdesivir was now the only treatment licensed for Covid-19. Unfortunately, Remdesivir was a very controversial drug with a litany of side effects, and to discerning doctors, it didn't appear to do any good.

Plus, hydroxychloroquine was not to be used with Remdesivir, as it negated the effects. So a drug that was very effective against Covid-19 negated the impact of Remdesivir. Geoff couldn't help but be curious about that link, so he looked up who made Remdesivir. Before he even got there, he came across a company called Genentech. They had coded all the snake venom gene patterns and peptides!

But it got even weirder: it just so happened they also found nineteen toxic proteins.

He came across that because Gilead, the manufacturer of Remdesivir, had purchased the Genentech biolabs and took the employees! Geoff was on a roll and kept ploughing on down this line of inquiry. He found *a lot* more.

He rang Michael and said, "Wait till you hear this," before regaling him with all his latest discoveries and more.

"And snake venom attacks the nicotine receptors in the brain that causes the diaphragm to depress or partially paralyze, leading to trouble breathing," Geoff continued. "Guess what they know is very good at blocking snake venom from attacking the nicotine receptors?"

"Hydroxychloroquine," guessed Michael. "Yep, the stuff Trapp was telling people about since day one," Geoff said. "It gets worse. Venom is administered in exactly the same way as Remdesivir — via 0.9% sodium chloride infusion bags. Venom is injected into horses to make monoclonal antibodies and anti-venom.

"There was an article on patients being treated for Covid with Remdesivir called *Like Venom Coursing Through the Body*. The enzyme attacking the body's organs was the same as the enzyme in snake venom."
"This is wild, but it fits," said Michael.

"There's more wildness to come," added Geoff.

"Injecting Remdesivir for five to ten days causes a cytokine storm in the lungs of all animals, usually leading to death on day nine. A lot of what is being called Covid is venom poisoning mimicking a respiratory virus shutting down the patient's ability to breathe.

"That's why so many went downhill so fast when they went into the hospital with non-life-threatening symptoms or something else, tested positive and were put on the Covid protocol," said Geoff.

"On top of this, we know that people were given other inappropriate treatments like sedatives so they could shove and keep the ventilator tube down the throat. But the sedatives depress the system further, like Remdesivir, and ventilators take away your own ability to breathe, worsening the situation," said Michael realising that the protocol was even worse in light of these discoveries.

"Yes, that's it," replied Geoff. "The research also states that the nineteen toxins in snake venom target the weakest organs of the body: the pancreas in a diabetic, the liver in a hepatitis patient, and the heart in a cardiac patient.

"The mRNA vaccines isolated these spike proteins and has the body create them! Moreover, the mRNA for these proteins is more stable when administered with invasive and toxic magnetic substances, which adds further to the stress on the body.

"Then I asked myself how they spread the venom and caused the spikes before the vaccine?

"And then I saw something on the news that was very odd. The CDC had a wastewater surveillance tracker on the Covid website. They had thousands of testing facilities all over the US, and they were testing the water for Covid, claiming to predict an incoming outbreak three to four days later when they found it in the water," said Geoff.

And before he could get to the next part, Michael had already figured it out.

"That's reversed; if people are excreting it, they have already had symptoms and are expelling it from the body. So they knew because they put it there."

"Exactly. They were making synthetic venom in high amounts and putting it in the water. They were alerting the public to 'hotspots' to legitimise covid," replied Geoff. "The next wrinkle is fascinating too. When natural healers suck snake venom out of a wound and spit it out, it is well known that they can lose their taste and smell for up to twelve months!"

"Venom ingested orally causes this symptom. Every single symptom of snake venom poisoning correlates with what they call Covid-19," Geoff continued. "And the treatments made things far worse and often fatal."

"It's outrageous," added Michael. "Going back to what you said about nicotine receptors, I heard the doctors were flummoxed that smokers were the demographic least affected when logic would dictate they would be more at risk of respiratory issues. Is that because nicotine also blocks the venom from binding to the receptors?"

Never ceasing to marvel at his biological father's quick detective mind, Geoff replied, "Yes, that's what was happening. And that is actually another treatment that can be used: nicotine patches or gums."

"I was wondering why this was even called a virus, and I looked up the meaning of the words," Geoff continued, "and I found that corona means 'crown' in Latin and virus means 'venom'. So coronavirus also means the crown's venom, the pope's venom, or the king's venom, which could also be called king cobra venom. Of course, we all know about the triad of the deep state and how much serpent art is in the Vatican."

"Very interesting," said Michael. "It still doesn't change what we found before on the death rates from all causes not increasing until 2021 after the vaccines, and maybe an infectious version of the flu was released in 2020 too. But this does fill in a lot of the gaps, in my view." Michael paused for a thoughtful moment, then asked, "Have you relayed this information to the military?"

"Not yet, but I've a meeting with them tonight, and I will lay it out."

"Brilliant. I think this will help progress things much faster."

Geoff met with General Flint, Colonel Jeffers, and other officials later that evening. Their response was extremely positive; they knew the water was being used, but they didn't know precisely how. Now they had everything they needed for full disclosure!

Geoff also brought this to air immediately on his channel. He was contacted by Dr. Bryan Ardis, who had found the very same trail to venom! And, of course, Dr. Bing Lui had discovered this before either man.

Despite their discoveries, it still wasn't getting to mainstream media news, which once again proved problematic.

However, the bombshell disclosures off the mainstream were also gathering more speed, and Geoff's foray into the game had added momentum. Moreover, he had the credibility of coming from a recent mainstream perch, which blew everything open for many on the fence.

And that was creating a bigger problem for the Cabal. They needed enough people in a stupor to keep those in the middle thinking they were following the majority. However, many found it difficult to understand what was happening, and the situations were getting darker.

Awakened spirits like Denise were telling people that the White Hats were in control, as evidenced by Covid mandates suddenly being dropped and free speech advocate Elon Musk taking over Twitter, then Facebook, and planning to take over Netflix.

This didn't change the fact that more and more people were suffering health problems and fatalities from the vaccines. Food and fuel prices had skyrocketed, inflation hit ridiculous highs, and a nuclear war was being threatened.

The Truthers said, "The day is darkest before the new dawn," but what if things were just going downhill?

The world had been in this position before, with JFK and before 9/11. Maybe the Cabal had hatched another plan to thwart the White Hats.

Putin had just sent Russian troops into Ukraine. Geoff and others were reporting all the happenings from both sides.

Putin said he was overseeing a surgical military operation to remove biolabs, Nazis, and child traffickers. The Western media said it was the opposite — that he was bombing civilians and wanting to take over the country.

The commentators raised an essential question: Who to believe?

Priscilla was getting very nervous and decided to hedge her bets by going underground with Miguel. Brad was left to his own devices to deal with the public.

She didn't even tell him she was leaving. Her plan was to bide her time and see how things played out. In her mind, having Syed was leverage for a potential deal should she need it.

They had an underground location in Texas which was still undiscovered and unconnected to other tunnels. The amenities these DUMBS had wasn't to be sniffed at — they had technologies suppressed from the masses for growing food, cleaning the air, and creating natural light in indoor settings.

From just one cell, the harvesting ovens could make an organ of any animal they wished. Plus, they had greenhouses with perfect conditions and enough seeds to last for decades. The kitchens were like that of a top-class restaurant, with enough preserved items to last for years.

They had what they needed, plus entertainment rooms and a connection to the internet. Hence, Priscilla knew they could survive underground as long as they needed to.

She kept herself abreast of all that was happening while remaining untraceable. Syed was held in a couple of walk-through rooms with a bed, a table, a television, and a table tennis table he put up against the wall to play games with himself or against Miguel.

They treated him well; if a deal ever came along, it would favour them if Syed was still healthy and sane. Still, there were times Syed wondered if he might need to render Miguel unconscious as his only hope of escape.

However, even with the very low likelihood that he got the better of an Olympic boxing champion, he would still not be able to use Miguel's facial recognition to open the door. So he figured he just had to make the best of a bad situation and hope he'd eventually be freed.

Chapter 15

Truth Social, Twitter, and Facebook were now freedom of speech platforms no longer brainwashing the masses or banning channels giving an alternate view. With both sides of the story emerging, an honest debate was sparked between the Western mainstream version and the alternative.

There were videos of civilian buildings in Ukraine getting bombed to bits. Ukrainians left the country in droves, fearing for their lives, and famous Ukrainians joined the battle against Russia. On the other side of the coin, there was footage of Russian and Chechen soldiers freeing tens of thousands of children out of tunnels in Ukraine.

Russian forces released evidence of bioweapons uncovered in large labs funded by US and European countries.

Then the attention turned to the Western media. The war footage they were showing was the same recordings from wars in Ukraine ten years previous, wars from different countries, and even a reel from a well-known computer game.

Videos of Ukrainians saying they were being shot at and bombed by forces of their own country displaying Nazi symbols emerged. Was this in line with the same government that had been ruling its country despicably for a long time and, in one microcosm of the broader issues, had gunned down hundreds of protesters in Kyiv in 2014?

Many members of the public began asking questions, and Geoff was leading the charge.
It next emerged that the president of Ukraine, previous to his political career, had been in several mediocre movies and a couple of unspectacular TV shows in one of the poorest countries in Europe but was worth close to a billion dollars.

As Geoff described to his listeners, "To put that in perspective, Will Smith, who was in a huge TV series, thirty movies — many of the biggest in Hollywood for over two decades, and produced twelve films, is worth half that amount. A combination of the wealth of Will Smith and Leo Di Caprio is still less than Zelensky."

It also emerged that Zelensky's annual income as the sitting president of a struggling nation was $112 million a year.

"Have a search for Zelensky's net worth," Geoff recommended to his listeners. "If you can't see something very wrong here, may God bless your soul."

What on earth was going on?

Then when Geoff looked into Putin, it was obvious he had the arsenal to have easily levelled Ukraine in two days if he wanted to, but he did no such thing. He was also moving the Russian Ruble currency to be backed by gold.

Geoff said on his podcast, "Wait a second — backing your currency with hard assets is a move for the people. It means the banking cartel can't print money backed by nothing or loan you money they don't have and make you pay it back with interest. It means they can't use their Ponzi scheme that leads to crashes that the ordinary person pays for, widening the gap between rich and poor."

The Western media had lied about everything else; maybe they lied for decades about Putin's actions and character as well. Going by the evidence, it looked like he was the good guy here and was being truthful about the operation in Ukraine!

It wasn't long before China was doing the same thing with Taiwan, going in to remove biolabs and child trafficking hubs with surgical military precision. Of course, they were also 'sanctioned' by western nations, changed to a gold-backed digital currency, and demanded payment in kind for their goods.

With China and Russia being two of the biggest suppliers of energy and imported goods in the world, this move would have drastic implications.

Paying them with fiat paper money was very difficult as their currency was real and much stronger. The fiat money system was already in trouble, but now that was being drastically accelerated. The West was either going to completely collapse in short order or transition their own currencies to being gold-backed to avoid the fall.

In the meantime, truckers could no longer afford to fill their tanks to supply food and other goods.

The banking system was falling apart because the White Hats had taken over the FED and Central Bank in 2019, and they stopped printing money backed by nothing. The financial system of the elite had an inflation problem and no way to outrun it anymore; their currencies were losing more and more power.

The banks were hitting the wall as their system unravelled — people's pension funds were gone, stolen by those institutions. The bank gave shares for the missing funds, but those shares were no good because they were bankrupt. Within days, the world economy had flatlined like never before. It was toast.

Evergrande, the largest Chinese real estate company, was declared bust. Several massive hedge funds in the US were next. They were also based on Ponzi schemes and fake money backed by nothing. They were only there to serve the elites and steal from the average person.

The deep state worldwide was in huge trouble. Their only course of action was to start a nuclear war against Russia and China. There were still factions of the Cabal in those countries doing horrible things, but the majority control was now with the White Hats, who were removing these nefarious groups and also declaring war on the deep state in other countries.

The Corporation of the United States — the bastardised version they created after 1917 that had moved away from the US Republic and full constitution — was publicly declared bankrupt by Supreme Court Judge Clarence Thomas on the mainstream news.

In a press conference, fake president Joe Biden was forced to confirm this and resign in disgrace. The laughing hyena VP Carol Solis went with him. She didn't even want the job, and no one wanted her to have it either.

The position was offered to the Speaker of the House, Maggie Amato, but she declined. Who would have wanted to be a leader of a bankrupt company? Any policies and cheques you wrote would have meant nothing, as the coffers were empty.

There was a vacuum. The military had to step in with emergency governance and publicly appointed General McConville as commander in chief.

Maritime law and printing paper money had caught up with itself.

Bailouts weren't going to cut it this time. As Michael Clarke had put it, "You can't kick the can down the road forever; eventually, you will go off the cliff." This was the cliff.

But the Cabal knew this, which is why they had the 'Great Reset' planned to write it all off. They also had their 'Build Back Better' plan, which would dupe the public, and result in fewer senior citizens or handicapped 'useless eaters' as they disgustingly called them. Finally, they would blame the transition on a 'virus' that collapsed the world economy and use dangerous but plausible strategies like sedatives, ventilators, and vaccines to kill many vulnerable people, leaving them with more control and power afterwards. But this time, at a level where slavery to authority, lack of privacy, rampant human rights abuses, and social credit systems would be worse than ever.

It was a sick, slick plan that was being intercepted, but most didn't know which way this was going.

Geoff told his listeners to keep the faith, but even he didn't know how this would pan out. There were still many splinters of the Cabal, and even though they didn't have their heads anymore, they knew their system, their plan; perhaps they would be able to reform and create new leaders.

These were valid questions, especially when things were so bleak. Suicides were on the rise. Food was running out in the shops, as the supply chain was lacking. People were asking neighbours for food. It had been ten days, and no one could buy any new nourishment in that period. Many were running out of the kitchen stores they had. The military helped out by handing out emergency food packages in towns and villages.

Other corporation countries had gone bust, too. Most didn't even have a constitution in place anymore, as these were leased from the British Crown of the City of London territory. The Crown and the Vatican were also declared bankrupt because they had shares in all the countries they controlled.

People still didn't know if the Cabal would start a nuclear war.

Then all at once, air sirens went off, and everyone was in a panic. They saw things in the sky that were hard to fathom, like lightning, but they were drone strikes. However, civilians were out of the way at home.

Martial law was declared worldwide. The military ran the streets now.

People were in lockdown. They had no money and relied on rations for food. The military knew this was likely, so the farmers had been subsidised in the US and other countries since 2019 to keep producing.

The friendly troops stationed locally were starting to subsidise the truckers to get them back up and running. However, there was still a gap in time when food was scarce.

Geoff, Denise, and the kids were lucky to be in a military facility with stores in place. The complex also had large fields where they grew their own crops.

The Hurley family spent half their days helping the soldiers get supplies to the surrounding areas. This was happening from every base worldwide. By this point, the drone strikes had stopped.

Electricity was gone for three days straight, and the internet was gone for longer – Truthers speculated it was because the Cabal wanted to stop disclosure. Or perhaps the Cabal was taking over again, planning a war and putting their own digital currencies and social credit score system in place.

Everyone waited with bated breath, including Geoff and Denise.

Suddenly an emergency broadcast system went live. But who was responsible?

Was it the good or bad side? The first day of broadcasting went through the truth on Covid — that it was planned, released first from the Wuhan laboratory, the media was ensnared to create a hoax, and it was really a combination of venom put in the water supply by contractors of the deep state and a more infectious flu created by Cabal-run institutions.

It accounted for about 5% of the deaths reported as Covid, so they were similar to flu figures. And almost all cases of flu had been rebranded as Covid, a fabricated reality created by reclassification and damaging treatments.

It was stated that the overall death toll increasing by 15% worldwide in 2021 was linked to the vaccine rollout; that it was a dangerous experimental gene therapy, as even the creator, Dr. Robert Malone, had said before he was promptly booted off Twitter.

Geoff's Remdesivir and venom findings and *Watch the Water* by Dr. Bryan Ardis and Stew Peters were both aired to explain the detail about contaminated water and the despicable, insidious treatment protocols used in hospitals.

However, there would be antidotes for people before or after they experienced the side effects of the bioweapon vaccine.

Most of the population was staggered and near-catatonic, trying to take this in. Ordinary well-intentioned people had made a cataclysmic mistake. It was all out in the open.

Geoff said to Denise, "Finally! Now we can move forward as a population."

Sarah and Lawrence took it all in and proudly commented that Dad had been right all along.

The second day saw more total bombshells as the Dominion Voting Systems truth was laid bare, explaining how they had flipped elections worldwide for decades. Election fraud was rampant, and your vote meant close to nothing.

On the third day, it was declared that Donard Trapp had won the 2020 US Election in a landslide victory, and the proof was presented. All the ballots had been stamped and chipped without anyone's knowledge — a sting operation.

Donard Trapp declared that income tax was abolished as part of the Nesara documentation. The rightful leaders worldwide would also be put in place shortly, and Gesara documentation, very similar to Nesara, would be declared in all countries.

Every country had signed up for this. The heads had already been dealt with behind the scenes. In days, pensions would be returned to people's accounts because all stolen monies had been seized. Everything was okay.

All that happened with letting the old system collapse, Putin and Xi helping that over the line, even how it ended with strikes of cabal buildings, was all by design. Trapp and the white hats had put everything in place years ago with the world leaders; via threatening disclosure of their child trafficking or simply convincing good men that Nesara-Gesara could work. While Biden could barely find his way from the basement to the bathroom, Trapp had remained in control behind the scenes. It was all a show to reveal the evil of the Cabal, and ensure a transition that wasn't going to revert back to how things were before.

President Trapp also announced that he would step down and allow the re-election of a Nesara government in just two months, in which he would run for office. It would be a minimal government, with a minimum level of officials, and after it was in place, people would vote for policies, not people.

At this point, many were starting to celebrate that the war was over! The bullshit was over!

The Trapp haters were having massive difficulty with this because he was painted as a villain for many years when he was really a hero for the people. They had more to learn, but they would be fully convinced to let go of their Trapp Derangement Syndrome when they figured it out.

Denise was over the moon about this. She had stuck up for Trapp for years, having studied what he was actually doing and not what was being said.

The clean-up was still going on as the White Hats were rounding up as many of the fractured elements of the Cabal as they could.

It wasn't stopping the EBS from beaming into televisions and phones, though, and the populace would soon understand why.

The fourth day came with a parental warning, so Geoff and Denise kept Sarah and Lawrence away from this one.

This broadcast detailed child and human trafficking and the paedophile rings amongst high-ranking members of institutional networks like the Free Masons and their insidious blackmail methods. The conclusions of the Maxwell-Epstein trial were surmised, and it was revealed that Trapp was only friendly with Epstein in the nineties. However, once he found out what he was into and Epstein tried to grope a daughter of one member of the Mar-a-Lago Club in Florida, they were done.

Trapp's *modus operandi* behind the scenes was about stopping child trafficking; when he was in office, they had already arrested two thousand paedophiles or child traffickers. The controversial wall was about stopping the gangs from bringing in drugs and children for abuse.

After this reveal, many people had nervous breakdowns, given the level of pervasiveness outlined and the politicians and stars they saw on tape admitting their crimes. People they respected and loved were vermin, and Trapp was the one looking out for them and their children.

The fifth day went through the worldwide re-evaluation of currencies all backed by real assets such as gold — giving money back to the people that was fraudulently stolen from them in the old fiat currency system.

The sixth day detailed the technology patents that were repressed and held back. The Medbed space-age technology was revealed, and its miraculous healing was demonstrated, one of which was specific to reversing vaccine damage. It worked via frequency and light.

Denise and other healers rejoiced as the tech they had heard about for quite some time was now available. Her parents were strong advocates of freedom of choice, natural health, and real science and had not taken the vaccine. However, Geoff's adopted parents had taken the shot, and he was mightily relieved they would get effective treatment for it.

Free Tesla energy machines were brought to the public attention. They were announced to be in place and ready to roll out in days. The tech going back to Nikola Tesla had already been there to power whole countries with little difficulty, but it had been repressed. The internet was also reset to Starlink satellites and Internet 3.0. It would be free, much faster, more efficient, and an Internet of Value instead of an Internet of Things. It was blockchain technology, which was authentic and couldn't be re-scripted according to false narratives, Cabal wishes, or anyone's wishes, for that matter.

False and fake journalists could no longer rewrite history to suit their paymasters, create 'official fact checking' opinion sites for their goals, and dominate the search engines without challenge and debate. Freedom of speech was restored where there were clear and transparent debates; people were given all the facts, the big picture, and freedom of choice in how to think and act in their own lives.

The seventh day outlined the Nuremberg Code 2.0 trials for the crimes against humanity of the Covid plandemic and how everyone would be dealt with according to their level of complicity in the vast damage it inflicted upon society.

Geoff and the whole Truther community were excited beyond belief. They were vindicated and ready to help the change because many people struggled to accept it. They had so many questions, and they needed answers and guidance.

After seventeen days, things started to reopen. The money that disappeared from regular bank accounts was restored in new blockchain ledger accounts on the quantum financial system, and universal payments began to arrive; debts were forgiven under Nesara-Gesara; income tax was gone, and there was free energy and free internet.

The penny was dropping with almost everyone that Trapp was the good guy. The Dark Knight had returned; he had to make you think he was the villain to take out the real criminals of Gotham.

Geoff and the other big-name Truthers hosted a confirmation roundtable, as they called it, to remove any confusion as to what was happening.

They went through it all: the plandemic and who did it; the child trafficking and paedophilia; the quantum financial system, equal opportunity; new technologies, and so on.

For those not well versed or that hadn't been following the Truthers for long, this was confirmation that the Cabal had been overthrown. They were defeated, and the good guys had won! This was released on the EBS; such was its impact on the new internet.

People were rejoicing worldwide, hugging each other, kissing, drinking beer, and having one massive party; this was a New Year's Eve party on steroids, and it went on for weeks.

Many of the trials were broadcast, including the tribunals and the confessions. One of those was Brad Stewart.

Lucas Brevea's family and friends, the family of the journalist they killed, and the rest of the world watched as Brad confessed to his guilt in these crimes. He also admitted to using Malaysia as a child trafficking funnel after the natural disaster, abducting tens of thousands of orphans into paedophile rings and adrenochrome slavery, and making hundreds of millions in the process.

They asked him if he had any last words, and his face became demonic as he addressed the lens directly and said, "TACFA stands for Taking a Child For Adrenochrome," and he made a panda eye paedophile sign over his eyes.

He was hung on camera; the soldiers couldn't wring his neck quick enough. Some wanted to watch these proceedings, and some preferred to only hear about them. But the most important thing was that the truth was out.

Nearly all the Cabal players had been captured, assessed, and put through tribunals. All had lost their power and influence in the new system. However, some had escaped and were missing. Two of those were Priscilla and Miguel. And Syed was still missing.

5 YEARS LATER...

Despite repeated public calls for Priscilla to turn herself in and let Syed free, she resisted.

She knew any deal she could get was still worth a lifetime in prison. That didn't appeal to her.

She was holding out for the deep state to wrangle back at least some control, for her to quietly smooth out a deal and regain some kind of 'normal' life. In the last few months, she began to realize such a situation was now impossible.

The new world moved further away from Cabal structures and into the great awakening.
Miguel knew this too. They stewed in their own isolation and hopelessness.

Cafford was a very different place now. In fact, every city in the world was a very different place.

Sarah and Lawrence were seventeen now, and on this night, May 22nd, 2027, they were giving a talk on their plan for the new education system to a thousand people in the Tesla Arena in Austin, Texas. Their parents and all grandparents, including Martha, Michael, and Diana, were in the crowd, bursting with pride.

Lawrence took to the podium first. He walked out with a grin, wearing a lovely blue slim-fit suit. Watching his maturity and confidence to make this talk and presentation was deeply impressive. He was as calm as a sixty-year-old CEO addressing a weekly supervisory meeting with ten employees.

Shuffling his papers, he beamed a wide, beautiful smile out to the audience.

"My name is Lawrence Hurley. You are welcomed here tonight to discuss how far we have come as a race, one race of humanity where *all* lives matter, not just Black ones —" the audience chuckled " — and how we can continue our stellar progress. I'm proud to be Black, but I'm not attached to it, and it doesn't really matter; I am Lawrence. Ultimately, all of us were slaves under the cabal system, and they were the ones that engineered the racial divide. We are one human race now."

The audience applauded and let out a few enthusiastic whistles.

He looked up and paused for a moment.

"Let's detail all the magnificent changes in the world: Cars are running on water, and it is a magnificent advancement financially and environmentally."

He looked down at the crowd, and Geoff sat back, smiling. He gave his son an encouraging wink.

"Houses and buildings have free energy from Tesla towers, and the internet is free for everyone. Free, clean energy is in place; fossil fuels are no longer used, and pollution is almost non-existent.

"Climate change was a Cabal or New World Order hoax to make carbon dioxide a villain, create fear, and help usher in a cashless society. Of course, pollution was real and not good for anyone or anything on the planet. However, our symbiotic life form — and there are more of them than us — plants, require carbon dioxide and can even produce oxygen. Pollution, not some arbitrary carbon footprint, was a problem.

"I remember seeing a Twitter post last year that my dad showed me dated 2021, and someone said, 'If there was only a way to turn carbon dioxide into oxygen,' and the reply from someone was, 'Yeah, they're called trees, dummy'."

The crowd laughed heartily, as climate change had been debunked a few years back — the planet had been two degrees colder in the last fifty years.

Lawrence continued, "When Trapp pulled the US out of the Climate Accord, it was for these reasons, and because the US was paying the most and getting the worst sanctions despite other large nations producing far more emissions. It was not because he didn't want a cleaner planet; that was always his plan. He had also already spent $150 million cleaning the oceans around the US. He just wanted to do it the right way to work for the people. With the free energy and fuel plans, we are doing that now."

Lawrence was in a flow and enjoying himself.

"People no longer have to pay bills for energy or transport or income tax. The tax they pay is 15% on non-essential items, and that is plenty to run the country on without the Cabal dipping their filthy hands in here, there and everywhere. All the stolen money is also being given back, and you have true equal opportunity, as abundance is the norm."

Lawrence let the people digest this for a moment; rolling from one huge achievement to another would be overwhelming for the listener and the presenter.

"Everyone is following their true passions. Huge companies don't exist anymore, and the economy is community-based again. People support local businesses and farms. Our food is unprocessed, local produce."

He took a breath. "I'm now going to hand you over to my sister, Sarah Hurley." Lawrence began to depart the stage as Sarah came on. They met in the middle and hugged each other.

The crowd gave Lawrence a large round of applause.

Sarah strode forward. The pretty petit Latina had come so far, but she still had that innocent, beautiful, strong spirit. She looked to Geoff and Denise, and they gave her encouragement with their smiles.

"My name is Sarah Hurley from Cafford, Texas. Like my brother, I'd like to welcome you all today to mark this special rise of humanity." She smiled at the crowd, her brown eyes, vibrant skin, curls and most of all, her soul, capturing the crowd's hearts immediately.

"Continuing from what Lawrence had said, we also have almost no crime now. Instead of a plan for AI to replace our jobs, they do the menial jobs we don't want. Along with affluence, it allows us to follow our passions and bring creativity, enthusiasm, and love to the world."

Geoff thought how proud he was of her, how she was so strong, mature and intelligent up there.

"Our Q-phones act as an unhackable voting system on the blockchain, where we can vote for policies and not people, at the community, town, and national level. This is a profound advancement."
She looked up, allowing people to assimilate just how wonderful a time we had moved into.

"Journalism is now real and truthful, or it doesn't resonate with fully developed people that ask questions. If it's not truthful in an integrated sense, constructive and resourceful, then it simply can't survive anymore; people are too wise and see through it."

"Here, here!" somebody shouted from the gallery, followed by applause.
Sarah smiled.

"Our health care system is finally rational and healthy, based on food being thy medicine and letting medicine be thy food. We also use herbal medicines, plentiful safe remedies, and modern technologies like Medbeds, which do incredible things, even curing chronic illnesses, terminal illnesses, and vaccine damage!" Sarah exclaimed, her voice getting more emotional and fervent as she finished her sentence.

People applauded appreciatively, as this one was incredibly pertinent to the final phase in bringing down the Cabal.

"And finally, something very dear to my family: education is being completely reformed. As soon as Nesara emerged, my father, Geoff, started his learning centres based on drawing people out on their own perceptions, developing their senses as the root of executive thought, and engaging the whole brain.

"He focused on what makes a human perceptive, brilliant, and eager to learn. And everything he used in his methods brought that out. He called it Quantum Learning and Education.

"And now Lawrence and I will roll that out into every school in the world. It is our belief that this is the cornerstone of what allows humans to flourish, continue on this path, and not return to the dark times. So my dad's humanitarian project of these learning centres will now also happen right in the education system because it has been so valuable!"

The crowd got on their feet to applaud Sarah and Lawrence, who had been ushered back out. Their stories had been well documented in recent years — for them to be so mature, happy, and developed that they could give back and empower others was truly a sight to behold.

There were many tears. It was a seminal moment for humanity to finally be in this position.

"Let's start the party!" Sarah shouted into the mic, unveiling a DJ from behind the curtain that the teenagers had arranged. It was to be a great night. He switched from the inspirational instrumental of the last piece to the party tunes, and the celebration began.

After a while, Sarah asked Geoff for his car keys to get something, and he quickly gave them to her.

"Wait, I'll come with you," he said, remembering the car was parked a few minutes down the street.

"Daddy, I'm a big girl," replied Sarah, smiling.

He thought about it for a second, feeling he had to give her more independence and said, "Okay," grinning back at her.

She walked outside and went down the street. It was dark, but the streetlights gave some illumination. As she passed by a turn-off for a small road, she felt a shudder — like someone was following her. She sped up.

The street was quiet, and she was nearly a hundred yards away from the hotel. There was no one around when she heard someone say, "Sarah… Freeze — don't move!"

She turned and was faced with a dishevelled Miguel Vasquez, obviously drunk, but not so much that he couldn't aim his gun. He was just past the corner of the side street junction about thirty yards away.

"You remember me," he said.

"Yes," said Sarah, visibly nervous but holding firm.

"Your father ruined my life. After suffering for so many years, I made easy money; I deserved the power and the good life," said Miguel.

"You killed people, kidnapped children, and sold adrenochrome. You don't deserve shit," said Sarah bravely.

"F%*k you, little bitch, I do what I have to do! You were just lucky — until now. I'm going to count to five and watch you suffer so I can tell him all about it. Your dad will wish I killed him instead."

He started counting.

"One... two... three..." Sarah was fighting the fear and closed her eyes. "Four... five —"

The gun fired.

Sarah couldn't work out why she wasn't falling to the ground. She felt her torso and head with her hands and opened her eyes. She was fully intact.

But Miguel was not.

Just as she wondered if Miguel had shot himself, a woman emerged from the side street, gun in hand — Priscilla Stewart.

"Hello, Sarah."

"Hello," she replied, knowing who this woman was only through stories and media articles. But her reputation preceded her.

"I was an innocent little girl once — before I was passed around at Hollywood parties. I went the wrong way, and you went the right way."

Sarah thought she had killed Miguel because she wanted to hurt Geoff herself. But maybe...

"Miguel told me what he was going to do. He was pure evil, and he had to be put down."

She paused; Sarah still thought she was done for.

"At least I've done some good in the end. Syed is also in the Cathedral Church at Westbank, Silverback in Texas, ready to get back to his family."

Though her features remained hard and stoic, tears streamed down Priscilla's face — she couldn't fight them any longer.

"I had a vivid dream a decade ago. I didn't pay much attention to it at the time because I didn't know what it meant. I dreamt that Lightworker No. 17 would get me in the end. He only did it with truth and love. That was the most dangerous thing to the shell of Priscilla Stewart. There is no hope for me in this life; I've done too many horrific things."

And she put the barrel to her head and pulled the trigger, dropping to the concrete beside Miguel.

Sarah fell to her knees and put her hands on her face in relief. People were coming out of the hotel now; the gunshots had alerted them that something was wrong.

When Geoff saw Sarah, he sprinted to her and threw his arms around her. "Are you okay?"

"Yes, I'm fine, Dad," she replied. "Just a bit shook up."

It was finally over.

They held each other like the first time Geoff had taken her in his arms. But this time, she was different; she was healed and knew exactly who she was. She was brave, strong and ready for the future ahead.

Lightworker No. 17, the concept described by Priscilla, shone so brightly now. It had young leaders all over the world ready to take humanity forward into truth and love, awakening its full potential.

Sarah was one of those leaders. She was reminded of something her father said to her over and over in 2022, which had proven true: "Nothing can stop what is coming." So much had already been done, but it was only the beginning.

Exciting times were ahead.

PLEASE LEAVE A REVIEW ON AMAZON. This really helps the book show up on recommendations and searches. Thank you. ☺

Published May 2022
Copyright © 2022 Brian Timlin
All rights reserved. Published by Brian Timlin.

Paperback version available on Amazon.com and worldwide stores (if having trouble finding it on Amazon search, then go to lightworker17.com for the exact links).

Audiobook version available on lightworker17.com

The quantum learning program discussed in this book is soon to be available.

Sign up on:
quantumlearning.info
to be on the notification list.

No calorie counting is the diet for you if you want to be able to eat as much as you want and still get to your ideal health and body.
Sign up today on:
nocaloriecounting.com

Made in the USA
Columbia, SC
01 August 2022